He shook his head slowly and closed his eyes. "Oh, my God," he said softly, "they've done it. Don't you see? Now that they've got us recorded, they can resurrect us any time they like. If we die in battle, they can still bring us back for the next war—or even later in the same battle—and we'll never know anything is wrong. Even if we quit the program or desert, they can just create another one of us to take the place of the one who left."

There had to be a way out—and he had to find it fast.

Also by Stephen Goldin

THE ETERNITY BRIGADE

by
Stephen Goldin

FAWCETT GOLD MEDAL • NEW YORK

THE ETERNITY BRIGADE

Published by Fawcett Gold Medal Books, CBS Educational
and Professional Publishing, a division of CBS Inc.

ISBN: 0-449-14336-8

Printed in the United States of America

First Fawcett Gold Medal printing: May 1980

12   11   10   9   8   7   6   5   4   3   2

dedicated to
Owen & Eclaré Hannifen . . .
for friendships and favors

prelude

Hawker knew war in all its perverse permutations. He knew the killing and the pain. He knew the endless waiting in darkness for the enemy attack to begin, that helpless frustration when his fate was in the hands of others. He knew the swift battles, with quiet death and meaningless destruction flaring all around him. He knew the quiet and the noise, the calm and the panic. He knew the hatred for the enemy, the scorn for his own superiors, the mystical friendship for his comrades-in-arms. He'd faced the paradoxes of combat and hacked his way through the overgrown jungle of its eternal contradictions.

He was a master at the fine art of mass killing. His original training in slaughter had been on members of his own race, but he had long ago broadened his education, to the point where he could kill any intelligent creature his superiors told him was an enemy. Numbers were insignificant; he could kill thousands at the impersonal touch of a button or execute an opposing sentry with his bare hands. Means and motives were immaterial. His superiors had molded him into what they hoped was the best fighting machine possible. Just point him in the right direction and let him do his job.

If Hawker had any opinions of this, his superiors had long ago stopped asking him what they were. He was a creature living solely for war; he had no other purpose. No one knew this better than Hawker himself. There might be peace when he closed his eyes, but there would be fighting when he opened them again.

This occasion seemed little different from the countless others that had preceded it. There were bright lights and noises; Hawker could tell that even with his eyes closed. The ground shook with the force of explosions, but they were either mild or far away. There was no immediate threat, but the situation could not be good.

He prepared himself for the training probe, that sharp mental stab into his mind which, in a fraction of a second, could implant all the background material he'd need to comprehend the current situation. He knew from past experience that the information would flash through his brain in an instant, the mental equivalent of playing a tape recorder back at far greater than normal speed. When the probe was gone, he would be dizzy for a moment, and then anything he needed to know about the current troubles would be at his fingertips.

But the probe didn't come. Hawker stood in his place, muscles tensed, but nothing happened for almost a minute. Then there was a string of profanity uttered by someone in front of him. Most of it was in a language Hawker couldn't understand, but he was fluent enough in the art of imprecation to recognize the pattern perfectly. Annoyed that they'd changed procedures on him *again,* Hawker opened his eyes to face reality once more.

He had to blink, at first, at the brightness of the room. All around him he could sense his fellow resurrectees reacting in a similar fashion. There were rumblings and muttered curses, the rustling sounds of small movements multiplied hundreds of times. There was an acrid smell in the air, a smell of something burning, perhaps something that had once been alive. Despite the burning, though, the room was cold and Hawker was naked. That was the part he disliked most. He had long ago given up being self-conscious about his body—most of his comrades were from races that didn't care how naked humans looked, anyway— but he hated the feeling of vulnerability that came with the lack of clothing. Anything covering his body—be it as simple as a toga or as complex as a personal force field—would make him feel safe, but this nudity was uncomfortable.

As his eyes adjusted to the brightness, he took in his surroundings with a professional detachment. He was standing in a crowd of other resurrectees, perhaps as many as two hundred. A third of them were humans, male and female, the rest of various races. All were oxygen breathers, all were from planets with similar gravities and environments. Little details like these could tell an experienced soldier like Hawker more about the situation than his superiors would have guessed possible.

He knew, for example, that the world he'd be fighting on was basically Earthlike; he could breathe and move around without too many restrictions, which was at least a small blessing. The mixture of races made it seem more like a civil war than a war of expansion or conquest; in the latter, high command preferred to use platoons that were homogeneous because it was easier to instill in them a feeling of racial antagonism. In a mixed group like this it was counterproductive to stir up feelings of alien prejudice.

Since high command had gone to the trouble of selecting members of races that could survive in the

9

same habitat, Hawker knew that this was likely a battle on a relatively small scale. For larger actions they would all be issued battle suits of one kind or another, suitable for creatures from any environment. There was also the implication that this side was losing the battle, or at least poorly equipped. High command would seldom select a ragtag bunch like this unless there was no other choice.

He reached these conclusions without conscious thought. He had fought so many battles in so many wars that the conditions of fighting were second nature to him. It hardly mattered any more; nothing did. Winning and losing were merely opposite sides of the same coin, and he'd lived with pain and deprivation so long they were as much a part of him as his left arm. Even death itself was scant respite; he had probably died hundreds of times by now, though fortunately the resurrection process spared him the memories of those incidents.

The room they were in was large and drafty, brightly lit with a diffuse glow from walls, floor and ceiling. There were many doors to both the left and right, while the entire front wall was a holographic screen. The screen was filled with symbols and lines, a surrealistic map of some place Hawker couldn't even guess at. The symbols made no sense, but they rarely did, to him. Hawker was no strategist or tactician. He was a fighter.

A sergeant stood before the troops. It was an alien, tall and barrel-chested with arms looking powerful enough to tear a man in half. It wore an unfamiliar uniform, with insignia Hawker couldn't identify, but there was no mistaking that it was a sergeant. Even though the title of sergeant had disappeared centuries ago, along with all the other rankings as Hawker had first known them, the role of a sergeant remained unchanged. Someone had to goad the fighters, instruct them, lead them into battle. Titles could change, beings could change, but sergeants went on forever.

Even as Hawker was looking about himself, sizing up the situation, the sergeant barked an order in some language Hawker did not understand. There was no mistaking the command, though. The entire room snapped to attention.

The sergeant looked them over with the same air of disdain sergeants have always affected. Then, when he was satisfied that the troops were in hand, he lectured them in the same incomprehensible tongue he'd first spoken. Hawker stood there, naked and cold and progressively more annoyed at the bureaucratic fuck-up that created this farcical situation. The troops weren't even separated according to language, and no translator sets had been provided! Hawker had taken hypno implants of at least two dozen languages at various times, and this one still did not fall within any of them. The situation in this war must be very bad indeed for high command to screw up this badly.

The sergeant spoke for twenty minutes, making frequent references to the holographic map behind him. Sometimes he spoke matter-of-factly, sometimes in a bellow of exhortation. Hawker stood in place like a good soldier, listening to every incomprehensible word and not even bothering to make sense out of it. He'd long ago given up on that. War never made sense; you just blundered through it any way you could.

During the sergeant's speech, the ground continued to shake. The enemy bombardment, if that was what it was, grew closer. Neither the sergeant nor the troops took any notice of it, but there was plenty of commotion outside the doors on either side of the briefing room. Running footsteps, shouts, practically an odor of panic seeping in under the cracks. Things were not going well at all.

None of that was Hawker's concern. His only job was to fight, and it didn't matter whether his side won or lost. The fighting was all that counted, and it would continue to the end of time. The merry-go-round wouldn't stop, and there was no way to get off.

11

His briefing finished, the sergeant dismissed the troops. Those who had understood him turned to the left and began filing out the doors on that side. Those who hadn't—and Hawker was far from the only one—followed the others' example. No one spoke much until they were through the door, out of the sergeant's immediate sight. Then a flood of babble broke loose.

"Anyone here speak English?" Hawker yelled into the general din. When there was no response he asked again, then worked his way down through the list of other languages he spoke with some degree of comprehension. Finally, when he had worked his way down to Vandik, he got an answer. "Here."

Hawker and his answerer kept shouting at each other in Vandik, closing the gap between them by fighting the crush of confusion on all sides, until they finally drew together. Hawker found himself confronting a female humanoid who came barely to his shoulders. She, too, was naked, but covered with a yellow-green downy fur. Hawker tried to remember the name of her race, but found he couldn't. They had been enemies at one time in the distant past, but had long since become allies.

"Could you understand what he said?" Hawker asked in his imperfect Vandik.

The female answered in an accent so thick he could barely make out what she said. Her grammatical structure, too, seemed strangled—although his knowledge of Vandik was centuries old and God only knew what had happened to the language in the interim.

"Is civil war," she said. "Is being this town fighting on all sides around. Bunker is this in which we are. Is will be fighting up top. Is must for us to hold off fighting for six hours. Is reinforcements will be coming at then. Is now for us to go get uniforms and weapons. This way."

Sorting through her speech, Hawker translated freely that they were currently in a bunker beneath a besieged town during a civil war. They had to fight a holding action until reinforcements could arrive—hopefully—six hours from now. That might explain a lot about the desperate atmosphere within the bunker and the slipshod conditions of the resurrection.

Hawker followed his tiny compatriot to the supply line, where uniforms were being doled out by laconic quartermasters. When his turn came, the being in charge gave him no more than a quick glance and reached behind him onto a shelf. He thrust the uniform and mess kit into Hawker's face and brushed Hawker aside to deal with the next man in line.

The uniform was a chocolate brown, one-piece jumpsuit with a pressure seam up the front and a red armband on the left sleeve. Hawker struggled into it, hopping first on one leg and then the other while being jostled by the other soldiers around him, all struggling to get into their own uniforms. He found that the jumpsuit was at least a size and a half too large, and almost found himself wishing this were a world with a hostile environment; at least the army took slightly better care to see that battle armor fit the wearer.

The only place where the size of this uniform was crucial was in the gloves; he'd be handling weapons, and he didn't want the excess material getting in his way. He pulled the gloves down as tightly as he could, making a slight tuck at the wrists to hold the fabric in place. The fingertips were still too long, but there was little he could do about that right now. Maybe if he was issued a knife he could cut the tips off altogether.

He fastened the mess kit to his waist and hurried after the woman he'd spoken to. He found himself standing in another line—this time for weapons disbursement. Two other soldiers had gotten into line between her and him, though, and he had no languages in common with either of them, so he could only stand impatiently and wait for his turn at the head of the line.

When he finally reached the front, the clerk asked

13

him a question. Hawker shook his head to indicate he couldn't understand. Nodding, the clerk half turned and gestured at the rack of weaponry behind him. Obviously Hawker was being given a choice of what he wanted.

Unfortunately, Hawker didn't know the precise conditions under which he would be working. He didn't know how close he'd be to the enemy, nor what their arms or defenses would be like. He'd have to choose general-purpose weapons, ones with the broadest possible application, and hope to use them to his advantage. His choice was limited, too, in that there wasn't much selection. His side, the forces defending this town, were obviously pressed to the wall, and were trying to hang on with the scantiest of resources.

Of those weapons with which he was familiar, he chose four grenades, an energy rifle, a wide-dispersion laser pistol and a pair of throwing knives. He would be prepared to fight anything coming within a hundred meters of him; beyond that range, it was someone else's concern.

Dressed and armed, now, he looked around to see what came next. People were organizing themselves into squads of ten. Hawker looked about and found the alien—a Spardian, he suddenly recalled—who had talked to him in Vandik. Her group was not yet complete, so he went over to join her. If worst came to worst, he'd at least have one member of his squad to talk to.

The leader of this particular squad was a human, but Hawker quickly established that the two of them had no language in common. Once again the Spardian was pressed into service as a translator, informing Hawker that their squad had been assigned to defend Sector 14 against possible breakthroughs by enemy troops. Hawker nodded. There wasn't much more he needed to know; he could take his lead from the rest of the squad.

When everyone was outfitted, the sergeant reappeared and said a few more words—probably last-minute instructions and/or words of encouragement. No one really listened; each squad was busy trying to make itself into a fighting unit rather than the random assortment of individuals it actually was. Perhaps the sergeant himself finally realized he was hindering more than helping, for he shut up abruptly and let the squad leaders do their job.

There was little enough time for that. All too quickly, the troops were pointed to the elevators and brought to the surface, where they would be dispersed to their particular sectors.

Hawker's first glimpse of the surface confirmed all his suspicions to date. The town they were defending was in bad shape; in fact, to all appearances it was lost already.

The sky overhead was dark, despite having two suns above the horizon. Clouds of black smoke hung over the city, evidence of fires wrought by enemy weapons. Although the air on this planet should have been breathable, the stinging sensation of smoke made it far from pleasant. There were tears in Hawker's eyes, and he wished there'd been gas masks available; rubbing at his eyes with the backs of his hands, he followed the rest of his squad to their designated sector.

All about them was rubble and desolation. Hawker had no idea what world he was on, what the original inhabitants had been like or how splendid their town had looked before falling to the ravages of this war. He could only see the end result: no building over four stories stood intact, and even the smaller ones had windows shattered by the constant bombardment of enemy artillery; large impact craters dotted the streets, hindering progress; vehicles abandoned, overturned, burned; dead bodies lying everywhere, some killed directly by enemy fire, others indirectly by being trapped under a collapsing building. And nowhere, other than his fellow troopers, could Hawker see a sign of life. Everyone capable of fleeing had already

15

deserted the city, leaving the opposing armies to decide the issue.

Let the soldiers fight it out, the citizens said by their actions. *Then tell us what the outcome is.* At times like this, Hawker often wondered what was the difference between cowardice and common sense.

The squad moved quickly through the empty streets, crouched low to avoid possible gunfire and taking cover behind deserted buildings along the way. Overhead, an occasional ball of blue flame would drift lazily through the sky. Hawker had never seen anything quite like them in battle before, but he hardly had to be told they were dangerous. His guesses about them were confirmed when one of the blue fireballs brushed lightly against the top of a building several hundred meters away. The structure promptly exploded, knocking the entire squad to their knees and showering the area with tiny bits of rubble, hardly more than a fine dust. Hawker instinctively covered his head, but he needn't have bothered; the blue fireballs didn't leave pieces big enough to cause any damage.

Their sector, it turned out, was an area of some ten square blocks near the outskirts of the inner city. The neighborhood had been oriented toward small businesses and shops, with few tall buildings and only a scattering of residences. As a result, it had fared better than some other, more important target areas. Only a couple of structures had suffered even minor damage, there were no casualties lying about, and the streets were quite passable.

Probably too passable, Hawker thought, surveying the scene with a professional eye. *The enemy could march a battalion through these streets, and all we've got is a ten-man squad to stop them.* He was already making mental notes of the most effective places to use his grenades to block the streets, should it be necessary.

They came to a halt and the squad leader broke

them down into two-man teams, each to patrol its own area within the sector. Since the Spardian was the only squad member Hawker could communicate with, he found himself teamed up with her again. They said little as they marched out to their post, at the most forward area of the sector. Hawker surmised his squad leader wasn't happy having someone he couldn't talk to, and had purposely assigned him to the front lines. Hawker was the most expendable person in the group.

He and the Spardian woman scouted their area and quickly found a secure vantage point in a narrow stairway leading down to a cellar. Peering over the top they had an almost unobstructed view of the street in both directions, while being reasonably safe themselves. With that accomplished, they settled in to wait.

He tried to talk some more with the woman, to find out whether she knew any more of the situation than he did. Their mutual command of the Vandik language, however, was only good enough for the most basic communication, and the woman was not very talkative anyway. Perhaps she resented being sacrificed at the front lines merely because she was the only one who could communicate with Hawker. She told him tersely that she, like he, was a resurrectee, and that the sergeant had only sketched the situation briefly. Then she reverted to sullen silence, implying that Hawker should do the same.

Hawker settled back against the wall and waited for the enemy to make its move. He'd learned long ago that a soldier has to cherish any quiet moment he can find. From the way this battle seemed to be going, things wouldn't be quiet for long.

He pawed through the mess kit they'd given him, looking for a cigarette. It was, by now, a vain hope; he hadn't seen any tobacco for centuries. There were other drugs to act as mild stimulants or euphoriants, but he'd never found them quite the same. *Damn! You wouldn't think it was that hard to duple a fucking cigarette, would you? All they'd need was one, to get*

17

the pattern right, and they could duple everything from that.

He sighed. The army never did anything right; why should he have expected them to start with that?

There were three tubes of the pasty stuff they called food. Each tube was a different color, and each had a written description of what it was. The descriptions were naturally in a language Hawker couldn't read. He wasn't particularly hungry at the moment—resurrection always re-created him at a state roughly halfway between lunch and dinner—but he'd learned to grab a meal when he could. The attack might begin at any moment and last for hours, with no chance to snatch a bite while the fighting was going on. Hawker sucked on the tubes of paste, again reflecting on how uncaring the army was. It would have been just as easy for them to duple good food as it was to duple shit like this. But what did they care whether Hawker's taste buds were happy? He was probably going to die soon anyway.

Two of the tubes filled him up, and he was debating whether to open the third when he saw his partner tense. He hadn't seen any motion upstairs himself, but the Spardian was facing the opposite direction. Hawker quickly stuck the unopened tube back in his kit, fastened it securely to his belt and took up his energy rifle.

Any animosity the Spardian had felt toward him vanished now. They were a team whose lives and continued well-being depended on how well they could work together. The alien woman spoke a few words into the commer on her wrist, to let the squad leader know something was happening here, then raised her own weapon in readiness. Cautiously she crept up the stairs until the top of her head was barely even with ground level. Hawker was content to let her take the lead in these matters; his spirit of adventure had evaporated long ago.

The Spardian motioned for him to come up close

18

behind her. When he had done so, she whispered for him to stay there while she ran to a vantage point across the street, where she could get a better view of what was happening. Hawker nodded comprehension and brought his rifle up, ready to cover her during her charge, if need be. The woman braced herself, then darted out from cover onto the street and across the way to a recessed doorway where she would be safe. The instant she left, Hawker was up with his rifle ready to fire, aimed down the street where his partner had been looking. But he saw nothing, and the Spardian made it across the street without drawing any enemy fire.

Hawker lowered his rifle, but did not relax. Something had spooked the Spardian, and he was not about to take chances. He peered through the smoky gloom that pervaded the city, even here in this untouched neighborhood, looking both ways along the street for the slightest signs of trouble.

There was a movement back in the direction from which they'd come. Hawker spun, rifle at the ready once more. A tall, thin figure was making its way through the haze toward the Spardian. It was not any member of their squad, that Hawker knew for certain. A memory sparked in his mind, an image of an army of these gaunt figures charging up a hill at him—quite unmistakably the memory of an enemy.

The Spardian was busy watching the front; she wouldn't see the creature approaching her from behind. Hawker thought to yell out a warning, but didn't want to betray both of them to any enemy within earshot. Lifting his rifle, he fired one quick bolt at the approaching figure, and the alien toppled to the ground, dead.

Hawker's partner saw the flash of his rifle and turned in time to see the victim fall. At first she froze; then, after checking the front to make sure she wouldn't be seen, she left her doorway and ran back to the dead body to check it out. She knelt beside it for a moment, then shook her head and ducked for cover once more inside a storefront. She spoke into her wrist commer again, and this time her voice came out of the unit built into the fabric of Hawker's sleeve. "Why did you that?"

"That was a . . ." Hawker strove to remember the name of that creature's race. "A Cenarchad. We fought them not long ago."

"Is being fifty years past. Cenarchads to us are allied." Her tone made it clear she thought him almost as bad a menace as the enemy troops out there.

"Well how the hell was I supposed to know?" Hawker exploded. "I was trying to save your fucking life. You sure as shit didn't bother telling me how to tell the difference between friend and enemy. If you don't want any more fuck-ups, you damn well better explain a few things."

The Spardian was quiet for a moment, probably translating his outburst into terms she could understand and then holding in her own temper. When she did speak, her words were well modulated and controlled. "Is being civil war now almost one year whole. Other side leaders copying our records, duplicating our people. Old knowledge is ungood—is friends, enemies on both sides."

Hawker paused to consider. If the enemy did have a copy of this side's records, the battlefield would be utter chaos. "How do we know who to shoot, then?" he asked.

"Is look at armband. Red is us, blue is they."

Hawker looked at the colored band on his left arm. Thinking back on it, all the uniforms issued in the bunker had red armbands. Checking more carefully, he could see that the band was just loosely basted on. "What's to keep someone from changing armbands?"

Across the street, he could see the Spardian shrug. "No one liking being shot by own side in accident." She paused. "Not even Cenarchads."

Hawker ignored her sarcasm. True, it would probably

20

be easy enough to change armbands and infiltrate the enemy lines—but imagine the irony of returning to your own side and being shot as the enemy. It was probably being done, but Hawker had no stomach for that double-sided game.

"*I sometimes think that's your strongest asset.*" It was Green's voice coming back to him after all these centuries. "*You have no imagination. You see only straightforward, without looking to either side. If there's an enemy there, you shoot. You don't worry about peripheral issues. People with imagination waste too much energy thinking about incidentals. Keep it up, Hawk, even if they kid you. You're really the strongest of the lot, when I think about it.*"

Poor Green. Hawker had a sudden recollection of that final image, of Green in his arms, begging not to be forgotten. *I still remember you, David,* Hawker thought. *That's one thing I won't let them take away, no matter how long I live.*

Whatever the Sparidan woman had seen—or thought she'd seen—there was nothing on the street now. She and Hawker waited in their respective niches on opposite sides of the thoroughfare for half an hour, with no signs of further activity. Far away, on the other side of the city, they could hear the fireballs exploding and the buildings tumbling. But there was too much distance to make it sound real; from here, there were no sounds of gunfire, no screams of charging soldiers shouting obscenities at one another, no wailing, moaning or smell of death. Hawker was beginning to think he'd lucked out this time.

Then it all came at once, a swarm of blue fireballs falling like hailstones. Hawker hardly had time to spot them before they were down. The first three hit in the street, jarring the ground like a powerful earthquake and biting huge holes in the paved surface. Hawker was knocked sideways against the wall, so hard that it knocked the energy rifle out of his hands. He stooped to retrieve it and was jarred by a second

21

explosion, even nearer. He scooped the weapon up blindly and raced out of the stairwell. That was no place to be when the buildings came tumbling down like Jericho.

But the street was no better. Volley after volley of the fireballs came in, and there was no defense against them. Buildings on the other side of the street were already demolished; Hawker could see no sign of his partner. He was looking around for a place to run, a place to hide, when a fireball hit the building right beside him. The top stories exploded in a rain of dust, but the lower levels, jarred beyond endurance, began to collapse.

Hawker dove back into his stairwell, just as the building tumbled down around him, burying him beneath a mountain of debris.

part 1

earth

Hawker was one of the early ones. The auditorium hadn't been crowded when he sat down, but as ten o'clock approached the seats began filling up. Since nothing was happening up front, Hawker found himself constantly turning in his seat and craning his neck to look over the later arrivals. He was hoping there might be someone he recognized, someone to sit next to him and maybe talk with later about whatever this mysterious assignment was.

But the army was just too big, and he couldn't possibly know everyone, or even a significant fraction of the people. Whatever obscure qualifications the army had used to pick the men for this briefing, Hawker fit them and his other friends didn't. It was a bit of a letdown, and it made him nervous. He still didn't know what this was about, and their making him sign that secrecy oath before he could attend only made it seem that much more ominous.

At a minute before ten there must have been close

23

to a hundred men in the auditorium, although the room could have seated twice that number. The seats on either side of Hawker were still vacant. Then, at the last second, a sandy-haired young man made his way down the row and asked whether the seat on Hawker's right was taken. Hawker admitted it wasn't, and the fellow sat down.

They both rose to attention a few moments later as a captain entered the room and stood on the speaker's platform in the front. The captain asked them all to be seated again, and spent the next minute fidgeting through a sheaf of notes on the lectern before him. He was a thin man with a prissy Hitlerian mustache—a desk jobber, Hawker surmised, who'd probably never been near a gun in his life. By contrast, most of the audience looked to be front-liners—none of whom were much impressed by officers who shuffled paper. Hawker could almost read the collective thoughts of the audience: *What kind of shit do we have to sit through today?*

The man next to Hawker leaned over and whispered, "Well, at least it won't be another VD lecture—there's nothing secret about those."

Hawker nodded, and smiled in spite of his nervousness. He was wondering how he should reply when the captain began to speak.

"Is there anyone here who hasn't signed one of these?" The captain held up a form that looked like the secrecy oath Hawker had signed earlier. When there were no hands raised after a few seconds, the captain put the paper back on the bottom of his stack. "Good. Just remember what you signed. What I'm about to tell you is all classified 'Secret' at the moment. Whether you end up volunteering or not, you'll still be bound by that oath. Any man who doesn't think he can handle it had best leave now."

"When he says it that way," whispered the man on Hawker's right, "nobody *dares* leave."

The captain gazed out over the audience and, as

Hawker's neighbor predicted, no one got up from his seat. After a discreet pause, the captain continued once more, "Very well. Let me introduce myself. I'm Captain Dukakis, and I'm going to describe to you a project that will probably sound farfetched, but it's one we've given serious consideration and the army wants to give it a try. I must emphasize again that this is entirely voluntary, and no one will be forced to sign up for the program. I'm just going to tell you about it and let you decide for yourselves.

"As you all know, both from having been there and from reading all the criticism in the papers, the United States was badly prepared for the African Wars. We got sucked into it so quickly that there was no way out, and we didn't have enough well-trained men available. Part of the reason for those initial heavy losses was that our troops were inexperienced, and made stupid mistakes that a combat veteran would never have made. We started out off balance, and spent most of the war just getting back on our feet.

"In analyzing the problem, the Pentagon decided that the peacetime gap between Vietnam and Africa was a major factor. At the end of the Vietnam War we had a great number of experienced jungle fighters who could have been counted on to fight well in the similar terrain of Africa—but without any war to fight, and with a pacifistic mood taking hold of the country, they returned to civilian life and their accumulated knowledge and expertise were lost. Complicating this was the fact that the draft was eliminated for a while, so that even the combat veterans who did stay with the army didn't have that many people to whom they could pass on their skills. When the multiple crises hit us in Africa and it was time to fight, our troops made the same mistakes all over again. They had to relearn the entire art of fighting in a hostile environment against guerrilla forces—and the lessons were costly ones.

"The African Wars are over now, and we're once

again at peace. But how long that peace will last is anybody's guess. It could be a month, it could be a hundred years."

"I'll put my money on the shorter end of that scale," whispered the soldier on Hawker's right.

The captain continued his lecture, oblivious of the interruption. "Each of you men was carefully selected. Each of you saw fighting in Africa, and each of you served with distinction. Each of you served your one-year tour there and signed up for a second. This indicated to us a certain dedication to your duty and your country that we wanted for this program."

"All it indicates is we're too stupid to get the hell out while the getting's good," commented the soldier beside Hawker. He was careful, though, that his voice didn't carry to the captain.

Captain Dukakis was so engrossed in his notes that little short of an earthquake would have halted his progress. "We also had our computers search through thousands of personnel records, looking for people who exactly fit the profile we wanted. Each and every one of you in this room has already been thoroughly screened for the desirable characteristics."

The captain paused and looked up briefly from his notes. "How many of you are familiar with the word 'cryogenics'?"

The soldier next to Hawker put his hand up, along with a scattering of others. All told, there were perhaps a dozen. Hawker wasn't one of them.

Captain Dukakis was not happy with such a small show of hands, because it meant he would have to explain. He took a deep breath and buried his head in his notes once more. "Essentially, cryogenics is the science of supercold, of freezing objects down close to absolute zero. In this particular case, we're interested in freezing people."

Hawker was expecting another wisecrack from his neighbor, but saw to his surprise that the soldier was leaning forward in his seat, interested in hearing more about this.

"What we hope to do," Captain Dukakis went on, "is to reproduce artificially what some animals can do naturally. Bears, for instance, can hibernate during the winter and emerge in the spring all ready for action. We have found by experimentation that it's possible to freeze a person's body down to the point where he seems barely alive, and thaw him out again at a later date. In this suspended animation state, the subject does not age at all—at least, not perceptibly—and may be stored indefinitely; yet when he is quickened once more, he is as fresh as when he went in. His health is good, and there is no memory loss or brain damage. It's as though he went to sleep and just woke up the next morning."

The captain dimmed the lights at this point and showed a film. It was silent, choppy and badly exposed, but had not been intended as a commercial feature. Captain Dukakis narrated, explaining the experiments portrayed. The audience watched various animals—mostly rhesus monkeys and chimpanzees—being placed in casketlike containers hooked up to endless amounts of scientific equipment. The captain did not describe the freezing process in detail, but there were a few quick shots of the monkeys lying peacefully in their coffins. Then there were scenes of the monkeys being revived once more. The earliest experiments had been for a few days, then a few weeks; eventually the scientists gained such confidence that one chimp had been kept in hibernation for two full years and then revived without any ill effects.

"Of course," whispered the soldier on Hawker's right, "they're not showing us all the monkeys that died along the way."

Then the film went on to document the experiments done with human subjects, prison inmates who'd volunteered to undergo the hibernation treatment in

27

return for lessened sentences. Tests had so far shown that men could be frozen for six months with no ill effects whatsoever. Men were shown after their experience, walking and talking normally, taking various verbal and physical tests. Interviews showed that the men felt as though they'd only been asleep overnight, and were quite stunned to learn that six months had passed.

And, Dukakis pointed out proudly, not a single human subject was harmed by the experiment. The army, he was sure, had the process down cold.

He was quite startled by the mild laughter that greeted his remark. He hadn't realized he was making a pun, and it took a moment for him to realized what he'd said.

The lights came on again as the film ended, and Dukakis returned to his lectern. "This, as you may have guessed, is the army's answer to the problem of how to keep enough trained soldiers on hand during peacetime, without letting their skills deteriorate. By freezing our best soldiers at the end of one war and reviving them to fight in the next, we maintain a sense of continuity that is otherwise impossible to achieve. A man in the state of suspended animation can be expected to age about one day during the course of a year, so that even a gap of a decade or more is no hardship.

"You men have been selected to participate in this experiment, if you choose to volunteer. You would be placed in suspended animation until you are needed, then revived and sent out for a tour of combat duty. You would each be put in charge of a squad, so that your experience could be used to train newer soldiers in the field."

He paused and cleared his throat. "Let me run through the risks one more time. We have a perfect record with freezing men for up to six months. We propose to freeze you for what might be a considerably longer period. We will, of course, be monitoring each individual for signs of trouble, and revive him instantly if anything goes wrong. Nevertheless, there might be some slight chance that something could go wrong and we wouldn't know about it until we wake you up.

"When you are revived, you go into combat like any other soldier, and you face the same risks of death that you always did—except that you'll be more experienced than most of the people around you, which hopefully will give you an edge. After your tour of duty, you will be discharged with the army's gratitude for a job well done."

Captain Dukakis paused once more and looked out over the audience. "Are there any questions?"

"Yeah," said a soldier in the first row. "What's in it for us?"

"Oh, did I forget to mention it? There's a bonus of . . ." He shuffled through his papers to find the appropriate figure. ". . .of four thousand, seven hundred dollars. That includes the standard three thousand re-enlistment bonus plus a special seventeen-hundred-dollar hazard bonus. You get the money plus a three-week leave before reporting back to begin the experiments. We think that's eminently fair."

The audience was buzzing as the men started talking among themselves. The thought of having close to five thousand dollars to go on a three-week spree was tempting—and as for risks, they had certainly faced worse ones on the front lines in Africa.

After a moment's thought, the soldier next to Hawker raised his hand. Captain Dukakis waited until the noise in the room died down a bit, then nodded acknowledgment.

"What about our pay?" Hawker's neighbor asked. "Do we earn our regular salaries all during the time we're in suspended animation?"

Captain Dukakis looked uncomfortable. It was clear he'd hoped no one would think of that point. "It, uh, it's something that can be negotiated."

"It damn well better be. Sir."

There were quiet murmurs of agreement in the crowd as each soldier began computing how much he might possible earn while he "slept." The financial rewards were looking better every minute. To try to take their minds off that, Dukakis hastily recognized another questioner.

"You say we'll be frozen until there's another war," one man said. "What if there isn't another one?"

The remark drew a general laugh and assorted catcalls, but the soldier persisted. "No, I'm serious. What if there's a sort of uneasy peace from now on and no real fighting breaks out? Do we just stay frozen forever?"

"There is a definite maximum term," Captain Dukakis replied. "We would revive you in no more than fifteen years, whether there's a war or not."

"They probably couldn't afford more than that," Hawker's neighbor whispered. "I'd have to check a table of compound interest for exact numbers, but even if they only kept us out for ten years, we'd wake up with more than fifty thousand apiece—and we'd still be young enough to enjoy it, if we survived *that* war, too."

The number sent Hawker's mind spinning. Even with inflation, fifty thousand dollars was a considerable amount of money—and he wouldn't have to do any work for it.

Another soldier stood up with a question. "We're just ordinary sluggos. Why aren't you putting the jeebies into this program?"

That brought the audience back to attention. It was a most logical question. The Green Berets were the elite fighting force. It would make sense to freeze the best, rather than just plain old-line soldiers.

Captain Dukakis was aware that all eyes were on him, and he tried to frame his reply as delicately as possible. "The army had decided that Special Forces teams are versatile enough to be of immense value to us even during times of peace. There are always pinpoint missions where a little bit of force applied in the proper spot can achieve its goal quite well. The Special Forces are useful in peace as well as in war. . . ."

"While we're only good for cannon fodder." This time, Hawker's neighbor spoke loud enough to be heard throughout the room.

Dukakis stopped and glared at him. "I would not put it that way," the captain said slowly. "You men have all demonstrated a special aptitude for fighting in combat situations. You may have a variety of peacetime skills that would serve you well in civilian life, but there's never any shortage of those. What the army needs most from you are your fighting skills, both to help train new recruits and to provide an example on the front lines.

"I won't kid you. The chances are that when we revive you, it will be because there's a war going on, and you'll be in the thick of it. You've all been in combat, you know what hell it is. The army isn't Santa Claus—you'll be expected to earn those bonuses we give you. But—aside from the calculated risk of being frozen and revived—you won't be asked to face anything you haven't faced before."

"All our knowledge will be out-of-date," one man spoke up. "The army's always coming up with new weapons. What if we wake up twelve years from now and don't even know how to fire the guns?"

"We've conducted a few technological projections, to the conclusion that weapons probably will not change beyond recognition in the next fifteen years. There will be improvements, certainly—lighter, better range, more accuracy, faster firing, perhaps laser beams instead of projectiles—but basically you can expect a rifle will still feel and act like a rifle. You will each be put through a rigorous course in weapons of all sorts before being placed in suspended animation—part of the same course, incidentally, given to members of the Special Forces teams—in an attempt to so familiarize

31

yourself with weapons of all description that no matter what you're handed you will quickly be able to use it proficiently. We can't predict breakthroughs in new superweapons, of course, but we can do our best to make you all as versatile as possible."

Captain Dukakis looked around the now-silent room, searching for further questioners. "Anyone else care to comment? No? Very well, then, let me just add a few final words. After I leave you, you may feel free to discuss the matter among yourselves, but *only* among yourselves. Remember the secrecy oath; no one who was not in this room during this discussion must be allowed to overhear any references to the profect. If you don't know the rest of the people around you—and the chances are you won't—introduce yourselves and talk the matter over. It's a serious decision; we realize that. You don't have to make it today, either. You'll have the next two weeks to think it over. If you decide to volunteer, or if you have further questions, you can reach me in Administration B-224 during normal business hours. If there's anything urgent after hours, the guard at the front desk will know where to reach me. That will be all."

Captain Dukakis gathered up his notes and spent a few long seconds evening the edges before putting the pages back into their folder. He then returned the folder neatly to his attaché case, clicked it smartly shut, turned and walked out of the room without so much as a backward glance at the men he'd been addressing.

The silence lingered for perhaps five seconds after the captain had gone, and then burst with the rumble of two dozen separate conversations. The young man who'd been sitting next to Hawker now turned to him and said, "Well, at least part of his advice made sense; it is best if we introduce ourselves. I'm David Green."

"Jewish?" The question slipped out before Hawker could stop it.

But if Green was offended, he didn't show it. The smile on his face remained broad as he replied, "Only on my parents' side."

"Listen, I didn't mean to sound bigoted or anything. I just haven't known too many Jews."

"Relax. If you play your cards right I'll become one of your best friends so that whenever you're accused of . . . oh hell, there I go being a smartass again. Don't mind me, I sometimes talk too much for my own good. Everyone says so. What's your name?"

"Jerry Hawker. My friends call me Hawk."

"Pleased to meet you, Hawk." Green stuck out his hand and the two men shook solemnly. "Honestly, what did you think of the captain's little pitch?"

Hawker shifted in his seat. "I really don't know. It all sounds so fantastic."

"Fantastic?" said a voice from behind them. "It's far fuckin' out, that's what it is."

Both soldiers turned to look at the man who spoke. He was seated directly behind them, a big man cut from the heroic mold—dark hair, blue eyes, with a square-cut jaw and a ruddy complexion. "I presume you intend to take them up on the offer, then?" Green asked.

"Hell, yes. You have any idea what kind of tear you can rip up with four thousand, seven hundred dollars and a three-week leave?"

"To tell you the truth, I hadn't even begun to consider the possibilities. I don't believe I caught your name."

"Symington, Frank Symington. Everyone calls me Lucky."

"Glad to meet you. I'm David Green, and this is my old friend, Jerry Hawker."

Symington nodded at them and continued enthusiastically, "Yeah, I could really score with the broads. Come into a place waving a wad of bills, they'll do anything you want. After three weeks of getting drunk

33

and chasing pussy, I'll *feel* like sleeping fifteen years."

"Now that's the part I was giving the most thought to," Green said.

"Listen, I once crawled through a mine field dragging two wounded officers behind me. This? Nothing to it!" Symington dismissed all worries with a casual wave of his hand. "You saw the films. Nobody got hurt. They wouldn't *let* us get hurt. They need us—that's why they're freezing us in the first place, remember? They don't want us dead; just think how embarrassing that would be."

"Yeah, I'll be blushing all through the funeral."

"I mean for them. This thing is secret now, but nothing stays secret forever. If they let us die, their asses'll be in a sling when Congress finds out. They don't dare let anything happen to us—and I'm not going to let that get in the way of my three-week leave and that bonus."

"Shit, man, you are a goof." A fourth person joined their discusion, a short, stocky black with a scowl engraved on his face and a chip permanently soldered to his shoulder. "You really believe that pudding they're dishing us about freezing and thawing? They're handing you fairy tales, man. You think the army's gonna give you some bonus just for sleeping? They're gonna take it out of your hide one way or another, you gotta know that."

"Actually, the program does make sense, in a way," Green spoke up hesitantly.

"Oh, yeah?" The black man turned to him. "What kind of sense?"

"I've read about similar programs. People have been freezing themselves for years now. Mostly it's people who are dying of some disease we don't know how to cure now; they have themselves put into suspended animation until doctors find a cure. I've often thought they were being awfully trusting; what if the people in the future don't *want* to revive them? But I don't suppose they have any other choice. We do."

34

"Nobody's putting my ass on ice," the black man said firmly.

Symington was not ready to concede his argument, though. "Look—say, what is your name, anyway?"

The black looked at him distrustingly. "Thaddeus Connors."

"Well look, Connors, weren't you listening? Didn't you see the film? They know what they're doing."

Connors snorted. "I heard what the man *said*. That don't make it true. Fuck, if I believed everything a captain told me, I'd be buzzard shit by now. Ain't you learned yet, you don't volunteer for nothing?"

"Apparently none of us have learned that lesson," Green interrupted. "Dukakis said we all re-upped for a second tour of combat. I'd say that indicates terminal stupidity on all our parts."

Connors glared at him, his hands balling into fists. "Who you calling stupid, Jew-boy?"

Green self-consciously scratched the bridge of his nose. "Me," he said quietly. "And him. And him. And you. Everyone in this room seems to share a suicidal tendency. Can you blame the army for thinking we'd be foolish enough to sign up for this gig, too?"

"I'm telling you guys, it's no sweat," Symington insisted, taking some of the heat away from Green. "After you've run straight at a machine gun nest a couple of times, like I have, you stop worrying. What have you got waiting for you when you get out of the army? Me, my dad drove a rig, I always figured I'd end up the same. If I take this instead, I'm set for life. Even blowing the whole bonus on leave, we still get paid while we sleep. If we're out more than five years, that's a tidy sum. I could invest it, or go to college on some GI grant and get a *real* job." He looked pointedly at Connors. "Couldn't you use that kind of money?"

"Don't matter what kind of money a nigger's got," Connors said. "He's still a nigger."

"He doesn't have to carry it around on a big sign like you do," Green commented.

35

"I don't kiss no white ass."

"Nobody asked you to."

"Sure, you fuckers go ahead and fight if you want," Symington said. "Bash your brains out right here in this room, save the army the trouble. Me, I see the chance of a lifetime, and I'm damn well going to take it."

The discussion went on for another fifteen minutes. Hawker stayed silently in the background, saying not a word. None of the others asked for his opinion on the matter, yet all considered him a part of the group. Connors was constantly pushing both Symington and Green, as though hoping to start a fight, but neither man exactly obliged him. Eventually the black gave up in disgust and walked away, leaving the other three standing by their seats.

"Weird guy," Symington said, shaking his head as he watched Connors leave the room. "A loser from the word go. You can smell it on him."

"Not like you, eh?" Green said.

"Head on." Symington's smile would have dazzled a searchlight. "They don't call me 'Lucky' for nothing."

"And you really intend to go through with this?"

"Just put the paper in front of me and let me sign away. It can't be any worse than being pinned down in a swamp for three days, can it? We'll be rich by the time we get out. Come on, what do you say? Give me a couple of friendly faces to go in with."

Green hesitated. "I wish I could say yes, but I've never been that impulsive. I need more time to think about it. How about you, Hawk?"

Hawker had settled into the comfortable position of observer, and Green's question unexpectedly dragged him into the conversation for the first time. "Uh, I don't know. I need time to think."

Symington winked at them. "You're both in, I can see it. You just have to convince yourselves. You don't need any more bullshitting from me." He slapped Green jovially on the back. "I'm gonna go get me a quick forty-seven hundred bucks. See you guys in the deep freeze."

Green watched him go, then turned to Hawker. "You know," he said, "he may be the first guy I've met, in the army or out of it, who is exactly what he appears to be. No pretensions, no frills. He knows what he wants, and he's not ashamed to admit it. He's a bit churlish, perhaps, but still refreshing after all the hypocrisy."

"Do you think he's right?" Hawker asked. "I mean, about us going in after all?"

"I don't know." Green chewed thoughtfully on his thumbnail. "There are certainly plenty of reasons not to, and I can't think of a single convincing argument in favor of volunteering. But logic may have nothing to do with it. Each of us is a lifetime's result of forces we can barely comprehend. If we're pushed too hard, we can end up doing the strangest things."

He sat down and stared silently out into space. Hawker stood by for several minutes, waiting for something further to happen, but Green seemed completely lost in thought. At last Hawker turned and, without saying goodbye, walked away. Green didn't even seem to notice that he'd gone.

Hawker was seldom bothered by insomnia, but that night he had trouble sleeping. He could not get the ideas out of his mind, those vast amounts of money the army was prepared to pay for his cooperation. As Symington had said, what was there for him outside the army? Hawker had always been the quiet one, never making friends easily. He'd gone straight from high school into the army, and once in uniform and past basic training he went straight into combat. His father had died when he was sixteen, and his mother died while he was fighting in Africa. His sister had married a men's wear salesman, and already had one kid. There was no one to take him in; if he left the army, he'd be completely on his own.

Hawker didn't like being alone. It frightened him—almost as much as making friends frightened him. The army wasn't the same as friends, it was more like family. You didn't have to like family, but at least it was always there, and you knew you always belonged.

He didn't have to volunteer for the experiment. He could go career in the normal way, maybe serve out the rest of his life in the army and wind up as a sergeant in charge of some motor pool. It was a simple life, unpretentious—but Hawker had never been a man for pretension. He could make the army his life, surrender himself to it and let it make all the decisions for him. That thought warmed him somewhat. The army would be a snug nest in which to hide from all the loneliness of the outside world.

But the initial glow faded quickly. Now that the war was over, the mood of the country was changing. All the newscasters were talking about it. Moves were afoot to cut the military budget once more, to reduce the size of the standing army. The service could no longer afford to take in anyone just because he was a warm body; a man had to prove himself to be of longtime worth before the army would accept him on a career basis. He'd already heard of men opting to re-enlist and being told the army had no place for them. What if that were to happen to him? It would be the ultimate rejection, his newly adopted family booting him out of the house. What would he do in that case? Where would he go? Who would take him in?

Of course, the army had already made its preference known. They did want him—but in a way that scared him, for reasons he could not even have begun to explain. Oddly enough, he wasn't afraid of the freezing process itself; he had the simple faith in technology that came from knowing nothing about it. He had no doubts that he'd wake up again when the army decided to revive him.

What frightened him the most was what he would find when he *did* wake up. The world would still be there, his personal problems would still be there. What would he have gained? How long could he keep running away?

Of course, Captain Dukakis had said there'd probably be a war going on when he was revived, and he'd be expected to fight in it. There was the chance he might be killed, and never have to face the real world. Or maybe by then the army would be more receptive to keeping him in, so he wouldn't have to leave. If only there were some way to know that for certain!

Hawker lived with the problem for two days, keeping it bottled up within him. His acquaintances—he had no real friends—didn't notice any difference. Hawker had always been one to keep to himself; his quiet desperation now was nothing out of the ordinary. His appetite faded away to nothing, and at mess he pushed his food apathetically around his plate without even bothering to taste it. His nights were filled with fitful dozes, interspersed with long periods of wakeful nightmares. He could only lie on his back staring up at the darkness and hoping for relief from the torment.

He made only one attempt to talk his problem out with someone, when he set an appointment with the base chaplain. Hawker nervously shook hands with the man and sat down in a comfortable chair, but found himself suddenly tongue-tied. Captain Dukakis's repeated references to the secrecy oath would not leave his mind; the paper Hawker had signed told in great detail the punishments the army could mete out if he told some outsider about the project. Hawker could only stammer to the minister his general fears about the future and what he should do. The chaplain listened politely but, not knowing the actual details of Hawker's problem, could only give the most platitudinous advice: Hawker would have to have the courage to face his own problems, and should ask God's support for guidance in his time of trouble. Hawker left the chaplain's office feeling less sure than ever what he should do.

The next day, Hawker ended the torture by going to Captain Dukakis's office and volunteering to participate in Project Banknote. He was told his application would be processed quickly, and was subjected to the most thorough physical examination he'd ever had in his life. They took samples of everything, and ran him through a series of tests that left him tired and dazed. By late that afternoon he was told he'd been accepted; his three-week leave would begin Friday at noon, and his bonus money would be ready for him when he picked up his pass.

He left with a tremendous feeling of relief. The decision had been made; everything was now out of his hands. For better or worse, his future was secured, and there was nothing more he could do about it. He could simply drift and accept what came his way. That was how he'd always lived his life, and now he wouldn't have to change it. His appetite returned, and he found himself ravenous. He had three helpings at dinner, to the astonishment of his messmates, and for the first time in three days he slept soundly, without dreams.

As he walked to the bus stop with his pass and his money firmly in his pocket, he still had not made up his mind how he was going to spend his leave. He supposed he could go home to Kansas City and visit his sister—after all, he might not see her for years—but he hadn't yet written her to tell her he'd be coming. He thought of all the questions she'd ask, and wondered how he could field them without telling her any of the truth.

I'll call her when I get in, he decided. *If it's too short a notice and they can't put me up, I can always stay at a hotel.*

"I see you took the plunge, too." Hawker had been so intent on his own speculations that he hadn't even noticed the person coming up behind him until the

40

voice broke his reverie. Turning, he saw it was David Green.

"How could you tell?" Hawker asked defensively, a little resentful that his innermost secret was so obvious to an outsider.

"Well, what are the odds on both of us getting leave on the same Friday otherwise? Have you made up your mind where you're going?"

Just because they'd talked together for a while didn't give Green the right to ask personal questions. The other man was intruding himself, unbidden, in Hawker's life. "Thought I'd go home, see my family," he mumbled.

"Yeah, so did I—for about five minutes. Then I started wondering why bother with them? They didn't appreciate me when I was around, why would they care about me now? From the sound of your voice, you don't seem too sure about it, either."

Hawker made no reply, but merely continued on to the ramshackle little building that served the base as a bus stop. The place was crowded with other servicemen going on leave at the same time, waiting around for the buses that would take them into town. Hawker stopped and looked around, his indecision stronger than ever; one step behind him, Green said, "Well, what shall we do?"

Hawker was tempted to remark that he hadn't invited Green to be his companion when a figure two benches away began waving at them. "Over here, guys," he called, and Hawker saw it was "Lucky" Symington.

"I guess we've been spotted," Green said. "We might as well go say hello. Maybe he'll have some suggestions."

Hawker was feeling very uneasy, as though his entire life were being taken from him and pushed in directions he didn't want to go. He wanted to stop it, to tell Green, "No, I want no part of you and I want no part of Symington. Just go your own way and let me go mine. I hardly even know you, don't force your company on me."

Instead, he followed Green over to where Symington stood, smiling triumphantly.

"Hey, I knew you guys'd show up. Remember, I told you at the meeting, all you had to do was convince yourselves. I knew it then, I could see it in your faces. We're all gonna be good friends, I know that, too."

"And people accuse *me* of being a know-it-all," Green said.

"Hell, there ain't no two ways about it. Don't you worry, buddies, everything's gonna be fine. I'm lucky, and my luck rubs off on my friends. We're going to have ourselves a fucking good time."

"Where you headed?" Green asked conversationally.

"Las Vegas." Symington drew the words out so they lasted several seconds apiece. "That's the only place where the action's fast enough for me this time. I've got the money and I've got the luck, and I'm gonna set the town buzzing."

"What a coincidence," Green said. "That's just where we were going ourselves, right, Hawk?"

Hawker felt another portion of his life being preempted, but didn't know how to stop it. He tried to think of something to say, but Symington cut him off before he could utter a word.

"Hot damn, I like the way you boys think. I just *know* we're gonna make a team, like the Three Musketeers."

"One for all, and all for one," Green said, aping Symington's boisterousness.

"Now you got it!" Symington slapped Green on the back so hard he nearly knocked the smaller man to the floor. The bus arrived just then; they boarded and rode for half an hour into town. Symington kept up a steady stream of chatter all the while, alternating between his various heroic experiences in Africa and his future plans for Vegas. Hawker wanted a chance to think, some way of backing out of this involuntary associaton, but his mind could not concentrate with Symington blaring into it.

Once in town, Symington herded them all into a travel agent's office. Before Hawker could protest he found himself the owner of tickets on three connecting flights that would get him into Las Vegas by 2 P.M. Saturday.

There were still three hours to kill before their flight left, so the trio went down the street to grab a few beers. Symington continued his nonstop talk, and as Hawker became resigned to his fate, he found himself increasingly grateful; he was in no mood to do much talking himself, and Symington did not expect much more than an occasional grunt. Green kept up just enough of a conversation to keep Symington going; he was clearly amused by the big man's brash style, and viewed it as pure entertainment.

After the third beer, Symington disappeared into the men's room for a moment. The other two waited for him out by the bar. Checking his watch, Green was about to comment that they should start for the airport as soon as Symington returned, when suddenly, from the direction of the men's room, came a loud crash and the sound of voices raised in argument. Hawker and Green were on their feet simultaneously, racing to the restroom to see what was happening.

There were just two men in the bathroom: Symington and a black whom they belatedly recognized at Thaddeus Connors. There had been some sort of a scuffle; Symington had been knocked into one of the stalls and was now sitting, dazed but fully clothed, on the toilet. The door to the stall was halfway off its hinges; it had banged against the wall when Symington was knocked through it, causing the crash the people outside had heard. There was a two-inch gash over Symington's left eyebrow, slowly dripping blood down the side of his face.

Connors stood before the stall, facing Symington.

43

As Hawker and Green entered, Connors turned and the men could see he had a switchblade out and ready. Symington, in an awkward position on the toilet, was momentarily defenseless if Connors charged him with the knife.

"Steady, there," Green said, and Connors hesitated.

"What's going on in there?" came a voice from outside, probably the bartender.

"Block the door, Hawk," Green said quietly. "Don't let anyone in."

Hawker did as he was told, even as he was wondering why Green made that request. It would seem to him that the more people they had in here with them, the easier it would be to control Connors. Grasping the handle, Hawker pulled the door inward, even as the bartender was trying to open it from outside.

"I don't know what this is all about," Green was saying in calm, level tones, "but it can't be worth going to the stockade over."

Hawker then realized what Green was doing. If this fight were discovered, both participants would be taken away for questioning and probable disciplinary action. Symington's leave would be ruined, and there was a chance he might even be kicked out of the special program altogether. Green was trying to cover up the worst of the damage privately, before the rest of the world knew what had happened.

The bartender was tugging harder against Hawker's grasp. "Let me in there!" he shouted several times. When that elicited no response, he said, "Okay, wise guys, I'm getting the MPs." He left, and Hawker relaxed his hold for the moment.

Connors, meanwhile, looked like a cornered animal. His gaze darted back and forth between Green and Symington, never letting either out of his sight for more than a second. Symington was recovering from his daze, and was slowly pulling himself to his feet once more. His jaw was set angrily, and he looked as though he wanted to return whatever punches Connors

44

had given him. That wouldn't help matters any, and Green knew it.

"Don't try anything, Lucky," Green said. "It's not worth it."

"Shut your face, Jew-boy," Connors said. "This is between him and me."

"He's right," Symington agreed sternly. "I don't know what got him started, but I'm going to end it."

"You're both going to end it, right now."

"I don't take no shit from nobody," Connors said. His knife hand made small, slow circles in the air. The wrong word could set him off in any direction.

Green recognized that fact too. His words were carefully measured as he said, "I'm trying to save us all a lot of trouble. If you put that away, this whole thing ends here and now, not a word to anyone. If you try anything fancy, Hawk and I open that door and let the rest of the world come in. Are you ready for that?"

"I ain't scared of nobody," Connors insisted stubbornly.

"Of course you're not. But it isn't a question of being scared, it's a question of being smart. You think you can take on the entire U. S. Army? Plus the police department? You've made your point, Connors, whatever it is. But a smart man picks his fights a little more carefully. He makes sure winning is worth the effort. Do the smart thing, just for once, and put that knife away."

"Sure—and then the three of you beat the shit out of me."

"Hawk and I have no fight with you."

"What about him?" Connors pointed with the knife in Symington's direction.

"He won't do anything either," Green said. "We've got a plane to catch, don't we, Lucky?" There was a special edge in his voice as he directed the last comment to Symington.

Symington was silent for several moments. He obviously did not like quitting while he was losing, but

45

at least a portion of his mind realized the value of what Green was trying to do. "Yeah," he said at last. "I won't do anything. I've got to save my strength for Vegas."

"See?" Green said to Connors. "Just put that away and the whole thing's forgotten."

Hawker suddenly had to tighten his grip on the door as someone outside tried to pull it open. When the strength alone failed, there was a pounding and a voice called, "Open up in there. Military Police."

Green looked at Connors. "Well?"

Connors looked slowly around the room at the other three men, snorted and folded the blade back into its case. As the black man dropped the knife into his pocket, Green nodded to Hawker, who let go of the door.

Two MPs entered, each of them bigger than Symington. "All right, what's the trouble here?"

"No real trouble, officer," Green explained glibly. Taking Symington's arm, he said, "My friend here just slipped on a wet spot on the floor and fell against the door, cut his forehead a little."

"Must've fallen pretty hard," one MP remarked dryly, seeing the damage to the stall door.

"Lucky's a big guy. You know what they say, the bigger they are . . ."

"That true?" The second MP ignored Green and looked directly at Symington, whose forehead was still bleeding. The big man did a good job of counterfeiting his normal affability. "Sure is. Can't a guy even fall in the john without everybody making a federal case out of it?" He smiled and winked at the MP, who only grunted and looked over to Connors for confirmation.

Connors was obviously the most nervous of the lot. Hawker could see beads of perspiration on the black man's forehead, and his nostrils were still flared in anger. "Sure, he tripped," Connors said. "You can't expect no white man to have no coordination."

The bartender was pushing his way into the room

behind the MPs. "I heard yelling in here," he accused. "There was some sort of argument."

Green nodded. "Sure. We were trying to remember our first-aid courses, and we were arguing about the best way to stop the bleeding."

"Then why'd you hold the door closed?" the bartender persisted.

"It must have stuck," Green said with a shrug.

The bartender shot him an expression of disgust and turned to the MPs. "Are you guys going to do anything?"

"Why?" Green asked. "Is it against the law now to slip in a bathroom?"

The second MP, who was obviously the one in charge, looked the situation over closely. Green's story was weak, and the MP was not a fool. He knew some sort of disturbance had been going on—but he also had been at his job long enough to know that he couldn't arrest every GI who got into a fight. The situation had obviously cooled down, and wiser heads had prevailed; as long as no one was seriously hurt, he could see no reason to pursue the matter further.

"You'd better watch your step more carefully next time, buddy," he said to Symington at last. Then, looking over to Connors, he added pointedly, "Both of you." He turned and started to leave.

"What about my door?" the bartender protested.

Green reached into his pocket and pulled out a fifty-dollar bill. "Here, this should cover it," he said, stuffing it into the proprietor's hand.

"But . . ."

"Leaving wet spots on the floor is negligence," Green pointed out. "You should feel lucky we're not suing you for damages. Come on, fellows, we've got a plane to catch." With Hawker and Symington at his heels he left the men's room. They picked up their suitcases from the table where they'd left them and walked out of the bar, down the street and into the bus depot, where they caught a bus to the airport.

Not until they'd boarded their plane did Green speak to Symington. "Now, what was that little fracas all about?"

"I don't know," the big man said with a shake of his head. "That fucker's crazy, that's all there is to it."

"There must be more than that. Tell me everything that happened."

"I just walked in and saw Connors already there. I figured he must be on leave, too—and that meant he'd probably signed up for the project as well. I said, 'I see you changed your mind,' and he told me to shut up." Symington grinned sheepishly. "I guess maybe that's it. I didn't shut up. I kept after him, wondering what had made him sign up after he'd been so down on the whole idea. He told me to shut up again, then he pushed me, so I pushed him back. Then all of a sudden he hauls off and hits me, right when I wasn't expecting it. He knocked me backward into the door, and I guess I broke it. I yelled at him what in hell did he think he was doing, and all of a sudden he pulls that knife. Then you two came running in, and you know the rest." Symington shook his head again. "It was all so stupid."

"Some people don't like a big fuss made about it when they're forced to change their minds," Green mused. "It reminds them they were wrong the first time. Connors made such a big deal about being against the project at first that when you pressed him about finally joining up, it set him off."

He paused. "But I wonder what *did* make him change his mind. Most of us have to be pushed from behind by something in our lives, and he'd need a bigger push than anyone. I wonder what's doing the pushing." And it was a while before he engaged in any further conversation.

They spent the next day on a series of planes, getting to know one another better. They talked mostly about the immediate past, their experiences in Africa

48

during the war, their various likes and dislikes. Symington did much of the talking. He had a wealth of stories about Africa, many of them frankly incredible. "If even half his adventures are true," Green commented when Symington was away in the lavatory, "he'd be the most decorated sluggo in the whole fucking war."

By implied mutual consent, none of them talked about their families or their childhoods. It was as though they knew, on a subconscious level, that by committing themselves to this project, they were cutting themselves off from their past forever, and wanted to leave the ghosts buried where they were. There were plenty of other things to talk about; Symington alone could ramble on for hours without saying anything of importance.

Even Hawker managed to open up and talk a little. In fact, he spoke more to these new acquaintances than he could ever remember speaking to his oldest friends back home. Much to his own surprise—and quite against his conscious intentions—he found himself forming a friendship with these two comrades-in-adversity. He became more relaxed in their presence, felt less need to guard his psyche against their intrusions. He still could not match either of the others in volubility, but nonetheless he was drawn into the circle of intimacy that grew up around the trio.

By the time they reached Las Vegas, they felt they'd known one another for years. Green suggested that they check into a motel somewhere off the Strip to save their money, but Symington would have none of that. They were here to have fun, he insisted, and that meant first class all the way. Similarly, he insisted on a separate room for himself. "You guys can share if you want," he said, "but I plan on running the broads through like a cattle call, and I don't need you interfering, if you know what I mean." This was accompanied by a broad wink to assure they knew precisely what he meant.

They ended up staying at the MGM Grand Hotel. Hawker and Green did decide to share a room, while Symington went off on his own. None of them had ever been to Las Vegas before, but Symington fell immediately into the fever pace of a twenty-four-hour town. Hawker and Green were tired after their long plane flights, and slept for most of the first afternoon. By the time they awoke and went down to the hotel's casino, they found Symington playing the roulette wheel with reckless abandon, placing bets with his right hand while his left was clamped firmly about the waist of some pretty girl he'd already managed to pick up.

The pair wandered about the casino floor for a while, dropping some coins into the slot machines and sitting in for a few hands of blackjack, but not getting totally involved in anything. By the time they wandered back to the roulette table Symington had vanished, along with the girl, and they didn't press their investigation any further.

They went to the bar for a few drinks, had dinner, saw the *Folies Américaines* revue, then gambled some more in earnest before finally calling it a night at 3 A.M. and collapsing in their room. The next day they bought swimming trunks and sat out by the pool, lazily soaking up the desert sun. That was where Symington eventually caught up with them again.

"Close your eyes, fellows," he said as he approached them. "I've got a surprise for you."

Obligingly, Hawker and Green closed their eyes until Symington told them they could look again. The big man had brought with him a trio of beautiful women, absolute knockouts in their skimpy bikinis. "I never did properly thank you for saving my ass back there in the bar," he said. "I just thought this was one way to show my appreciation. Take your pick—except Laura here, I'm afraid I saw her first."

Hawker and Green were both speechless, so Symington, never one to abide a long silence, jumped into the breach. "Felicia, why don't you get yourself acquainted with my friend the Hawk over there? Maya, this is my friend David Green. Normally he talks a lot; I guess he's just struck dumb by how beautiful you are." As the girl named Felicia moved over to stand beside Hawker's chair, Symington brought Maya over and set her gently down in Green's lap. "There, isn't that better?"

Felicia was rubbing her long-nailed hands through the hair on Hawker's chest in an erotic pattern that instantly produced the desired results. Self-consciously Hawker crossed his legs to hide the growing bulge in his trunks.

Hawker's embarrassment, though, was nothing compared to Green's. That young man's face was brick-red, and he made a great effort to keep his hands firmly on the arms of his chair and away from Maya's tempting flesh. "Uh, Lucky, this is very kind of you . . ."

"Think nothing of it, ol' buddy. I always repay favors."

"It's just that I, uh, right now that is . . ."

"Don't be so shy, Dave. You don't want Maya thinking you're queer, do you?"

If anything, Green's blush only deepened. "I, uh, I forgot I already made another appointment." He lifted Maya off his lap and stood up. "If, uh, if you'll excuse me . . ." He backed away a few steps, then turned and walked quickly back into the hotel.

Symington was left with his mouth open. "I'll be damned." Turning to Hawker, he added, "You don't suppose he really *is* a fag, do you?"

Hawker was equally puzzled by their friend's behavior. "I don't know," he said. "I didn't think so. He seemed perfectly normal. I don't know what got into him."

With a characteristic shrug, Symington dismissed the problem from his mind. "Oh well, that just means there's more for us, doesn't it?" He put an arm around the deserted Maya and pulled her closer to him. "I

51

never tried it with two at once before; it might be kinda fun. Have fun with Felicia," he waved back at Hawker as he led his two women off to his room.

Hawker was worried about Green, but Felicia's expert ministrations soon made him put the thought to the back of his mind. He was a little concerned, as he led the women back to his own room, that Green might already be there and he knocked self-consciously before entering. But Green was not there; Hawker and Felicia had the room and the afternoon all to themselves.

Afterward, Hawker made sure to give Felicia a generous tip, even though he was sure Symington had already paid her well. Felicia smiled and thanked him, and told him that she stopped by the hotel every couple of days if he should want to see her again. After she left, Hawker returned to his bed and slept soundly for several hours.

It was after dark when he awoke. There was no sign that Green had returned to the room. Now seriously worried, Hawker set out to search for him. He checked the casino and the restaurants without success. A waitress in the bar said Green had spent most of the afternoon there, running up an enormous tab and getting progressively drunker. She remembered him staggering out several hours ago, and he hadn't been back since.

Hawker checked the lobby and the casino again, but there was still no sign of his friend. If Green had wandered off to one of the other hotels along the Strip, there would be no way of finding him until he decided to reappear. Hawker was half ready to make the rounds of the city anyway, but decided to give the grounds one more search. On a hunch he checked out by the pool, and that was where he spotted the lone figure sitting motionless in a deck chair staring into the surface of the water.

Hawker came up slowly behind him, and saw that it was indeed Green. The young man had a drink in his

52

hand, but was staring intently into the swimming pool as though trying to fathom from it the secrets of the universe. He looked up as Hawker reached his side, then returned his gaze to the water.

Hawker pulled up another chair and sat down beside his friend. For a long time, neither man spoke. The night was warm and quiet. Finally Green tired of the silence. "I suppose you think I'm homosexual."

"I don't know," Hawker shrugged.

"Sure, why not? That's the logical assumption, isn't it? I'll bet that's what Lucky thinks."

"He asked me if I thought you were," Hawker said. "I told him I didn't know."

"There's a lot of things you don't know, isn't there?" Green raised his glass to his lips, then put it down again without drinking from it. Taking a deep breath and letting it out again, he continued, "Well, I'm not. So there. But it might simplify a lot of things if I were."

Hawker accepted that with his usual silence.

Green let the quiet reign for a few more minutes before breaking it again. "We're all being pushed, Hawk. We're all being pushed into this damned project, and there's not a damn thing we can do about it."

"No one forced us to volunteer."

"The push was made a long time ago," Green said, shaking his head. "Before we ever knew what was happening. Except for someone like Lucky. I really think he *enjoys* this kind of crap. A natural-born volunteer. He's going to die in action with a smile on his face.

"Connors, too. Something pushed him hard. He didn't like it. Probably fought it like a wildcat. No use. That's why he blew up at Lucky. He was mad at himself for being pushed, and had to let it out somewhere. Lucky just got in the way."

Green paused and looked straight into Hawker's face. "And you, my little sphinx. You're the major mystery. Something pushed you, and I can't read what

53

it was. You look like you're drifting, but you're pushed just like the rest of us. Wish I knew why."

Hawker wanted to explain the fear he'd felt at being forced out on his own, the anxiety at taking responsibility for his own life, the dread of making decisions. It was all much simpler, he wanted to say, when the choices were made for you; then you could just accept it and not have to worry.

But the words refused to come. He was never comfortable with words, and especially around someone as smart as Green. He didn't want to look like a dummy, so he preferred to say nothing. With any luck, most people would interpret his silence as wisdom rather than stupidity.

Green kept staring at him, and Hawker was forced to turn away. After a few minutes, the other man said, "Well?"

"Well, what?" Hawker asked.

"Aren't you going to ask me?"

"Ask you what?"

Green exploded. "Ask me what's pushing *me,* you moron! Aren't you interested? Don't you want to know? Don't you have even the faintest shred of curiosity? God gave you a brain, the most magnificent computer ever devised, to set you apart from the chimpanzees and the orangutans; are you just going to let it go to waste? Don't you even care what's going on around you? Don't you care what makes things work? Don't you wonder, even a little bit, why people do the things they do?"

Hawker was dazed by the sudden outburst. "I . . . I always sort of thought that was none of my business."

Green relaxed again, and then began laughing uncontrollably. "You are one of a kind, you know that?"

"I don't see what's so funny," Hawker said, hurt that the other man would be laughing at him.

"You wouldn't," Green said, and continued laughing.

Spurred to anger by his friend's callousness, Hawker

exploded a bit himself. "Yes, damn it, I wondered. A guy like you could have it made it civilian life. You're smart, you could go to college and make something of yourself. Doctor, lawyer, politician, I don't know—something big. For me and Lucky, the army's the best thing that happened to us, but I never could figure out what you were doing here. I figured that was your business, though. If you wanted me to know, you'd tell me, otherwise it wasn't right to ask. But you have no right to laugh at me, just because I respect your privacy."

Green stopped laughing, and wiped the tears from his eyes. "I wasn't laughing at you, just at this whole preposterous thing. Forget it. Forget I ever mentioned the subject." He tried to stand, and got halfway before sinking back into the chair. Hawker got up and helped his friend to his feet.

"Thanks," Green said. "I've been drinking a lot on an empty stomach. That's not good for me. What do you say we get some dinner and go to bed?"

"Fine."

After a quick snack at the restaurant they returned to their room. Hawker helped his friend undress, and both lay down in the darkness on their respective beds. Hawker, though, wasn't tired; his nap after the afternoon's activities had left him feeling wide awake now. He lay on his back, staring up at the ceiling. Through the darkness, he could tell that Green was awake, too.

Finally, Hawker said, "What *is* pushing you, David?"

Minutes went by without an answer, and Hawker began to think he must have been mistaken about Green's being awake, or else that the other man was too tired—or too upset—to answer him. But then suddenly Green replied, in a near-monotone, "My father is an Orthodox rabbi."

"Oh?"

"Yeah." More silence, then, "I don't suppose you really know what that can mean. I'm my father's

55

youngest son and his biggest disappointment. He told me so, constantly. 'Davidka,' he'd say, 'you are the failure of my life, the ultimate frustration of all I've worked for.' He said that even before I was ten years old. Some accomplishment for a little kid, huh? I'd hardly had a chance to do *anything*, and already he was convinced I'd betrayed him. I could never be smart enough or clever enough or good enough. Not that he didn't push me to try—but he was always careful to stick his foot out in front of me to make sure I'd trip. With his support, there wasn't a thing I couldn't fail at.

"You mentioned before you thought I could go to college and maybe become a doctor or a lawyer. I've got one of each as older brothers. I've got another brother who's a cantor. I think that made my father happiest of all. Me, I can't even carry a tune."

He paused and coughed a couple of times. "Everything in the house was very strict. My mother in particular made sure of that. Between her and my father, I didn't have a chance. She was the one who set my attitudes about women. *Goyisha* ... that is, Gentile girls were *traif,* not kosher. There was something unclean about them, as though they all had some slimy social disease all over their bodies. Only good Jewish girls were worth loving, and even then I had to wait until I married one. I got the impression, somehow, that non-Jewish girls never bathed, or used Pigshit #5 cologne, or something equally disgusting. Funny thing is, I'm told I'm the exact opposite of most Jewish men. To them, Gentile girls are a turn-on; they marry nice Jewish girls and carry on with Gentiles. Not me; I'm spoiled for life.

"I tried once, during the war. I was on leave with some of my buddies over in Africa—Salisbury, I think—and we went out and got drunk. I could barely stand up, but my friends steered me into a whorehouse, one of those cheap black places on the edge of town. The building was run-down and filthy, and the girls

56

hadn't bathed in several weeks. The room smelled of sweat—Negro sweat. I couldn't do anything, and I broke down and cried. My friends thought it was because the girl was black, so they pooled their money and took me to a fancier white bordello. I couldn't do anything there either. I ended up vomiting all over the bed—hardly the most comforting experience for a young virgin, right?"

Hawker didn't answer, and another long silence ensued. Finally Green spoke again. "I entered the army to get away from home. Isn't that hysterical? There I am, running away from the authoritarianism of my parents, and where do I go to hide? The most authoritarian system in the world, the army. So you see, I must be more mentally defective than any ten Marine Corps boots combined. And *that* is what's pushing me. I keep hoping that maybe, if I play Rip Van Winkle long enough, the world will change beneath me to something I can live with."

"I'm sorry," Hawker said at last, when he was sure his friend had finished. "I didn't know."

"Of course you didn't know. I didn't tell you. But that's why Lucky threw me into such a tailspin when he brought those girls over. I just couldn't face anything like that again. It's so hard looking into the mirror and knowing what a complete and utter failure I've made of myself."

Green stopped talking again, and it took Hawker several moments to realize his friend was crying. Hawker lay in bed for a time, not sure how to handle this development; then finally he threw the covers back, got up and crossed the room to where Green lay. Taking his friend in his arms, he held him tightly until all the tears were gone and Green had slipped off to sleep. Hawker left him then, at peace at last, and slipped out of the room to get himself a drink.

Green spent most of the next day nursing a frightful hangover, but once that was behind him he returned to his old cheerful, sometimes cynical, self. By some implied understanding, neither man mentioned their talk of the night before; the subject was as closed as two friends could ever make it. Nonetheless, Hawker knew they had turned a corner in their relationship. Before last night, they had been friends by convenience, two people thrown together by similar circumstances making the best of their awkward situation. Now, though, that had evolved into a deeper feeling. Hawker felt actual concern for Green's welfare, an admiration and liking stronger than any he'd experienced except for some old boyhood friends. He could tell, too, from the look in Green's eyes that the feeling was returned. There was trust, now, the feeling of intimacies shared and nurtured.

They saw Symington occasionally as the big man dashed to and fro through this playground city. Hawker at least found a chance to take Symington aside and tell him—without going into details—that Green's refusal of the girls was a personal problem that had nothing to do with being homosexual. Symington, easygoing sort that he was, accepted this explanation without question.

For the most part, Symington was too busy to care. He was always either chasing women or gambling—or both—and seemed to be having more success with the former. At one point, after a week and a half, he came to Hawker and Green asking for a stake to help with his gambling, and the two were convinced he had squandered his entire bonus already. He repaid them, though, the next day—with interest—and never brought the subject up again, so they could never be sure what his situation really was.

For Hawker and Green, though, the time passed more quietly. They went to all the big shows along the Strip, seeing star performers they'd never thought they'd see in person; they gambled a bit, losing somewhat more than they won and writing the losses off to experience; they spent some time in the bars, watching basketball games on TV and arguing with other sports fans; and they lounged about the swimming pool, soaking up the sun and getting a modicum of exercise. They avoided any deep, personal discussions; that one night had been more than sufficient for both of them. Much of the time they didn't talk at all, and when they did it was of superficial matters. The one subject that was completely off limits was Project Banknote. The future would hit them fast enough—they were here to forget it in the meantime.

The problem was, neither of them could forget it—and as their hours of freedom ticked away, they were oppressed by the knowledge that soon they'd be leaving the safe, familiar world behind them, venturing into a future as frightening as it was uncertain. During the second week of their leave, they found themselves talking less and less. Each man immersed himself in contemplation of what the future held for him—and neither could quite bring himself to discuss the problem with the other.

Although the desert sun shone brightly, Hawker began to feel as though he were walking underneath a perpetual raincloud. The artificial gaiety and the forced frantic pace around him began to ring hollow; he found himself smothering in a blanket of gloom he could not lift.

With a week still to go on his leave, Hawker packed his gear together and took off by himself, leaving behind only a brief note to Green, saying he'd see him again in a week, back at the base. Then Hawker took a taxi to the airport and bought a ticket on the next flight to Los Angeles.

Hawker had never been to Los Angeles before, and knew no one there. In part, that was the charm the city held for him. For his one last week in the real world, he wanted to bury himself in anonymity. He'd heard about the L.A. mystique, and thought this was a perfect opportunity to experience it firsthand.

He got a room at the Holiday Inn, just north of Hollywood Boulevard. The weather was gray and overcast—unseasonable, the desk clerk said, but Hawker hardly noticed. The leaden skies matched his mood only too well.

Over the next several days he roamed Hollywood at random. He had originally intended to go all over Los Angeles, but the city's large size made that impossible. Instead, he spent his time wandering the length of Hollywood Boulevard, drinking in its diversity and yet still feeling unfulfilled at the end of each excursion. Bookstores and record shops, boutiques and emporia, even famous names implanted in stars along the sidewalk—nothing could lift the depression that had settled over him. He walked amid the bright lights and the chattering people like a premature ghost, in the world but not of it.

When he walked at night he received numerous solicitations from both men and women; he ignored them all and walked on. On his second night in Hollywood he encountered a prostitute he couldn't easily get rid of, a woman in her forties with lipstick so garish on an overly whitened face that she looked almost like a clown. For some reason she attached herself to Hawker and would not leave his side. Resigning himself to the inevitable, he took her back with him to his hotel room, but despite the best efforts of both of them, he found himself impotent. At length angered by his inability, he chased the woman out of his room, then cried himself to sleep on the bed.

The world around him became progressively less real, a scene of shifting shadows. He had come here, subconsciously, to say goodbye, but the world seemed to have already left without telling him, leaving him alone in an emotionless void.

Three days before his leave was due to expire, he saw a dime on the sidewalk. He stopped and stood over it, mindless of the people who pushed by him on their hurried way. The small circle of silver became a

60

mystic token, symbol of an entire world he was departing forever. Already it was considered an insignificant piece of change, but he remembered receiving a dime as a kid and buying himself some candy. The dime was a solid link to his past, but what of the future? What if there *were* no dimes when he awoke? What if there were no money at all, and everyone used credit cards or something? What if there was nothing familiar when he woke up, and he found himself facing a world of alien complexities? He had been frightened enough of the world he knew; could the future be any less terrifying?

He stared at the dime for half an hour, until a little boy noticed what he was looking at and ran over to pick it up. The kid ran off with the coin and Hawker, jolted out of his reverie, returned slowly to his hotel room.

He spent the remainder of his leave in his room, not even venturing out to eat. He turned on the television and sat hypnotized in front of it, blinking uncomprehendingly as a series of images paraded across the tube. His face grew gaunt, and bags appeared under his eyes. He dozed a couple of times in front of the set, waking with a start each time and returning to his meaningless preoccupation.

His strange ritual finally completed, he checked out of his room and prepared to return to the base. Unshaven and haggard, he looked like a derelict, though he still had plenty of unused bonus money in his pocket. Hawker didn't care what people thought about him. He had divorced himself from the present the only way he knew how, and was prepared to step into the future.

It turned out to be a longer step than he had counted on. He was not put into suspended animation immediately upon his return. Instead, he was placed in a separate barracks with the other volunteers, and was told there would be several weeks of special weapons training and physical testing before the experiment began.

Green was here too, as was Symington. Both were delighted to see him, and the threesome spent their first few minutes together thumping backs and swapping insults. Green and Symington both pretended they'd hardly missed Hawker at all; Hawker could see past the surface, though, to the concern Green had felt, and the relief that he now knew his friend was all right. But significantly, neither of the other two men ever asked Hawker where he'd gone or what he'd done. Each had probably gone through his own version of the psychological crisis, and knew there were some privacies it was not decent to intrude upon.

Of the ninety-three men who'd volunteered for the project, eleven did not return from leave. After twenty-four hours, they were listed as AWOL and dropped from the subject rolls. Hawker sometimes wondered about them, and whether their lives were better or worse for having made the decision they did.

But the army gave him little time just then for idle speculation. The volunteers were given a course in weapons use conducted by a Special Forces instructor who did not tolerate failure. They spent four hours a day in a classroom·learning the theory of weaponry, and eight more hours a day in the field putting their knowledge to practical use. They started with the simplest weapons—knives, bows and arrows, spears— learning not only their use but how to improvise them in the field if they found themselves unarmed. They spent long hours on the target range until each of them was adept at these before moving on to more modern armaments. They learned about guns, from the earliest to the most modern, including some of the more experimental computer-guided models and the laser rifles that promised to add new dimensions to warfare. Hawker and his comrades learned to disassemble, clean and reassemble every firearm in the U.S. arsenal, plus a number of captured enemy models. They saw films and demonstrations of artillery pieces, and practiced in conjunction with field artillery teams.

There was no way of knowing what kinds of weapons would be available to them when they awoke. The best way to deal with this, from the army's point of view, was to make each of the volunteers as versatile and proficient as possible. By the end of their training, each of the volunteers was a specialist in calculated mayhem.

Their schedule was so exhaustive that they had little time for private lives. Between meals, classes and field exercises, Hawker had little opportunity to talk with his friends. By the end of each day it was all he could do to crawl into bed and try to get a little sleep before the cycle repeated itself the next day.

Just as the recruits were congratulating themselves for surviving the weapons training, the physical examinations began. Each of them had been examined before being accepted into the program, and they thought the re-examinations were just a formality. They were wrong.

The army was fully aware that this cryogenic experiment was something that had never been attempted on this scale or for this duration. It wanted to make absolutely certain that each specimen was at the peak of health before committing him to the freezing procedure. Each volunteer was subjected to the same testing used on the astronauts both before and after a flight into space. Every major organ was tested several ways, with readings correlated by computer for any systemic weakness that might fail under the stress of suspension. Three more men were eventually washed out at this stage of the operation, although since it was not their fault they were not required to pay back their bonuses. The word seeped back that the army was retaining them as combat training instructors, and most of the volunteers left in the program felt a little jealous. The washouts got all the advantages of the program, and cushy jobs besides, without having to face any of the risks.

The men were given little time to dwell on the possibilities of washing out, however. The day after the final weeding, the men were told to report to the laboratory building immediately after reveille. They were shown the equipment for the first time—large white coffins with thickly insulated walls. Hawker had expected to see tangles of wires leading from each coffin, as had been the case in the original films they'd been shown, but the machinery was much too sophisticated for that. These boxes were designed to be shipped anywhere in the world within thirty-six hours, if an emergency arose; they couldn't be entangled with needless spaghetti.

When Captain Dukakis announced that they were all to be prepped for the "final phase" of the experiment, there was a low rumbling through the group. None of the men had expected things to be this abrupt. "Don't we even get a last meal?" someone asked nervously. "Even a murderer gets that!"

"You had your last meal last night." Dukakis was nervous and impatient himself. "We've found the process works best when the subjects' stomachs are empty—otherwise ulcers tend to form. If your bodies develop any nutritional needs while you're asleep, we can handle them intravenously. Now get moving."

The men were led into a waiting room and processed five at a time. Green and Connors were taken in the same group, each man ignoring the other's existence. It was another forty-five minutes before Hawker, his stomach rumbling, was led off to the prepping room.

He was forced to strip completely, and underwent several enemas to clean out his bowels. This, the nurse explained brusquely, was to prohibit any impactions of waste products in his system while he was in suspension. His penis would be catheterized as well, but that would be done after he was unconscious to minimize the discomfort. He was given a mild sedative shot and led to his own box—number 37, he noticed.

"Won't it be awfully cold?" he asked suddenly as he was climbing inside.

"You'll be asleep before you can feel any drop in temperature," the nurse promised him.

Hawker stretched out in his box and tried to make himself comfortable. After all, he'd be here, he'd be in this box, for quite some time; he didn't want to wake up after ten years with a kink in his leg. But no matter how he stretched out, the box was just the triflest too narrow to allow him any comfort. But, on reflection, he thought that might have been done intentionally. The doctors wouldn't want him turning even slightly in his sleep and upsetting their instruments, so they'd make the fit as tight as possible.

Just as he thought he was settling in, the technicians around him began attaching instruments all over his body. One small disk was attached in the center of his forehead, two others at his temples, two more behind his ears, one on either side of his neck, one at the inside of each elbow, one at each wrist, four scattered over his torso and two at his groin. The sedative was beginning to take effect by now; Hawker watched the people work and felt only a distant detachment. He drifted peacefully off to sleep before the instrumentation was even completed.

The technicians and the nurses moved more quickly once the patient was fully anesthetized. They finished placing their instruments, monitored them for several minutes to make sure they were all in working order, inserted a catheter to empty Hawker's bladder of the last drops of urine and finally, when all was in readiness, they lowered the transparent cover over coffin number 37 and moved on to the next subject.

Hawker slept.

If there were dreams—or any brain activity at all, for that matter—they did not register on the sensitive instruments that monitored his condition. For all practical purposes, Hawker was a corpse in a cryogenic

65

coffin. Pulse, respiration, brain waves, metabolic rate, all the normal systems used to register signs of life showed readings so close to zero as to seem negligible.

Those same vital signs, though, were monitored constantly by a series of computers, wary for even the slightest deviation from the constant value. Those computers, in turn, were monitored by other computers, which were checked by human beings. The army was risking a great deal on this experiment, and wanted nothing to go wrong. There were fail-safes and redundancies built into every step of the process. The condition of those men in the boxes was monitored more closely than humans had ever been monitored before.

Captain (later Major) Dukakis even made personal inspection trips down into "the Vault" to observe the men himself. Peering through the transparent coffin lids, his eyes searched in vain for any telltale signs of trouble. But as the days turned to weeks and the months to years, there was no trouble at all. Everything, for once, went exactly as planned.

Hawker slept—and outside his sleep, the world moved as usual.

His first sensations on awakening were of warmth and light around him. His skin was tingling oddly, like the pins-and-needles feeling when a foot goes to sleep, only all over his body. He thought about scratching, but he was so tired that he was loath to make the effort just now. The sensation wasn't that uncomfortable. He would just lie here for a few minutes and gather his strength.

He tried rolling over on his side and his muscles, sore from long disuse, protested. He drew in a sudden gasp, and then realized what all this meant. If he were still in the suspension coffin, there wouldn't be room to turn over. And if he were still frozen, he wouldn't be able to think all these things.

He tried to open his eyes, but even that was too much effort for now. All he could do was lie in bed and think. He didn't feel any different from when he lay down in the coffin; surely he couldn't have been asleep for very long. The project must have been a failure for some reason, and they'd awakened him prematurely. There was a certain amount of disappointment in that thought, but even more relief. He disliked the notion of being connected with something that flopped, but on the other hand he wouldn't have to face the future he'd feared, either. The army could scarcely blame him for the failure; he'd done his best. Maybe they'd give him the option of being a training instructor and let him stay in for life.

After a while he finally pried his eyelids open, and had to blink back the tears until his eyes could get adjusted to the room's brightness. When he could look around, turning his head slowly against neck muscles that protested every movement, he could see he was in a large ward with many other men. All were lying still in their beds, covered by sheets and blankets, as he was himself. Everyone, himself included, was being fed intravenously from glucose bottles hanging beside the beds. His mind was still a little too fuzzy to count the other beds, but there were a lot of them. He was not an individual case, then, a single accident within the program. The army had thawed out most or all of the other volunteers as well. That did not speak well for the scientists behind Project Banknote; someone's head was likely to roll because of this. Not for the first time, Hawker was glad he didn't have to take responsibility for a mistake.

Even the minuscule exertion of looking around him was wearing, and he lay back on his bed, exhausted. He closed his eyes, and was asleep again before he knew it—a natural sleep, for a natural duration; and if there were any dreams this time, he did not remember them.

He awoke again to the sound of someone walking up to his bed. A hand reached under the covers to touch his arm and feel for a pulse. He opened his eyes suddenly and looked up into the nurse's face.

The nurse was a middle-aged, heavyset lady with gray-blond hair and a professionally concerned expression. She was wearing a tight white uniform that was unmistakably medical, though her short hair was cropped in an unfamiliar style. The mere fact that a nurse was still recognizably a nurse brought Hawker a sense of relief. Some things hadn't changed while he'd been "away"; whatever time in the future this was, he would not be a complete stranger to it.

The nurse saw him looking up at her and smiled. "Hi," she said in a pleasant voice. "How are you feeling?"

He struggled to return her smile. "Weak," he answered, and his voice was hoarse and scratchy. "Tired," he added as an afterthought.

"Weak I can understand, but as for tired you've already done your share of sleeping. Although," she added, half to herself, "too much sleep can make you tired, too." She checked his pulse against her watch, and jotted the figures down on the chart at the foot of his bed.

"How . . . how long did I . . ."

The nurse shook her head. "Don't worry yourself about details right now. Just rest and gather your strength. The major will be in to brief you tomorrow, as soon as everyone is awake and recovered." And with that she moved off down the ward to check the rest of the patients.

Hawker watched her make her rounds, until finally she left the ward. Then he noticed one of the other patients half propped up on his elbows, looking at him. The man was on the other side of the room, about two beds down. Hawker tried to remember who he was, and the name Johnston came to mind.

"You won't get any straight answers out of her," Johnston said. His voice was weak, but a little better than Hawker's. "I've been awake for two days now, and nobody wants to tell me anything. I think they're afraid of something."

"Maybe they're afraid to shock us," came the voice of another man, Pastorelli. "Maybe they want to wait and tell us all at once, so rumors don't spread."

"I think maybe the whole thing was a failure," Hawker volunteered. "It sure didn't *feel* like I slept too long."

Johnston smiled. "Yeah, maybe that's it. Maybe they flopped, and now they're scared to admit it."

Hawker looked around the ward, taking in some more details. There were twenty beds in here, ten on each side of the long room. About half the patients now seemed to be awake to some degree. From his limited vantage point, Hawker couldn't see either Green or Symington in the room; they must be in other wards. He was disappointed at not being with them at this time of confusion, but he wasn't really worried. They were probably all right; for all he knew, they could be in the very next room.

The temperature in the ward was very warm, but whether it was summer or whether the hospital chose to keep the temperature up in the room, he couldn't tell. The other men in the ward who were awake were talking among themselves, exchanging theories on what had happened and how long they'd been asleep. Hawker didn't contribute further to the conversation. It was clear, after listening to what the various parties had to say, that no one *knew* anything. All they had to go by was guesses and opinions; to Hawker, such things were worse than useless. The nurse had said some major would be in tomorrow to brief them; he could wait until then. For the moment it was sufficient to know that he was alive and in good health; he'd worry about the rest when the time came. Right now, he needed his sleep.

Every man in the ward was awake by the next day, and everyone—Hawker included, though he didn't show it—was intensely curious about the experiment's outcome. All eyes went to the door when Dukakis entered the room. The recruiter for Project Banknote was in a major's uniform now, but that meant little; the promotion itself could have come at any time, and the men needn't have been suspended for more than a week or two to have missed it.

But it was Dukakis himself that caused the men to stare. The man had aged perceptibly. His face was lined, now, and his hair was graying at the temples and sideburns. He was twenty to thirty pounds heavier and there was a slower, more tired feeling to his walk. Hawker began to feel nervous again. Those changes hadn't come about overnight, and he realized that perhaps his initial thought was wrong, that perhaps the experiment wasn't such a failure after all.

Dukakis walked slowly to the center of the room, turning so he could look at each of the men who were staring at him. There was a smile on his lips, but it never reached to his eyes.

"Hello again, men," he said. "First of all, I again want to thank you for taking part in this experiment. The army has already learned a great deal, and we expect to learn still more in the future with your continued assistance.

"To cover the subject that I'm sure is uppermost in all your minds, let me say first that Project Banknote has been an enormous success, far exceeding our most optimistic expectations. The group of you was kept in suspended animation for eleven years, five months and thirteen days, and it took a mere three days from the time of taking you out of your suspension chambers until this present moment."

A startled gasp went through the room. Although Dukakis's appearance had given the men some warning that time had passed, none of them was quite prepared for the actual amount. Almost a dozen years had slipped beneath them. And yet none of them felt any different, or even as much as a day older than they had when they settled into their coffins.

Dukakis paused to let the basic facts sink into the men's minds. When he had their full attention again, he continued his briefing. "You have all survived the most unknown phase of the experiment—more than survived, in fact. Each of you, and all your colleagues in the other wards, appears to be in perfect physical condition. You've all mentioned experiencing weakness, but we anticipated that; even though your minds don't notice any time discrepancy, your muscles do. There's been eleven and a half years of disuse to overcome, but we've established a program of physical therapy and calisthenics that should mold you back into fighting shape in less than two weeks. Once that's accomplished, we'll be moving into the next phase of the experiment.

"As you recall, the main reason for conducting this program was not to see whether men could be frozen for indefinite periods of time; that had already been pretty well established by earlier experiments. No, we had you suspended because we knew that sooner or later there'd be another war, and we'd need good trained fighters to help us in the initial phases, until more of our draftees can become battle-hardened. That war is here, and you're going to have to prove yourselves in battle once again. The army is hoping you'll do as well there as you did in the suspension tanks."

"Who are we fighting, sir?" one of the soldiers asked.

A portion of the old Captain Dukakis showed through, the man who hated having his well-rehearsed spiel interrupted. He turned and glared at the man who'd asked the question, then had to recalibrate his mental processes to answer it. "The situation is very complex," he said slowly. "You'll be given a much more thorough briefing on the exact political nature of the endeavor in due course. For right now, let me just say that there is a civil war in China. The incumbent government is being challenged by a reactionary clique of Maoist/Leninists. The Russians stepped in to help the rebels, so we ended up being forced to help the official government."

"You mean we're fighting to save Communists?" One of the men, Litwak, thought this was incredibly funny, but his humor was lost on Dukakis.

"I see nothing to laugh at," the major said. "And I doubt you will either, once you're dropped into combat. This is a hard and dirty war, as bad as any action you saw in Africa. It had already been going for nearly two years before we became involved, and the casualty rate is very high. Fortunately, according to our agreement with the Chinese government, the troops we provide will be mainly for support; their own soldiers will do most of the actual fighting. Still, we thought it best to activate you and see how you do under actual field conditions. Don't expect a picnic over there; neither side shows the slightest bit of restraint or mercy to the other. The atrocities make My Lai and Katumbwe look like Sunday school outings."

Dukakis paused. "My portion of this particular experiment is over. I doubt you'll be seeing me again." One soldier started clapping, but Dukakis stared him back into silence. "Starting tomorrow, there's more hard work in store for you. As I said, lots of physical therapy and calisthenics. There are also a few new developments in weapons that you'll have to familiarize yourself with—nothing you can't handle, though, in view of your special training.

"You'll find you can talk about the project openly, now. The secrecy was lifted a couple of months ago, when we were debating whether to use you in this war. Everyone knows the sacrifices you made, and the courage it took to make them. In some circles, you're even being regarded as heroes. People are only now beginning to appreciate the applications of these suspended animation techniques to civilian life. You

72

helped make it possible, and the United States is grateful.

"In two weeks, you'll be shipped out to China. You've been in battle before, you know what to do. Just acquit yourselves as well in the field as you've done so far in the laboratory and I know that the army—and I personally—will be proud of you."

Dukakis saluted smartly twice, once to each side of the room, then turned and walked down the center aisle and out the door. Behind him he left a silence that lasted well over a minute as the men considered what he'd told them, and how their lives would be affected—both by the war and by their eleven-and-a-half-year isolation from the world.

That evening, while the glucose tubes were still in their arms, the soldiers received their first meal since awakening: lukewarm chicken broth and a dish of lemon Jell-o. The men started an uproar all at once; if they were heroes, they should eat like heroes. They'd been cheated out of a big "last meal" before being frozen, and they felt that their first meal after waking should be a little more impressive. The nurses listened to the complaints with a minimum of tolerance, and continued to serve the food as ordered.

Despite their protests, the volunteers found they had trouble eating even as basic a meal as this. Their digestive systems needed time to readjust to real food, the nurses told them afterward. It was all perfectly normal, and had been anticipated. By the next day, most of the men would be eating normally again. In the meantime, less than half the men were able to finish the meager servings they were given, and some ended up vomiting what they'd eaten. Hawker himself had eaten three quarters of his meal, and paid for it the rest of the night with a painful series of stomach cramps that kept him from getting much sleep.

The meal the next morning was virtually the same,

except for the addition of tea. After breakfast, the nurses removed the soldiers' IV tubes; most of the men were fed up with bedpans, and the nurses spent a large percentage of their time helping the volunteers walk to the lavatories at either end of the ward.

After that, the patients were placed on gurneys and wheeled to a large physical therapy room—actually a gym that had been converted for this purpose. They lay on tables and were placed at the mercy of machines that stretched and bent them in more ways than they knew existed. All of them were sore and exhausted by the time they returned to their ward for lunch, but they were not allowed to sleep. After the bland midday meal, each man got a small TV and headset, and they watched a videotaped briefing on the background of the Chinese civil war.

There had always been factionalism within the Chinese Communist hierarchy, the briefing officer explained, and as a result the country went through periodic violent upheavals. By the middle of the 1970s, the moderates had gotten into power, and were noted for placing the improvement of their country above ideological purity. With a few major and explosive lapses, the moderates had held control of the central government ever since—but the militant Communists, who believed in their doctrine with religious fervor, were seldom happy with the course the moderates charted.

Running as a parallel thread through modern history was the antagonism between the two major Communist superpowers, China and the Soviet Union. Border incidents had flared between the two almost since the Chinese Communists' takeover at the century's halfway mark. There had been reports of occasional fighting over the years, but the harshest sniping of all had been on the propaganda front, where each nation accused the other of the most disreputable behavior. There had always been the threat of all-out warfare, but until recently it hadn't materialized.

74

Now the Russians saw their opportunity. The Chinese militants were stronger than they'd been for years, and intelligence reports indicated they'd been making life hell for the ruling moderates. When the moderates finally clamped down, the militants appealed to Moscow for aid. The Russians were actually being *invited* into China by a revolutionary group that needed their assistance. The Kremlin leaders saw this as a perfect chance to drive a solid wedge into their enemy's territory and at last gain the upper hand in their decades-long war of nerves with China.

Their only consideration, of course, was how the United States would react. The United States had been playing off the two Communist superpowers for years, and would not look favorably on a Russian effort to tilt the scales. The Russians tested the waters and elicited an angry U.S. response, but judged that America was not willing to commit itself fully to China's defense. After months of indecision, the Russians stepped in on the side of the Chinese militants.

Now all the pressure shifted to the United States. As long as Russia and China had been evenly balanced, America could let things ride and drift with the political currents. The Russian invasion changed all that. If Russia succeeded in this power grab, they would end up ruling the largest empire in history, encompassing nearly a third of the human race. They would become an enemy more formidable than even the United States could effectively counter. There was strong pressure to step into the fighting on the Chinese government's side.

This pressure was countered, though, by an ideological pressure within the United States. To step in and preserve a Communist government seemed counter to American politics of the last sixty years. There were conservatives who loved nothing better than the thought of Russia and China fighting among themselves, hoping they'd knock each other off and leave the United States free to step in and pick up the pieces. President Livingston, himself a conservative Republican, wavered for nearly two years while pressure to intervene—coming from both the left and the center—grew ever stronger. The decisive factor, finally, was the Soviet nuclear strike—accidental, they claimed—against Shanghai. The United States could not remain neutral after that, and so, with great reluctance, President Livingston committed the nation to a military alliance with the Chinese government.

There would be further briefings, the men were told, about the nature of the fighting in China and the extent to which America had committed itself to aid its new ally, as well as briefings on the new weapons systems developed during their period of inactivity. But this briefing had lasted most of the afternoon, and it was now time for dinner. There was only so much these men could be expected to absorb so soon after their emergence from suspended animation.

The next day began the same way, with a painful physical therapy session. The men were feeling much stronger, however, and afterward they were led into an exercise yard, where they were reunited with the rest of the volunteers from other wards. There was great rejoicing when people saw that their friends had also survived the experiment; even the normally taciturn Hawker let out a whoop at seeing Green and Symington again for the first time since his awakening.

The three friends compared their waking experiences, which were basically similar, and complained about the food. Green remarked that the "chicken broth" was an insult to chickens the world over, and that his grandmother would spin in her grave if she knew he'd been drinking it. The men were allowed little time for chatting, though; a tough old drill sergeant named Jenks—whom everyone promptly termed "Jinx"—came out and set them a series of calisthenics that drove them all to the brink of physical exhaustion. The men could barely make it back to their wards under their own power at the end of the session.

The days passed in a regular progression. The men were introduced to the new weapons, including the laser rifles and the satellite-guided bullets, whose trajectories could actually be altered by instructions from a spy-satellite overhead for pinpoint accuracy against the enemy. The men took these developments in stride; what mattered to them the most was that there had not been similar great advances in the army's food preparation technology.

By the end of the two weeks, Hawker felt he was in better condition than ever before in his life. He was fully recovered from his hibernation and in perfect health. His fears about this project had melted away to the point where he was actually looking forward to combat duty. It was something he knew, something he could cope with. The world was no stranger than it had been before, despite his earlier fears.

The only negative note was sounded by Green early in their second week of recuperation. During a short pause in the exercise period, the young man looked around the yard and frowned. "Hawk, how many of us were there the morning we all got frozen?"

"Seventy-nine, I think. Why?"

"That's what I thought. There are only seventy-seven of us here now, and as far as I can remember that's all there's been since we woke up. I wonder if anything happened to the other two."

A chill went down Hawker's spine. The army had been emphasizing how pleased it was with the success of the project, and how it had exceeded all their expectations—but nowhere was it stated that the project was free of mishaps. Had two men actually died during the experiment, or had they perhaps merely been awakened early because of some malfunction of their equipment? It was a question he never learned the answer to—and to make matters worse, no matter how hard he strained his memory he could not remember which two men were no longer a part of the group. They had simply vanished from his universe as though they'd never been.

Hawker's mind was flexible. During his previous combat tours, dozens of people had drifted in and out of his acquaintance, never to be seen again. And, after nearly a twelve-year gap, he would have to get used to the fact that there were many things in life that had passed from his acquaintance. After a while, he ceased to think of the missing men. They were just statistics; let the army take care of them.

At the end of the two weeks, when the volunteers had fully recovered from their long sleep, they were sent to China as promised. Once there, their group was broken up and disseminated among other outfits. The whole point of the experiment, after all, was to put these combat veterans into units with greener troops, thereby passing on the benefit of their experience; there was little to be gained by keeping them together.

The night before they were separated, Hawker, Green and Symington went out together on the town. Wartime Beijing was a strangely subdued city; unlike the African metropolises of the previous war, it had not yet discovered the lucrative business of catering to the needs of soldiers on leave. Symington, though, had an instinctive knack for finding the places with the most action. The three friends drank well into the night, swearing their undying friendship for one another and vowing to get together again when this war was over. None of them really thought they would, though; they knew too well the odds against the three of them surviving the coming war. Even if they did all live through the experience, the army had a million ways to keep friends apart. When they separated, it was likely to be for keeps.

Hawker joined his new outfit the next day. It was a convoy detail escorting shipments of arms and supplies to outlying districts. Hawker and the team assigned to him were supposed to ride shotgun and make sure the equipment was delivered to the proper people—or, if an ambush developed, to blow up the trucks and make certain the supplies did *not* end up in enemy hands. Hawker was given the authority to kill as many of his men and destroy as much of the convoy as necessary—and that scared him.

He was scared, too, by the responsibilities of command that were suddenly thrust upon him. There were officers above him in this unit, and theoretically his influence was small. But practice turned out to be another matter altogether. When it came to combat experience, the officers were as green as the ordinary sluggos—and *they* were fresh out of boot camp in most cases. Everyone in the outfit knew that Hawker was one of the "sleepers," and he was looked upon as the Old Man of the group. It was startling to realize that technically he *was* the oldest man in the unit, beating out even the captain by several years even though he looked no older than most of the other recruits.

Hawker was ill at ease with his new position. He was constantly being asked for advice—and for a man who hated talking as much as he did this was almost physically painful. He could not simply answer with a few well-chosen words; it was his duty, he knew, to provide instruction with his advice. He had to let the others know why things were done one certain way and not another, and he often had trouble elucidating his reasons. He had developed an instinct for survival in enemy territory. Certain things *felt* wrong—but how could he put that feeling into words?

His position within the unit was awkward, too. The officers above him felt he undermined their authority because the men went to him for advice instead of to them—and also because they sometimes had to consult him themselves, which was humiliating. The other recruits resented him because he was one of them, but slightly better. Physically he was as young as they

79

were, but he was given preferential treatment that they would have liked themselves.

Because of his unique position, Hawker had no friends within his outfit. The other men's hostility never flared into open fights or insults, but Hawker could feel it tangibly nonetheless. He ate alone and was never included in the friendly byplay that made life at the front barely tolerable. As far as anyone was concerned, he was a man from outer space, hated and respected at the same time.

Hawker's convoys had little contact with the enemy— a few firefights and skirmishes, but only a couple of minor injuries, no casualties and no serious threats to the safety of the convoy itself. Whether this was due to his expert precautions, or whether he just had a cushy assignment, he couldn't say—but he knew he could never dare relax as long as he was here, because *that* would be the moment things went wrong.

It was, naturally enough, his last convoy that hit the big trouble. The convoy was nearing its destination, a small base guarding a mountain pass, and everyone aboard was thinking how good it would be to reach the end of the line so they could dump their cargo and return home the next day. Return trips were, if no less dangerous, then certainly less burdensome. Home base also had bathing facilities lacking in the outlying areas, and that in itself was no mean consideration. The men got tired of their own sweat very quickly.

It had started to rain, and the trucks were having a hard time pulling their loads up the steep slopes along roads that were little more than dirt tracks. Suddenly, in the distance ahead of them, they could hear the repeated sound of gunfire. The trucks stopped instantly and the men reached for their rifles, but they realized almost at once that the shooting was not directed at them. It came from their destination, the small firebase ahead. The enemy was attacking it in strength, trying to capture it while it was low on supplies and perhaps get into position to take the supplies for themselves.

The convoy's captain called ahead and received a harried description of the situation. A savage bout of dysentery had reduced the effective manpower to almost half the complement, even before the attack. The base had the advantage of position—it was well fortified on top of a hill—but that was about all. The Ruchinks were charging in waves, taking heavy casualties in a determined effort to capture the base. The bad weather was impeding satellite assistance, and other attacks elsewhere along this line were keeping air retaliation busy. Unless additional ammunition from the convoy could be delivered quickly, the firebase was likely to be overrun, giving the enemy free access to the valley beyond.

The convoy captain looked at Hawker, then made a decision on his own: the convoy would move forward and try to reinforce the firebase at all costs. Hawker did not speak up or object to that plan; he wasn't even sure that he should, since he had no better idea in mind himself. But it did seem that driving straight into the face of danger was not the safest course open. He gripped his rifle tighter and prepared for action.

They had almost made it to the base when they saw some forms approaching quickly through the gloom. The men in the front trucks raised their weapons and prepared to fire, but held up long enough to establish that the soldiers were government troops fleeing the base. The fortress had been overrun, and the enemy was approaching quickly. This entire valley would belong to the rebels by sunrise.

The captain had a tough decision. There was no room for his trucks to turn around on these narrow mountain roads, and he could scarcely order them to back downhill in the rain. At the same time, moving forward was suicide. Reluctantly, he decided to make a stand where he was. He radioed back to headquarters, informing them of his predicament and begging for help. Headquarters was noncommittal, saying they would do what they could, when they could. The convoy was on its own.

The captain gave orders for his men to leave the trucks and take up positions in front and to either side. At the same time, he gave orders to ready the convoy for demolition, should the Ruchinks overcome them. These supplies must not fall into enemy hands.

Hawker didn't bother worrying about those considerations. While it was true he had the authority to order the trucks blown up, there were still a captain, a lieutenant and several sergeants ranking above him to make that decision. As long as any of them was alive, he could let them have the responsibility. He was particularly responsible for making sure the men behaved well under fire, and this was his first real opportunity to test himself and them.

The refugees from the captured fortress came in waves, now. Some of them were fleeing so fast that they ran right past the convoy's barricade, but most slowed their flight and ended up joining the lines of defense. The additional support made Hawker feel slightly more confident, but the situation would still be rather touchy. Everything depended on how badly the enemy had depleted its own troops in taking the base; if the Ruchinks were too badly hurt themselves, perhaps they wouldn't follow up on their victory and keep their opponents on the run.

Perhaps. Hawker had learned by now not to live on such fragile hopes.

As he'd feared, the rebels did want to pursue the battle and keep the loyalists running. Even before Hawker could catch sight of the enemy, his comrades at the other side of the line had opened fire on the advancing soldiers. The rainy atmosphere was soon peppered with the sound of gunshots, and Hawker could hear stray bullets whizzing past his location. He told the men around him to hold their fire until they had a clearer target—but it wasn't long before the

82

enemy came into view, advancing slowly through the gloom of a drizzly dusk.

The fighting continued on and off for half an hour, but it was very clear to Hawker that it was little more than a holding action; the Ruchinks had superior manpower, and were just waiting for the proper moment to regroup and make their decisive charge. Unless the convoy could be reinforced by airstrikes from home base, there was little to prevent their position from being overrun—and home base was still diddling around about committing themselves to support this rearguard action. Hawker had been in the army long enough to know when he was being considered expendable—and he didn't much like it.

The battlefield suddenly grew ominously still as the Ruchinks ceased firing for several minutes and drew back slightly from their forward positions. The captain and lieutenant conferred, then sent the word out over the walkie-talkies: the enemy was probably preparing for its big charge, and the convoy had only one major trick up its sleeve. When the rebels came rushing in, the convoy would blow up the trucks, hoping to cause enough confusion to allow the men to escape.

Nothing was said about the pattern of retreat. Hawker correctly surmised it would be every man for himself.

The charge came moments later, hundreds of Ruchinks—looking dirty and ill-clad, but very well-armed—running down the hill through the rain, screaming and shooting as they came. Hawker and his fellows fell back, as ordered, drawing the enemy into range. Then, with blinding suddenness, half the hillside exploded into day.

The trucks had been rigged ahead of time to provide a dazzling display of pyrotechnics. They exploded in sequence rather than all at once, providing almost a full minute of blasts that shook the ground and lit the

83

countryside as bright as the noonday sun. Hawker hit the ground and buried himself face down in the mud, counting the explosions—one for each truck. Rocks and debris tossed skyward by the blasts pelted down on him, and even after the last truck had blown he waited several seconds before gettting to his feet again and looking around to get his bearings.

The scene was chaotic, to put it mildly. Soldiers from both sides were lying dead in the road, having been too near the trucks when they exploded. Still others lay dying or injured—and from what Hawker had seen of this war so far, there was little concern about tending the wounded. Most of them would probably die, slowly and painfully. Of the rest, many were still recovering from the shock of the blasts. If ever there was a time to escape, this was it.

Crouching low to hide himself in the tall grass and boulders alongside the road, Hawker began his awkward run from the scene of the battle. Home base was more than fifty kilometers away, but he didn't think he'd have to travel that far on foot; there were advance patrols out constantly, and if he could hook in with one of them he could ride the rest of the way home. Everything depended, though, on his staying alive between here and there.

He tripped over something lying hidden in the grass, and nearly went sprawling; only quick reflexes and a good sense of balance kept him on his feet. He looked back to see what had upset him, and saw that it was a body dressed in a U.S. uniform. That in itself was no indication—rebel soldiers frequently dressed in captured uniforms to fool the loyalists—but the man was also black, which almost guaranteed his being on Hawker's side. The enemy forces were mostly Chinese, aided sometimes by Russians who were white or Eurasian; any blacks were sure to be Americans.

The man at first appeared dead, and Hawker started to move on when the fellow moaned softly. Torn between the desire to run and the impulse at least to

84

check the extent of the other's injuries, Hawker stood still for a moment. Then his humanitarian instincts won out, and he moved to the black man's side. "Take it easy," he whispered. "Don't make any noise, or they'll spot us. Let me see how you're doing."

He rolled the man over on his back, and recognized him almost immediately. It was Thaddeus Connors.

Connors was bleeding from a bullet hole in his abdomen. He'd lost a lot of blood already, and the wound showed no signs of closing. His face was contorted with pain and it was unlikely, in his condition and in the fading light of dusk, that he recognized Hawker. He tried to talk, but the pain was too great and he could only gasp a couple of syllables.

"I've seen men live with worse," Hawker said, reaching for the first-aid kit at his belt. He remembered the all-too-brief lecture on the items in the kit, including bandages coated with their own coagulant to retard bleeding. "Just press the bandage against the wound," the instructor had said, "and hold it there tightly until the bleeding stops. If it takes more than two minutes, move on—the patient's beyond your help."

There was little light left to see what he was doing—just the rapidly fading light of a rain-soaked day and the distant fires of the burning trucks. Hawker ripped off the paper covering and held the bandage tightly to Connors's stomach. Whatever the chemical was, it seemed to work; the bleeding stopped in less than two minutes, and Hawker used some of his kit's adhesive tape to secure the bandage in place. Connors had passed out in the meantime and Hawker, kneeling beside him, sat back on his heels to think what he should do next.

He owed nothing to Connors, beyond what any human being owed to another. The man had always been hostile to him—and dangerously so in that men's room incident. Hawker didn't like him, and his mind could make a good case for abandoning the man right here beside the road. He'd already done more than his share by stopping the bleeding; he'd perhaps saved Connors's life. He had his own welfare to consider; why jeopardize himself to aid a man who'd been nothing but trouble?

There was not a single good reason—except that Hawker had been raised with the belief that one had to help one's fellow man. For all his belligerence, Connors was still a colleague—and he was one of the few remaining people from Hawker's own world of the past, one of the few who could understand the special problems of being dissociated from normal time. For that alone, Connors was valuable to him.

Hawker pondered the problem. They certainly couldn't stay here if they hoped to escape. Even if the rebels didn't see them during the night, they'd have almost no chance of avoiding detection tomorrow. Their main hope was to be far enough away from here by morning that the enemy would have to spread out more to conduct a search.

The night would be both blessing and hindrance. Its darkness would give Hawker and his patient cover to slip back toward home base secretly; the rebels' night-time detection equipment had never been very effective. If they could make reasonably good time during the night, they could find someplace to hide and sleep during the day.

On the other hand, traveling at night would hold its own hazards for them. There were large stretches of ground between here and the base that had been mined by one side or the other; it didn't matter whose mine he stepped on, the end results would not be pretty. The road itself was safe; it was regularly swept clean of mines. But staying directly on the road meant being more easily spotted by enemy snipers. . . .

Hawker shook his head as he found his mind traveling around in circles. He would have to improvise some form of compromise, traveling near the road to minimize the risk of mines, but not so near that the enemy would spot him.

Looking down at his patient, he could see that Connors's eyes were open again. The man was conscious and breathing a little more easily. "Feeling ready to move?" Hawker asked him. They'd already tarried here far too long; the enemy troops would be advancing soon to snatch as much territory under cover of darkness as they could.

Connors gave a short, bitter laugh. "Ain't no good, man," he said. "I'm dead."

"Naw, you're only lazy, just like all you niggers."

That did it. Hawker could see the spark of fire returning to Connors's eyes. "Motherfuckin' honky bastard," he said. "You just get me on my feet and I'll show you who's lazy." He grabbed Hawker's upper arm to use as a crutch, and pulled himself up so hard that Hawker was almost yanked off balance. Connors made it to his feet, though, and stood for a moment swaying unsteadily. He was obviously weak from the loss of blood.

"I figured we could walk back to base," Hawker whispered. "You can put your arm around my shoulders and lean on me. . . ."

"Fuck that shit! Thaddeus Connors don't lean on no white man."

"Suit yourself. But we've got to get going now, or the Ruchinks'll be crawling up our asses."

Hawker led the way, bending over and walking parallel to the road but about twenty meters from it. Connors followed much more slowly, but too proud to take any help. Hawker felt frustrated that, despite the ever present peril, they couldn't move any faster than a wounded man could stagger. Time after time, the thought occurred to him that he could travel better alone. He could find a safe hiding place for Connors and go on until he reached safety, then send a team back for the man. But no matter how tempting the idea, he never once mentioned it. Connors was his responsibility for the moment. He might hate that fact, but there was little he could do to change it.

Connors stumbled and fell several times, but each time Hawker came over to help him up, the other waved him away and struggled back to his feet himself. Although Hawker had been proud of his little stratagem for getting Connors moving, he was now beginning to wonder whether it was entirely wise. It would be of little use if Connors walked himself to death rather than admit he needed Hawker's help.

Hawker estimated they'd covered about four kilometers when Connors fell and could not get to his feet again. Sitting beside his fallen companion, Hawker tried to make it sound as though stopping here had been his idea all along. "I think we're far enough from the battle to be safe for the night. We'll rest here till dawn, then find a place to hide during the day. We can travel some more tomorrow night."

There was no answer; Connors had already passed out. With a sigh, Hawker moved a few meters away and found a comfortable spot where he could lean against a small boulder. He unslung his rifle from his back, set it on automatic and laid it gently on his lap. Leaning back against his rock, he closed his eyes and allowed the fatigue of the day's tensions to wash over him. Like most soldiers, Hawker had learned the knack of resting whenever he could grab the time; within minutes he had fallen asleep, leaving the worries and insecurities until the next morning.

He woke with the first light of dawn and sat still for a moment, allowing the recollections of the previous night to filter back into his brain. His body was stiff from having spent the night on the cold ground in an awkward position. After looking around to make sure he would not be seen by any Ruchinks in the area, Hawker stood up and stretched his muscles, then went over to check his patient. Connors was still unconscious.

Hawker next checked their environment. They had made it down the mountainside during the night, and were now in a field a dozen meters from the road.

There was not a person in sight; nothing moved except a few birds circling lazily overhead. The sky had partially cleared after the night's rainfall; patches of blue sky showed between the clouds. Perhaps when the sun came up it would actually be warm. Hawker looked forward to that; his uniform was still cold and soggy from last night.

There was a drainage ditch off to the left. It would provide the best cover around here during the day. With great difficulty he lifted Connors up under the arms and dragged him slowly across the ground to the ditch, then eased the man down into it and crawled in himself. Only then did he feel reasonably secure.

He hadn't eaten anything since lunchtime yesterday, and his belly was loudly reminding him of that fact. He did have some protein tablets in the survival kit on his belt, but he was reluctant to take them yet. He didn't know how much longer he'd be stranded out here before he could reach the base, and he might need the tablets more desperately later. He'd gone hungry before in the army; he could stand another day or so before resorting to the pills.

Water was another matter. The drainage ditch contained several large muddy puddles; the water didn't look very appealing now, but it might later. His canteen was about half full, and he noticed that Connors had his canteen, too, though Hawker didn't know how much it contained. With any luck, they'd have enough fluids to last them until they reached help.

Connors awoke shortly after sunup. He still seemed very much in pain, but was resolved not to show it. The two men stared silently across the ditch at one another for several minutes before Connors broke the silence. "You're a sleeper too, aren't you?"

"Yeah," Hawker said.

"Thought I recognized you. You're the dude who hangs around with Fuckface and the Jew-boy, right?"

Hawker said nothing, afraid of being unable to hold back his temper. He disliked having people say nasty things about his friends—particularly people whose lives he'd just saved.

"Always the quiet one. Why'd you let them sucker you into signing up for this shit?"

Hawker shrugged. "I don't know. It just felt like the thing to do."

"Stupid," Connors said, shaking his head.

Hawker could contain his anger no longer. "If you're so fucking smart, how come you're here?"

"Mind your own fucking business." The wound had done little to improve Connors's congeniality. The two men didn't speak the rest of the morning.

By midafternoon, though, Connors's condition became more serious. Though the sun had broken through the clouds and was warming the ground, the wounded man was taken by a shivering fit. He squirmed in the mud and clutched his stomach, his teeth chattering audibly. Hawker moved over to his side. "Let me have a look at that."

"I'll be okay," Connors insisted.

Hawker ignored the other's protests and bent over for a closer examination. The wound had not reopened, but the area immediately around it was looking pale and puffy. He touched the region experimentally and Connors cried out in pain.

Hawker pulled back and frowned. He was no medic, and he wasn't sure what to do now. Checking his first-aid kit, he found a packet of pills labeled "general antibiotic," and another couple of pills that promised to be strong painkillers. He gave one of each to Connors, who was by now shivering so badly he could barely swallow them. Hawker remembered reading somewhere that wrapping a person in blankets was supposed to help—but he had no blankets, only the clothes each of them was wearing. Even if Hawker were to strip and wrap his own clothes around Connors, it would do little good; the clothes were still pretty wet from their soaking the night before. He left Connors

90

as he was, and returned to his spot a few meters away where he could watch the other's progress.

Despite the pills, Connors only seemed to get worse. His shivering fits increased in intensity and his moaning grew louder. He drifted in and out of consciousness and thrashed about on the ground, sometimes so violently that Hawker had to come over and restrain him to prevent the man from hurting himself. Connors began mumbling to himself, too—quietly, at first, but as his fever mounted his voice grew in volume until Hawker could not help overhearing the delirious ravings.

"I killed him!" Connors cried out during one fit of convulsions. "My God, I killed the bastard!"

Hawker moved over and held him steady. "We've all killed people," he said soothingly. "It's not fun, but that's what war's all about."

Connors sat up suddenly and stared into Hawker's face. His eyes were wide open, the whites glistening and his pupils reduced to a pair of black pinpoints. There was a mad, uncomprehending quality about them that sent a chill up Hawker's spine.

"Not pigs, man, we don't kill pigs!" Connors's voice was harsh and rasping.

Hawker was so startled by Connors's sudden action that it took the words a few moments to settle into his brain. "A cop?" he asked. "You killed a cop?"

"I had to, man. He was coming at me, had a gun. I had to."

"Where was this? When?"

"Detroit. I was seventeen." Connors closed his eyes and began another series of convulsions. "No, keep him away, I won't kill him again. Gotta run, gotta keep running." He started screaming, and Hawker had to cup a hand over his mouth to shut him up. It would do them no good at all if enemy soldiers heard the shouts and came to investigate.

The fit eventually wore off, as the previous ones

91

had, and Connors lapsed back into unconsciousness. His delirious revelations, though, gave Hawker something to think about as he sat there resting in the ditch, not quite daring to sleep for fear of discovery. Connors's raving may simply have been nightmares induced by this fever, with no basis in reality at all. It was hard to put much credence in anything the man said while he was in this condition.

But if it were true, if Connors actually had killed a policeman in Detroit during his youth, it would answer a lot of questions. He would be on the run, hiding out in the Army during a war. The army was a large impersonal machine where it was easy for an individual to get lost. And since there was no statute of limitations on murder, Connors might be afraid to leave. It was fear of being forced into the outside world that had prompted his volunteering for the experiment, despite the fact that he thought it was stupid and dangerous. Being forced into the program against his will, he would be sensitive about his reasons—sensitive enough to draw a knife on Symington when the latter innocently remarked on it in the rest room of that bar.

There was no doubt about it. Connors had a temper that could lead him to murder, and he was sensitive about something. That was a dangerous combination. Perhaps, Hawker thought, he should have left Connors back there at the convoy anyway, and saved himself and everyone else a lot of trouble.

He had started this course of action, though, and he had to follow it through. Hawker was not an imaginative man, and once set upon a path he followed it doggedly until its conclusion. He made himself responsible for Connors's safety, and he couldn't abandon him until either Connors was dead or the two of them had been rescued.

Connors's fever broke shortly before sundown, and by the time the sun was an hour past the horizon he was awake and coherent once more. He seemed to have no memory of what had happened during his delirium, and Hawker was reluctant to bring the subject up. If it were true, and Connors thought Hawker knew his "secret," God alone knew what he might do when both were safely back at the base.

Instead Hawker knelt beside his patient and said, "Feel like taking a little walk?"

"No," said Connors. "But I will anyway." He rolled over and got slowly to his feet under his own power. If anything, he seemed slightly stronger for having undergone his ordeal than he was last night, giving Hawker hope that they might cover more ground tonight.

They set off, walking at a slow but steady pace, and Connors seemed to be making a genuine effort to keep up with Hawker's impatient strides. Hawker kept a careful watch on the other man's progress, and insisted on frequent rest breaks whenever he thought Connors was being pushed too hard. At one point during the night they passed a small cluster of farm buildings, but they did not dare approach. There was no telling which side of the conflict the inhabitants were on, and Hawker preferred the calculated risk of staying outside to the unknown hazards of approaching these people.

Even with their frequent stops and slow pace, Hawker estimated they had covered about ten kilometers when the sky began glowing in the east. They found their shelter this time in a bombed-out shed. This area had seen much fighting in the past few months, and was sparsely inhabited. Connors slept most of the day, and Hawker dozed fitfully off and on, waking abruptly, rifle in hand, at any slight sound around them.

Connors was worse again that night. The pain of his wound, combined with the food deprivation and the strenuous activity, made him barely able to stand. He was in so much pain, in fact, that he raised no objection when Hawker came over and slid Connors's arm around his shoulder, letting the black man lean on him as a crutch. Even so, they could barely travel three kilometers when Connors collapsed again, and Hawker knew they would go no farther tonight. To make matters worse, the fever had returned. Hawker gritted his teeth in despair and frustration that he might have been able to get Connors this far only to have the man die anyway because Hawker was unable to give him the specialized care he needed.

Hawker must have dozed, because he suddenly found himself waking up with the light of dawn in his eyes. It wasn't the light that had awakened him, though, but a sound—the distant sound of an automobile engine. He checked his rifle and rose slowly to a half-crouch. He was about forty meters from the road at this point, and he looked cautiously along its length in both directions. There in the distance he could make out a small convoy of jeeps traveling slowly down the bumpy trail. They were coming from the direction of home base, and as they approached Hawker could see the markings that designated them as U.S. government property.

Standing up fully, he started waving and yelling in an effort to attract their attention and flag them down. The driver of the front jeep spotted him and said something to his companion. This second man suddenly raised his rifle and fired at Hawker. The bullet whizzed just past his ear.

Cursing, Hawker dived headlong to the ground, but not quite in time. There was a sharp pain in his left leg as a bullet hit his thigh, and the pain was compounded by the sharp impact as his belly hit the earth and the breath was knocked from his lungs. He almost blacked out, but managed to hold onto consciousness. He had dropped his rifle a few meters away when he fell, and he crawled back to retrieve it. The jeep had accelerated and left the road, and was almost upon him, but there had been no further shots since the one that hit his leg.

"Hold it, Corporal, he's one of us," he heard the

driver of the jeep say to the man who'd done the shooting, just as Hawker managed to pick up his own rifle and fumble it around in his hands so that it was pointing in the jeep's general direction. Then, to Hawker, the driver added, "Take it easy, pal, we're on your side."

"Fucking great way to show it," Hawker said through clenched teeth. Nevertheless he lowered his rifle and relaxed on the ground. The two men leaped out of their vehicle and ran over to him.

"Sorry, buddy," said the corporal who'd shot him. "I thought you were Ruchink. The area's crawling with them, and we were told to look out for ambushes."

Hawker looked into the corporal's anxious face. The kid was barely older than he was. *How'd he get to be a corporal?* Hawker mused, despite the pain. He swallowed back the first two retorts that came to mind, and said merely, "My friend over there's hurt pretty bad. We were in the supply convoy they overran a few days ago. Been trying to get back to base."

The two men ran over and checked Connors, confirming that he was still alive but in bad shape. They called in men from another jeep in the convoy, and Hawker and Connors were both loaded into the back of one vehicle and dispatched to the base.

Hawker remembered little of the four-hour ride. His leg was throbbing, despite the painkiller they gave him; all the pill did was make him woozy. The fatigue from his arduous trek and the lack of food for the past few days also contributed to his condition. He merely stared up at the sky, fading in and out of consciousness at irregular intervals.

Back at the base he was put in the hospital, where they removed the bullet from his leg and kept him in bed for a week. After that, he was permitted to walk around with a crutch for another couple of weeks while the doctors argued at what point he would be fit to return to light duty. He was informed that Connors had pulled through, thanks to his efforts, and one of the nurses told him privately that he'd been nominated for a medal for his heroic actions. Hawker wondered, a bit cynically, whether he'd also be eligible for the Purple Heart for being wounded in action.

The war ended the day before he was scheduled to be released from the hospital.

As the fighting ended, the rebel militants were left in control of the northern portions of Manchuria and Inner Mongolia, which the official Chinese government ended up ceding to them as an independent state, much as Outer Mongolia had been for decades. While there was still much bitterness between the two factions, the Chinese government felt the price they'd paid had secured something of value: a hostile, but still independent country to act as a buffer between themselves and the U.S.S.R. The Russians were pleased to have whittled away part of their major antagonist in the Communist world, but the cost in Russian lives and arms had been astronomical. The United States, at comparatively small cost to itself, had regained a certain uneasy stability in Asia.

In short, while no one was happy with what had been done, all parties were at least satisfied with the results—for now.

Hawker, meantime, was out of a job, and viewed the peace with mixed feelings. He had never liked war, had never enjoyed the prospect that someone he didn't even know was out there eager to rip his guts apart with a shrapnel grenade; but the thought of facing civilian life was almost as terrifying. He was right back where he'd started at the beginning of this experiment, facing a hostile world without sufficient resources or knowledge. The situation was even worse, in fact; the world was now twelve years older, and at the rate it had been changing who could tell how different the outside world would be?

A week after the war ended he was shipped back to the States in an enormous plane—larger than any he'd ever seen—with more than a thousand other servicemen. Everyone was tired of the fighting and glad to have survived. There was singing and swapping of stories; cigarettes and marijuana were passed around freely. But Hawker, as was his wont, kept apart from the rest. He wasn't one of them; he was a stranger out of time. He'd hoped to see Symington and Green, but neither man was on this flight. Hawker had no way of knowing whether either was still alive.

Back in the United States, the troops were housed in temporary quarters while their paperwork was processed. Hawker was in no hurry. He hoped that now, with all this experience behind him, the army would strongly consider letting him go career. They'd find some position for him—after all, there was always something that needed doing in the army.

Four days after his return, he saw a notice requesting all participants in Project Banknote to report for a special meeting the next day after lunch. His spirits rose instantly. For one thing, this would be a chance to find out whether his friends were still alive; for another, it would let him know specifically what the army expected of him now that the experiment was over. He arrived early for the meeting and took a seat near the back door of the room so he could see people as they entered.

This room was far smaller than the large auditorium in which he'd first heard about Project Banknote; there was only seating for forty people at most. Of course, that did not mean much; perhaps most of the sleepers were still over in China, or perhaps some of them had been shipped to other bases. But as people straggled in one or two at a time, Hawker found himself scanning their faces anyway for a sign of Green or Symington.

They showed up together, and greeted Hawker with happy shouts. In a three-way flurry of conversation, each of the friends tried to inform the others of his activities during the war. The stories were confused, at first, but Hawker learned that Symington had seen lots of action with an artillery division along the western front; Green, on the other hand, had been assigned to a clerical quartermaster's job through some error in paperwork, and hadn't seen a moment's action the entire time. Hawker and Symington were ribbing him when the briefing officer entered the room and interrupted their reunion.

They had been expecting Major Dukakis, but the officer standing before them introduced himself as Lieutenant Dickerson and explained that he was now in charge of recruitment for the suspended-animation program. He started his speech by thanking the men once again for participating in the pilot program; it was their efforts that made Project Banknote such a resounding success. Although sleepers had sustained almost a fifty percent casualty rate, that was to be expected—after all, they'd been sent into the toughest assignments because of their previous experience. They had all acquitted themselves admirably, however, and as a result the army had cut back on the "inexperience factor" that had plagued it in the African Wars.

Having proved that suspended animation could work on a limited scale, the army was now ready to initiate the process at large. If less than a hundred battle-tried veterans had made such a difference to the fighting, imagine how much better a thousand would be, or two thousand, or a hundred thousand. The army was prepared to put as many people in suspended animation as would volunteer for the duty. There would be an active recruiting drive among the returning China veterans and, as before, bonuses would be offered. The bonuses would not be as high as they were originally—after all, the process had now been successfully tried, and the risk was far less—but there was still the incentive of being paid while sleeping.

Naturally, Dickerson said, he would not dream of making a recruiting pitch to these, the original sleepers. They had already served their country well in two wars, and had earned their rest. Still, he added, if any

98

of them chose to sign up for a second term of suspended animation, he would personally see that they received priority treatment.

Hawker felt a queasy feeling in the pit of his stomach, but it took him some time to work up the nerve to ask his question. "What if I wanted to go career without another term in suspended animation?" he was finally bold enough to ask.

Dickerson hesitated. "Well, that would depend, of course, on the individual case. We'd have to test you to see whether you have any of the particular skills we need. You see, one of the reasons for expanding the sleeper program is to cut back on the cost of maintaining a standing army during peacetime. We will always need specialists, men to have on hand in case of a temporary emergency—but the ordinary fighter is another matter. If we can—I hope you'll pardon my bluntness—if we can freeze him when we don't need him and thaw him out when we do, the savings to the taxpayers will be phenomenal."

"Why is that?" Green asked. "It must be awfully expensive to keep those coffins maintained, and to monitor them constantly to keep the sleeper alive inside. How can you save *that* much money this way?"

"It's the same as in business," Dickerson said with a cold smile. "When you deal in large volume, the cost goes down. Project Banknote was terribly expensive to start and maintain. We had to design the 'coffins' from scratch, build each one individually, work out the computer maintenance programs, provide surveillance to ensure that nothing went wrong—oh, a million different things, all for the sake of less than a hundred men. But the costs don't go up that much if it were a thousand men instead. The only significant difference is the increased number of storage boxes. The same computers can check a thousand men as easily as they check a hundred. Building a facility to house a thousand coffins isn't ten times as expensive as building one to hold a hundred. The more people we can encourage to sign up for this program, the cheaper the per-capita cost becomes.

"Compare that with the cost of maintaining a nonsleeping army. Ordinary soldiers have to be fed; you could probably finance the entire sleeper program just on what the army spends for meat in a single year. Ordinary soldiers have to be clothed; I won't bore you with statistics on how much the army pays for uniforms each year. Ordinary soldiers have to be housed; I know you all joke about how crude the barracks are, but they still have to be built and maintained, they still have to be heated, they still need the electric bill paid. Ordinary soldiers get sick and need medical attention, drugs, recreational facilities. Ordinary soldiers are constantly in motion, and the army has rivers of paperwork flowing to accommodate them.

"All those factors are minimized with an army in suspended animation—and, without fighters who need services, we can dispense with the vast proportion of the army that provides them. We can eliminate thousands of cooks and quartermasters, doctors and nurses—and especially clerks. The paperwork on a soldier who's asleep is minuscule.

"One of the problems of a modern army is that, for each soldier who actually goes out and fights, it takes three or four more behind the lines just to support him. It's bad enough to put up with that in wartime, but why should we have to do it during peacetime? With the sleeper technology, we won't have to. The more volunteers for suspended animation we get, the more effective the program will be. The army expects to save millions of dollars each year once the plan gets going."

Dickerson paused and looked back at Hawker. "That's why we can't automatically promise career positions. We'll still need specialists of various sorts—we can't cut back on weapons development, for example—but we already have more than enough people in the general categories, and we'll be phasing *them* out as rapidly as possible once the sleeper program is a success."

Hawker's heart fell. Other than fighting, he had no special skills that would make him useful to the army. Unless he chose to sign up for another term of suspended animation, he'd have to go out and face the real world.

Green could tell he was depressed, and after the meeting he and Symington took Hawker out for some drinks to cheer him up. Hawker bared more of his soul to his friends that afternoon than he'd ever done before, telling them about his fears that he couldn't compete out in the real world because of his lack of skills. Green refused to be depressed, however; he pointed out to Hawker that their salaries had been accumulating while they slept, and that they were all rich men. Among the three of them, they should have well over $100,000—more than enough to invest in a business of their own. Instead of worrying about skills that would keep them going in the open market, they could become bosses and *hire* people with the necessary skills.

The three of them made a pact while sitting around the table drinking beer. They would pool their resources when they left the army, go into business together and form their own company. They drank several rounds of toasts to their mutual success, and by the time they split up that evening, Hawker was feeling much more optimistic about his prospects for the future.

His optimism lasted three days before it began dissolving. He, Green and Symington all received their discharges at the same time—and along with the discharge came a statement of their accumulated earnings, less than a third of what they had originally calculated. In checking the error with the paymaster, they were told merely that, because of ever spiraling inflation, the United States had finally revalued the dollar downward, and that the new money was worth more than the old, even though they had less of it. Green did his best to explain the economic theories behind the move, but it all sounded like double-talk to Hawker. It didn't matter to him that the things he bought would also—at least in theory—cost much less than he was used to; all he really cared about was that the government had promised him so much money, and had used some fancy footwork to pay him less.

The three friends found that their combined fortunes under the new monetary system came to slightly less than $40,000. Still, Green refused to be dismayed. It was buying power that really counted, he assured the others; compared to the rest of the population they should still be well off, and the opportunities for investment should still be good.

Shortly afterward, as they were being processed to leave the army, they learned of another change. Each was asked to pose for a photograph that would appear on his identification card. When they questioned this, they were told that every U.S. citizen now had to have an ID card before he could get a job or qualify for any kind of government aid. So many illegal aliens had been entering the country that an unforgeable means of identification had become a necessity, even over the cries of the civil libertarians. Normally, some proof of citizenship was required, but being veterans of two wars, the requirement was waived in their case.

After giving the information, they were each handed a small plastic card with their picture on it and a thumbprint on the back. Green looked his over, and a shiver suddenly went up his spine. "What does yours say under 'Race'?" he asked Hawker.

Hawker checked. "There's a 'C.' I guess that's for 'Caucasian.' "

Green nodded, and frowned down again at his own card. "I've got a 'J.' Three guesses what *that* stands for."

He turned to the corporal who'd given him the card. "Why is my card different from theirs?"

The soldier looked at the card, then back at Green. "You *are* Jewish, aren't you?"

"Yes, but . . ."

"It was decided that Jews are a race as well as a religion. It's been that way for five years now. Nobody argues about it."

"But why do you even have to list race at all?"

"It's mostly just for, um, what's the word?" The corporal snapped his fingers a couple of times. "Demographics, that's it. Besides, you should consider yourself lucky. You're listed as a minority, and you get all sorts of breaks."

Green stood silently for a moment, staring at the card, then turned and walked out of the room. Symington and Hawker were right behind him. "What's the matter, Dave?" Symington asked. "It's not that big a thing to get upset over."

"Maybe not," Green said. "But I can't help remembering what I heard about Nazi Germany. One of the first things they started was the internal passport, and every Jew had a big 'J' stamped on his papers. You know what *that* led to."

"Shit, that can't happen here," Symington said. "This is America, for God's sake. Anybody tries to hurt you, I'll break his arm personally. I ain't forgetting how you helped me in that fight in the bar." He put a long arm around Green's shoulders and pulled the smaller man closer to him in an affectionate hug.

They got some of their money in cash, and were told the government would send them the rest as soon as they had a permanent mailing address. Symington also picked up a small box that had been held in security for him. When his friends asked about it, he opened it reluctantly to reveal a display of fourteen medals.

"My God!" was all Green could say, and Hawker

stood speechless. Both men had privately been wondering whether Symington's endless tales of heroism were true; the box of medals made it quite obvious they were.

"You must have one of everything in there," Green continued for a moment.

For the first time in their acquaintance, Symington looked embarrassed. "I never asked for the fucking things, they just kept giving them to me. Look, fellas, forget you ever saw them, okay?" He closed the box and struggled for a smile. "I only use them to impress the broads, anyway."

Nevertheless, Hawker and Green came away from the incident with a new respect for their friend.

The trio packed their few belongings, and left the base as civilians for the first time in nearly fifteen years. Each of them was more nervous than he would have cared to admit; none of them knew what they'd encounter once they'd left the sheltered confines of the army.

The bus that took them into town was small, lightweight, and ran on battery power rather than gasoline. Green said he'd been expecting vehicles that rode on cushions of air rather than tires, but adoption of that innovation was still apparently in the future. The bus traveled slowly under electrical power, but the driver explained to them that the gasoline shortage had made the switch to electricity almost mandatory for public vehicles. There was little enough gasoline for private consumption, and driving was seriously curtailed.

"That's okay," Symington laughed. "Our driver's licenses have all expired, anyway."

Green, however, noted the scarcity of traffic on the highway around them, and said nothing.

They checked into a hotel in town, and were amazed at the prices. Each of them could have his own room for just four dollars a night. A good steak dinner in the hotel restaurant was under two dollars. Most other prices were similarly reduced—the ominous exception being that gasoline was advertised at thirty cents a liter, where it could be found at all.

"At these prices, we can live like kings!" Symington exclaimed happily.

Green cheered up a bit for the first time since getting his ID card. "I told you it's all relative. Even though we seem to have less money, we have the same buying power we'd have had if there hadn't been any money conversion. We can still buy our own business." That news made them all feel better.

They argued over dinner as to what they should do next. Green took over as the brains of their outfit, and insisted they go to New York. "That's where all the money is, that's where the best deals are made," he told them. "If we want to make something of ourselves, that's where we have to go. Besides, I've got an uncle who's an investment counselor—if he's still in the business. He'll help us get the best deal for our money."

They went to a travel agent the next day to arrange their transportation. One of her first questions was whether they had the proper travel passes, a question that stumped all three of them. They had never heard of such a thing, but when Green told the woman that they were all sleepers just released from the army she gave them a broad smile and said she'd do anything she could to help them.

Travel passes were necessary for anyone entering the bigger cities these days, she explained. Ever since the Energy Riots, the government had to make sure that terrorists and troublemakers were kept out of the major metropolitan centers; city life was too fragile a thing to entrust to chance. Anyone visiting New York had to have a valid reason for going, and a government-certified pass before he could enter—otherwise he was forced to stay outside.

The fact that Green had relatives in New York was deemed reason enough for going, and his friends were allowed to accompany him. The travel agent copied down the numbers of their ID cards—which turned out to be their old Social Security numbers, except that Social Security had been abolished several years ago in favor of something called National Assistance—and promised to expedite their travel passes. They didn't have enough money to fly to New York, since they wouldn't get their back pay until they had permanent mailing addresses, so she arranged bus tickets for them, to be effective as soon as their papers came through. She estimated it would take two days—four, at the most—and told them to check back with her.

The three friends returned to their hotel slightly stunned. So far they'd barely gone twenty kilometers from the base, and already they'd encountered monetary devaluation, national ID cards and travel restrictions. They could hardly help but wonder how many more surprises this modern world held in store for them.

It took them eight days to reach New York. Three of those were spent waiting for their travel papers to clear the government offices, and the other five were spent on the road. The electric buses they rode were slow and cumbersome, and stopped at each state line for inspection. They got used to taking out their ID cards and travel permits at border crossings to flash at inquisitive state troopers. At the Pennsylvania border, there was one passenger who'd boarded the bus just recently, and whose ID card failed to satisfy the border patrol. He and his luggage were removed, and the bus drove on without him. No one else aboard the bus thought to make any fuss about it, but the incident shook Hawker, Green and Symington a little bit.

Again, there was little traffic on the road around them. The nights were dark and quiet, and sleep was easy as the bus drove through the darkness—until Green realized that they were passing through a densely populated part of the country and that there should have been *some* lights of civilization around them. The energy shortage must really be bad if cities turned off their lights at night. That thought made it harder for him to sleep.

Their arrival in New York reassured them temporarily. The city looked hardly changed from when last Green had seen it. Traffic still clogged the streets, gasoline-powered traffic; there was so much congestion that it seemed to belie the energy crisis that had such an impact elsewhere in the nation. New Yorkers bustled about with the same callous unconcern they'd always shown. Clothing styles had changed a little, but not to excess: women wore much more austere, harshly cut business suits, and more men wore turtlenecks rather than ties.

Green set about the arduous business of tracking down his family after such an extended absence. His parents were no longer listed in the phone book, and a call to the synagogue yielded the information that Rabbi Green had retired seven years ago and moved to Miami. His Uncle Sid, the investment counselor he'd been counting on to help them, had died three years ago, and the people currently at that telephone number knew nothing of where his widow had gone. Of his brothers and sisters, only one—Benjamin, the doctor—still lived in New York, but the nurse at his office explained he was on vacation for the entire month, and wouldn't be back for two weeks.

In desperation, Green took his friends down to his old neighborhood to look for some acquaintances. There were still a few boyhood friends and neighbors, and even a cousin he'd almost forgotten about; people gathered around him and marveled at how young he looked but other than learning some more details about how his family had dispersed, he accomplished little that day.

Dismayed, the men checked into a cheap hotel in Greenwich Village while they decided what to do next. Green went to buy a newspaper, and was shocked to

107

see how drastically the *Times* had shrunk in size, down to a mere thirty-six pages—and most of those were want ads. He called the public library, explained his situation, and asked why the paper was so thin. The librarian explained that the newspaper industry had run afoul of the energy crisis; it simply required too much energy to pulp the paper, print up copies and then distribute them to homes and newsstands. Most people these days received their news over special channels built into the cables that serviced their TVs— a much more energy-efficient method of information dispersal.

The three friends read through the abbreviated paper during dinner, checking the classifieds thoroughly. The "Employment Opportunities" section was abysmally small; the energy shortage had apparently caused massive job layoffs throughout the economy, and people were scrambling for any kind of work at all. The only jobs listed with any consistency were those requiring some technical proficiency or advanced degree that none of them had.

The "Business Opportunities" section was barely more encouraging. There were plenty of businesses available to be bought—including an astonishing number of gas stations, garages, sales routes and delivery services—but most of them were businesses that none of the three knew the faintest thing about. How could they expect to run a restaurant or a laundromat against cutthroat competition in these harsh modern times? They were starting with a disadvantage of ignorance on several levels, and they were all deathly afraid of throwing away the one advantage they had—their accumulated savings—through their inexperience and lack of knowledge. Even Symington's normal cheerfulness was muted; he didn't feel *that* lucky to risk a business venture that could only end in disaster.

Green read through what little there was of the straight news, and became even more depressed. Not that there was any one item that was particularly bad—and that, in fact, was what disturbed him the most. The reports were filled with generalities, with scarcely a hard fact anywhere in them. Although he could not have said for certain, Green grew suspicious that the news was being censored in subtle ways to downplay the seriousness of any particular bad tidings. The travel agent had, after all, mentioned Energy Riots; perhaps the government didn't want people being stirred up that much any more by bad news, and so smoothed out the rougher spots in the day's reporting. It was an ominous thought, but one he couldn't push from his mind once it had entered.

Early the next morning, before they had a chance to decide what to do, they received a call from a news reporter who had tracked them down. She wanted to do a story about them, she explained—three latter-day Rip Van Winkles, and what their particular problems were in adjusting to the modern world. Hawker was skeptical about the idea, but the other two talked him into it. A little free publicity would never hurt them, they said. Perhaps someone would see the story and offer them some help. It was worth a try. They told the reporter to come over and, while waiting for her to arrive, they phoned several business consultants and investment firms, lining up consultations for that afternoon.

The reporter seemed eager to help them, and in fact was happy to concentrate on all the problems they'd faced in current-day America. Her questions emphasized how they intended to cope with situations such as the energy crisis and unemployment, and what they intended to make of themselves. It wasn't until after she left that Green realized why she'd done that; by making these three sleepers seem miserable in her story, the reporter was helping make her average reader feel that his *own* problems were comparatively minor. "There's nothing like someone else's suffering to make you feel better," he remarked cynically.

The interviews that afternoon were uniformly disappointing. The counselors were unanimous in advising the trio against going into business without knowing present-day economic conditions and how to compete effectively. Their best suggestions were to put the money into real estate or stock investments, but Green wasn't sure how good that was for them. The investments would be sound, but that kind of investment was more of a long-term deal, and the ex-soldiers wanted something that would keep them going *now*.

On a hunch, they stopped in at a library to get information about going to college on some GI loan and possibly furthering themselves that way—but the prospects were negative here, too. Many of the smaller colleges had been forced to close down when the crunch came—and those that were open had raised their admission standards. The trio's high school educations were more than a dozen years out-of-date; they'd have to go to night school for a year before they could make up enough of the difference to even think about applying.

The three of them drank heavily that night to relieve the oppression they felt growing in their souls, and they awoke early the next morning to the sound of the telephone ringing. The story of their plight had appeared in that morning's telenews report, and almost instantly they were deluged with offers of all sorts: offers of a spare room in someone's house, expressions of sympathy, even offers of marriage. There was one man who kept calling to insist: a) that suspended animation was anti-Christian, and b) that it was all a hoax, anyway. Hanging up on him did little good; he kept calling back, more strident each time than the last.

By far the most numerous types of calls, though, were the ones offering them business deals. Some people were eager to loan them ready cash now, using their accumulated back pay as collateral—probably, Green assumed, at frighteningly high rates of interest. There were many people who began by expressing their condolences, and quickly turned the conversation into a spiel to buy land in Alaska (guaranteed to be rich in oil) or to invest in some crazy fly-by-night company that seemed totally unsound, even to men who'd spent the last dozen years asleep.

"We've gotten on every sucker list in America," Green said bitterly after the third hour of uninterrupted telephone conversation. "We have no idea what's going on in the world, so everyone and his brother think they can take advantage of our ignorance." He threw the phone against the wall. "Well, I'm fucking well sick of it."

He stalked out the door before the other two could do more than stare at him. They found him a few hours later at a bar two blocks away, drunk enough to numb his pain and disillusionment. They put him to bed, and he slept until the next morning, right through the continuous barrage of phone calls that lasted until Symington finally had enough, and called down to the desk to tell them not to send up any more calls.

Green was quiet and thoughtful through breakfast the next morning. His eyes looked slightly sunken, and they had lost the bright luster of optimism. Symington tried to ignore the other's somber mood by keeping up a lighthearted banter about which of the waitresses would be best in the sack.

Finally Green interrupted with the quiet declaration, "I don't like this world very much."

Symington paused and looked at him. "Oh, come on, we've hardly even seen it. Just 'cause things are bad here doesn't mean they're bad everywhere."

"They are," Green insisted. "You don't have to drink a whole liter to know the milk's sour—just taste a few drops. If anything, things are probably better here than anywhere else. New York is like a dinosaur—you can kill it and the message still takes a year to reach the brain.

"There's a sickness in the country, or at least a

difference. It would have been one thing if we'd lived through it, gotten used to the changes gradually, as they happened. But getting hit with them all at once like this. . . ." He shook his head.

"Even if you don't like it here, where're you gonna go?" Symington said with a nervous laugh. "Australia? They've got an energy shortage there too, probably."

Green ignored him and turned to Hawker. "What do you think, Hawk?"

Hawker scarcely had to think. "I'm with you, Dave. You know that."

"Hey, you two aren't thinking of going through all that *again*, are you?"

Green blinked and looked back at Symington. "Why not? It's the easy way out of here, isn't it?"

"We've hardly even seen what the world has to offer. . . ."

"I have, and I'm not buying. There's no place for us here, Lucky. We're souls out of time, floating where we don't belong and unable to settle because we clash with the furniture."

"You think it'll be any better next time? Look how much trouble we're in after just twelve years."

"Why are you so against it? You were all for it, last time."

"Sure. Last time it was an adventure, something nobody'd ever done before, an easy way to pick up some big money. But we've proved our point. We don't have to do it again. Sure, things look bad now, but they're not hopeless. It's not like we're beggars or something. We've got enough money to stake us if we play the cards right."

Green sighed. "I just have to play the game differently. You want to gamble one way, I want to gamble another. The odds are lousy either way, but . . . I don't know, maybe I just don't have the guts to stick it out from day to day. Maybe I'm just an optimist, thinking there's a rainbow around the corner and tomorrow will be brighter than today. I'll try the way I know best."

Symington stood up, and Hawker thought he saw a flash of anger in the big man for the first time in their acquaintance. "You do that. Me, I'm heading out. New York isn't the only fucking place in the world. Things have got to be better somewhere else. Maybe that guy on the phone yesterday really had something, talking about Alaska. Not that I'd buy his fucking land, but I'll bet there's something there for a guy to do. Sure, it's a frontier, they always need people."

He gave them one last look, then turned his back and walked out of the restaurant.

Green watched him go. "Good luck," he said, too softly for Symington to hear. Then, turning to Hawker, he asked, "Do you think we're doing the right thing?"

Hawker shrugged. "I don't know, but it's the only thing I can think of, too."

"I wish I had his kind of courage," Green said, staring down into his coffee cup. "Lucky's the sort of guy who just plows ahead and refuses to admit he's beat. Me, if I see the game's lost, I look around for another one somewhere, one I have a better chance of winning."

He looked up again, the traces of depression almost gone from his face. "This time will be different, though. We know the ropes now, we know some of the mistakes we made and we can make sure they don't happen again."

"What mistakes did we make?" Hawker asked.

"The main thing is, we didn't take care of the money we were earning. We just let the army hold onto it, at no interest. Of course, the program was secret then, and we couldn't go to an accountant and ask him the best way to handle the matter. Now we can. We can have our paychecks deposited in a trust account, and let the trustees invest it for us while we're sleeping. If we're away for the same length of time, it could make

113

a substantial difference. I'll bet we could accumulate twice the money in the same period. Added to what we've already got coming—and using that as a starter —we could end up so rich that we'd never have to work again a day in our lives."

"If we live through the next war," Hawker reminded him. But Green had done with being gloomy for the day, and would hear no further criticism.

They spent the next week checking with more investment firms and banks, working out the arrangements for their trust fund. Finally they agreed to a pattern of investments that balanced high yield with security, and promised to make them very wealthy indeed if they slept for any substantial length of time. They further agreed that, if one of them should die, all proceeds would go to the other—and if they both died, the trust fund would go to Symington or his heirs.

That done, they went to the downtown army recruiting station to re-enlist. The sergeant at first was reluctant even to talk to them—the sleeper program was working well, and the army had little use for general recruits—but once they explained they'd been sleepers before and wanted to sign up again, he was delighted to take them on. They received their special bonuses—most of which went straight into the trust fund—and within a week they were back at their base preparing to undergo the ordeal of suspended animation once more.

They found the process greatly simplified this time. The physical examination they had to take was much less formal then previously, and there was no advanced course in weaponry. Apparently the army was confident enough about the suspension process that they didn't need to ensure every volunteer's being in perfect condition—and the weapons training before seemed to have been largely wasted. It would be far too expensive to give such training to the large numbers of sleepers involved in the program this time.

Within three days of arriving back at the base, Hawker and Green were back in their coffins, resting coldly and quietly until the army needed them once again.

Waking up was less traumatic this next time, too. Hawker remembered how weak he'd felt on his first emergence from suspended animation, and concluded that this must have been a sleep of a shorter duration. He was to find out, though, that just the reverse was the case; he and the other men had slept for nearly fourteen years. The army had learned from its previous experiment, though; while thawing the men out, before they even regained consciousness, their bodies were put through traction exercises to get the muscles back in shape, and they were given injections of hormones to improve muscle tone. As a result, Hawker merely felt tired, as though recuperating from a bad cold. The recovery period was shortened from two weeks to six days, and even that was probably an error on the conservative side.

The thought of another fourteen years stolen out from under him was more than a little frightening, but it was balanced by the comforting thought of the trust fund, and how it would have built up over the interval. Even with all the devaluations the government chose to throw at him, he would still end up with a sizable chunk of money to call his own.

On the third day after awakening, Hawker was reunited with Green, and the two friends greeted one another with unrestrained abandon. They agreed that they didn't look too bad for middle-aged men, and chortled to think that they were well into the twenty-first century and still young enough to enjoy it—providing, of course, they survived the war.

The next day brought them another surprise. They ran into another sleeper, and almost walked right past him before they noticed it was Symington. They hadn't expected to see him here under these conditions, and bombarded him with questions. Symington was sheepish at first, but under their persistent interrogation he admitted that they had been right—the world of fourteen years ago had not been suitable for people from their time. He had gone to Alaska and found that out the hard way, squandering most of his money in the process. Bitter and broke, and a year older, Symington had come wearily back to the army, which accepted him as though he were the prodigal son.

Hawker and Green were so glad to see him that they didn't even bother to rub his nose in the fact that they had taken precautions to shelter their earnings while he hadn't. They laughed and cried and, as soon as the doctors would allow, they went off and had some beers together for old times' sake. Symington regaled them with the horror stories about his year in Alaska, and they listened with the sympathy of true friends.

Hawker and Green tried to call their bank to find out how well their trust fund had done, but were told that outside calls were forbidden; this was an army camp in wartime, and the situation was tight. Similarly, mail service was also unreliable, and there was no way for them to learn how rich they were. It was frustrating, but they accepted the news philosophically. They couldn't spend the money yet anyway—they had a war to finish first.

While walking to the exercise yard, Hawker also looked into one of the other wards and spotted Thaddeus Connors there with some of the other sleepers. Apparently the black man was still on the run himself, from either the law or a guilty conscience. He shook his head and walked slightly faster, hoping Connors wouldn't spot him.

The war this time was completely different from anything the sleepers had expected. Both China and Russia were now allies of the United States, and the enemy was a conglomerate of countries from South

America and Africa—emerging nations of the so-called Third World. The prize of contention was the continent of Antarctica and, in particular, the wealth of resources it had lately been discovered to contain. The old-time superpowers desperately needed the resources to maintain their economic dominance over world industrial production, while the smaller nations saw this as perhaps their last chance to break the hegemony of the industrialized countries. This was not a tactical war, as the African and Chinese conflicts had been; this was a battle to the death for one side or another, and the direction of Earth's future lay in the balance.

Early in the war, the combatants signed a pact agreeing to ban nuclear action by either side. To the general public, this looked like an incredible concession by the superpowers, who had vastly more sophisticated weapons and delivery systems, and there were large protests in the United States against trying the military's hands. But those in command knew better. The Third World countries were much more desperate, and had absolutely nothing to lose by resorting to nuclear weapons. They could easily have infiltrated major cities in the developed nations and wrought havoc with primitive, homemade nuclear devices. As crude as that approach might be, it would be immensely disruptive to industrialized society —and the only way to counter it would be to render the entire continents of Africa and South America totally uninhabitable. That alternative presented problems of its own that were unthinkable. Both sides realized that the anti-nuclear treaty was a necessity for everyone's survival.

Hawker, of course, had no part in such esoteric planning. It wasn't his job to decide why the United States shouldn't just nuke the hell out of its enemies. He was expected to fight the way infantrymen have always fought—in the field under enemy attack, prepared to kill or die at any given moment.

The nature of this war's terrain forced him into some mental adjustments. His first war had been fought

117

in the steaming jungles of Africa, and his second on the plains and mountains of China. The battlefield this time was Antarctica, a land of frigid wastes and universal whiteness. It was a world of bitter cold and blustery winds that chilled him even through the heavily furred parka the army issued him. The only luxury was the pair of battery-heated gloves to keep his fingers warm so that he'd have no trouble handling his weapons in combat. Other than that, he had to suffer along with the rest of the troops.

He suffered for three weeks as his unit advanced over icy terrain that looked no different from the area all around them, yet which the brass insisted was vitally important. There were occasional skirmishes, but in general the enemy seemed to be falling back in front of them. They made great advances, but Hawker grew worried. This was a little too easy, and he suspected a trap. None of the officers asked his opinion, though, and Hawker would never think of volunteering it. He merely watched and waited.

The big attack came shortly before sunset. The enemy's forward lines, which had been routinely falling back, suddenly stiffened their resistance. At the same time, Hawker's unit found itself under attack from the flanks, too. They had been drawn into a classic box, which was rapidly closing around them, cutting off all hope of retreat. The ground rocked with the explosions of artillery shells, and even the onset of night did not bring total darkness; the constant flare of gunfire provided an eerie, if intermittent, illumination.

Early on during the attack, Hawker was hit by pieces of a fragmentation shell, making wounds in his right leg and the left side of his torso. He fell to the ground and was unable to move. The pain was excruciating, and he found himself wishing he would die and end the torment. He drifted in and out of consciousness all through the night, to the lullaby of death and destruction about him.

The shooting stopped shortly after dawn. Hawker lay quietly, thankful that the two sides were willing to let him die in peace. Then a squad of men came walking by. One of them kicked him in the ribs, and Hawker thought he was so deep in pain that his mind couldn't make sense out of their gibberish; then he realized belatedly that they were speaking Spanish. He had been picked up by the enemy.

After some small discussion, two of the men lifted him and carried him awkwardly to a waiting vehicle, where he was tossed in with other soldiers, some wounded, some dead. More bodies were tossed in around him, and then there was a long, jostling ride that only aggravated his injuries. He felt feverish despite the cold, and the edges of reality wavered at the corners of his vision. He was positive death would come at any moment to relieve him of his suffering, and his only regret was that he'd never spend all the money he'd earned while sleeping the past fourteen years.

The enemy doctors, though, had other ideas. This was still early in the war, before shortages of medical supplies became acute, and the Sammy staffs were honestly trying to be humane. After more than a week of wavering between life and death, Hawker finally landed on the positive side. Eventually he recovered without the loss of limbs or organs. But the war for him was effectively over. He was a POW until the end.

In this regard, he was quite lucky. Prisoners were treated much more fairly than they'd been in either Africa or China. The fact that he'd been picked up by the Sammies rather than the Freeks was also a fortunate break; the Africans still had a few primitive notions about the treatment of captured enemies.

Not that his life as a prisoner was easy. Food and supplies were always minimal, and the Red Cross packages were always too little and too late. As the war dragged on, food became even scarcer, and he sometimes went for days at a time without eating.

The prison camp guards were no less sadistic than others of that profession since the beginning of time; Hawker was beaten occasionally, but never so badly that it would show when a Red Cross inspection team came for a visit. There were three attempted escapes during his term in the prison camp, of which he was involved in two. None of them was successful, and all of them brought prompt and stern punishment.

Hawker spent three years in his prison camp until the war was officially declared over, with partitions drawn all over the continent of Antarctica, portioning out the land to all parties concerned. Then there was a round of negotiations before the prisoners could be released back to their own sides. After that, there was another week of waiting in Antarctica before Hawker's papers came through, transferring him back to the States.

While waiting to be shipped home, he attended a briefing that turned out to be a recruitment pitch for another indefinite period in limbo. But this time, the process would be much different than it had been before. Instead of being frozen down and placed in suspended animation, the soldiers' "life patterns" would be recorded and stored until they were needed.

"I know that probably doesn't make sense to you right now," the briefing officer said, "so let me try to explain. This is something on the very forefront of modern science—but it *does* work. I think you all know basically how television works. A camera takes a picture, and the image is broken down into a series of lines, which can either be stored or broadcast and eventually reconstructed into an exact duplicate of the original picture.

"In a similar manner, we've lately been able to break down actual physical objects and reconstruct them perfectly from the stored pattern. A special scanning device takes a three-dimensional 'picture' of every atom in the object, and its relation to every other atom. The scan is done so quickly that it's

120

practically instantaneous. The pattern is then recorded inside a computer. When we want to bring the object back, the computer bank simply tells us how much of each kind of atom we need. We adjust the mix in a chemical vat, and the computer impresses the electromagnetic pattern on the chemical mixture. In a matter of minutes, the original object is reconstituted exactly as it had been when it was recorded. It hasn't aged a day, it hasn't suffered any debility by being inactive for so long—it is, as far as anyone has been able to tell, exactly the same as the object before it was recorded."

There was a buzz of conversation throughout the room, and the officer held up his hands for silence. "I know this all sounds like the wildest science fiction to you right now, but just let me show you some holos of the process in action. I think you'll be amazed."

The "holos" themselves were amazing enough to Hawker, three-dimensional images projected onto a bare area of the stage. The images moved and spoke just as though they were real people and objects, and yet they could appear and disappear, run forward or backward, fast or slow, all at the whim of the projectionist. The entertainment industry must be having a field day with this, he thought, and then wondered idly what would have been the fate of the good old drive-in movie.

He and the other soldiers watched as the holos demonstrated a series of experiments. At first, common inanimate objects were placed in the scanners and dissolved into nothingness, only to be re-created moments later, looking the same as before. Then came a succession of test animals, from mice to chimpanzees. The animals appeared to be unhurt by the process and, to test their memories, creatures with special training in mazes were recorded and resurrected, with no loss of their memory. Finally, the tests were conducted on human subjects—most of whom spoke Spanish, and Hawker surmised that this was one fate of Sammy POWs during the recent war. It was frightening—and not a little sickening—to watch a man being reduced to a puddle of ooze on the floor of the scanner, only to be reconstructed later apparently undamaged. The man could not recall anything from the moment the scanner was turned on until the moment he was re-created—it seemed like just an instant to him, and he insisted he was the same person and that nothing had been done to him.

"You can imagine how excited we are about the new process," the officer said after the holos had concluded. "The benefits over the old hibernation process are obvious. There's no expensive maintenance program, no coffins to watch, no vital functions to be constantly checked. The patterns are stored neatly and safely inside the computer until we need them. The new system is much more mobile, because the reconstruction equipment is far easier to transport than a building full of delicate hibernation chambers. And best of all, from your point of view, there aren't any elaborate preparations to go through at either end of the process. You don't need physical exams, shots or enemas beforehand, and you don't need a week or two of physical therapy and calisthenics after you come out of it. As far as the subject is concerned, the process is completely painless and takes place between one thought and the next, in less than the blink of an eye.

"So, if you're feeling adventurous, if you really want to see what tomorrow is like, if you want to serve your country in the best possible way, there'll always be a place for you in the army. Think of us before you commit yourself to anything else."

To Hawker, the concept seemed ludicrous. The idea of being frozen in suspended animation—that at least had some semblance of reality to it. But this new system was just too bizarre for words. He was glad he and Green had set aside their trust fund. He would be independently wealthy by now, and wouldn't have to worry any more about signing up for future hitches.

The plane flight back to the States took a bare three hours, even from Antarctica, and yet still seemed like an eternity. On arrival, he was told there was a package for him—a large manilla envelope with his name scrawled across the front and Green's name in the upper left-hand corner. Hawker felt a thrill of excitement, to know that his friend had also survived the war. The envelope had a rectangular hard lump in it, and when Hawker opened it he found just a videotape cassette, with no other note or explanation.

He asked a few people and found he could borrow a cassette player from the base library. Curiosity about Green's message made him race to the library to play the cassette at his earliest opportunity.

He dropped the tape into the machine and nervously pressed the "play" button. The screen flickered to life. This was just a flat, two-dimensional screen, rather than the holo Hawker had been hoping for, but the color picture was sharp and clear. There was David Green, looking straight at him and smiling.

"Hi, Hawk," the image said. "I asked around about you and heard you'd been taken prisoner, so I figured there was a good chance you'd eventually get this message once the war was over and you came home. I tried waiting around for you as long as I could—I wanted to see you in person—but ... well, you'll understand when I'm finished.

"First, the good news—as little as there is of it. Lucky and I both came through the war okay. We went through our year of combat duty and then rotated to noncombat status. The army didn't want to let anyone go—not with a war on—but we were transferred Stateside to fill in backup positions and free other men for fighting duty. Lucky ended up as a cook— would you believe that?—and I ended up as a chaplain's aide, I guess because my father was a rabbi and they thought I might have some closer contact to God or something. At any rate, we're both alive and well— or we are when I'm taping this. I'm not so sure

123

what our status will by by the time you get it.

"One of the things that helped me get through the war—I'm sure it helped you too, thinking about it in the prison camp—was that trust fund we set up. Even with the devalued dollar as it was when we set up the fund, we'd still be rich enough to live off it comfortably for most of our lives. I tried writing some letters to the trustees at the bank, asking how the progress was, but nothing came through. Well, you heard their excuses before, about it being wartime and the problem with communications, et cetera. I never heard anything back from them all the time the war was on.

"As soon as the war was over, the army broke the news to us. While we were sleeping, there was a big scandal over paying soldiers for not doing anything. Seems a lot of other guys had the same idea we did, of trying to get rich while they slept. A lot of people thought that was unfair—after all, the army was taking care of all our needs, so why should we get paid for lying in a coffin? They raised a whole big stink in Congress, and the upshot of it was that sleepers had all their assets confiscated, everything they earned while they were in suspended animation—including everything they earned the *first* time, as well. I hear there's some guys trying to fight it in the Supreme Court as being both *ex post facto* and a breach of contract, not to mention being taxation without representation. I wish them luck, but with the way the country's going I don't think they've got a prayer.

"The fact of the matter is, Hawk, we're dead broke. They were generous enough to start our paychecks again when they took us out of deep-freeze, but that isn't worth shit in today's economy. Of course, they never bothered to tell us this until after the war was over. They probably knew damn well we'd never fight for them if we knew how they'd stabbed us in the back."

Green gave a weak smile. "I can tell you, we were pretty damn mad. Lucky wanted to bust some heads,

124

and it wasn't even *his* trust fund. Some of the other sleepers went a little crazy and ended up in the stockade. Me, I thought I'd play it smart and get even rather than get mad. But it isn't all that easy—you'll probably find that out for yourself.

"We thought things were bad in the United States after the China war. Let me tell you, that was nothing compared to what's going on right now. The place is like an armed camp. Nobody goes *anywhere* without travel papers—and it hardly matters if you've got the papers, because travel is so expensive you probably can't afford it anyway. If you're lucky enough to get a job—the unemployment rate has stabilized at twenty percent or so—you're practically stuck in it for the rest of your life. If you can't get a job, you get stuck on the welfare rolls, and I'm told almost nobody ever gets off them once they're on. The government does give you free dope to help you forget your troubles, but frankly I think almost anything is better than sitting around doped to the eyeballs day after day.

"The government is as close to a dictatorship as we've ever come. They still hold elections, apparently, but from the looks of things the candidates are all preselected for you. The news is heavily censored, so I couldn't see much of what was happening, but it looks as though the standard of living has dropped significantly. It's amazing how science keeps enabling us to do more and more, while society clamps in and lets us do less and less. I have a feeling something is going to explode somewhere along the line, and I'd just as soon not be there when it does. You can't press people too much further without something tragic happening.

"Lucky and I wanted to wait until you got back from the prison camp, and the three of us would decide together what we should do. But the army wasn't going to wait. It could be another couple of weeks before you come home, and the army doesn't want to keep us on salary. We've got an ultimatum: either we sign up for this new process they've got or they kick

125

us out into the real world and we have to fend for ourselves. Between the two, I don't really think there's much choice. We're damned any way we look at it."

Green looked uneasy, and glanced downward for a moment before looking back at the screen. "Lucky and I have decided to let them 'record' us, which means another jump into the future. As I said, I wish we could have waited for you, but they're getting pushy. If you do decide to go that way, things won't be so bad—we'll simply come out of the machine and there you'll be, only a few hours from when I'm recording this. If you decide to stick it out in the real world, I'll understand that, too. This new process of theirs is a scary thing."

Green hesitated and Hawker thought that would be the end of the message, but after a few seconds of silence the image spoke again. "I'm not at all sure about this 'recording' business. I mean before, when they were freezing us, it was still *us*, the same exact body that had just been put to sleep. Now it looks like they want more than our bodies, they want our souls, too. I don't know, maybe I'm getting too metaphysical. I've seen their films, I've read some of the literature, it all looks perfectly respectable. To all intents and purposes, the person they re-create is the person they recorded. But is it the *same* person, or just an exact duplicate? There was no question about it being the same when we were asleep, but—oh hell, I'm going around in circles. There's a very abstract philosophical point being lost somewhere in there, and I'm not a good enough philosopher to explain it. I'll bet some of the old rabbis who worked on the Talmud would have a ball with this. They could kick it around for centuries and still not come up with an answer. Maybe what I'm trying to say is, can they duplicate the soul as well as the body? What happens to the soul when the body's recorded? Is it recorded too, or does it fly away somewhere? Or do people even have souls at all? Maybe I'm worrying over nothing, maybe we aren't anything more than an organized collection of molecules."

He gave a deep sigh. "I don't know, Hawk. The more I think about it, the more sinister this whole nightmare becomes. Maybe we should get off the merry-go-round now, while we still have the chance. We've already tried escaping into the future twice in search of something better, and look what we've found. If we don't get out now, I don't think we ever will. We're just too different to fit in with life in the ever changing modern world—and it's only going to get worse. The pace of human existence is accelerating all the time. Have you ever heard the legend of the Flying Dutchman? That would be us, lost souls doomed to repeat our mistakes forever through history."

Green shook his head. "Damn, but I'm getting philosophical in my old age," he said with a bitter laugh. "I'd almost managed to forget all my doubts until I started this letter to you. If I don't stop now, maybe I'll talk myself right out of it—and life here in the twenty-first century is no picnic, that's for sure.

"That's all I have to say, I guess. Be careful, and don't let them railroad you into anything you don't want to do. Whatever you decide is fine with us—and Lucky and I both wish you an eternity of good luck. Take care of yourself, Hawk; you matter more than you know." And the screen went blank.

Hawker stared at the screen for many minutes after the message had finished, unable to move for fear the tears that had gathered behind his eyes would suddenly come welling out and embarrass him in public. Only when he was certain of his self-control did he stand up and return the cassette player to the library desk.

The next day, he was called into the administration building for a "counseling session." The counselor—a civilian, Hawker noted—tried to break the news about the seizure of sleepers' money as gently as possible, and Hawker did nothing to make it easier for him. Hawker acted properly indignant when the facts were

127

explained to him, and the counselor rushed to mollify him by showing the alternatives. The regular army had no room for him, the man said, but Hawker could always sign up for another hitch of suspended time, this time as a recorded pattern in the army's computer.

"What if I don't want to do that?" Hawker asked. "Who knows what you'd steal from me this time."

The counselor blushed and turned away to his computer console. He typed quickly onto the keyboard and had Hawker's dossier on view on the screen within seconds. He did a double take at Hawker's age, until he saw the note that Hawker was a two-time sleeper. He mentioned that Hawker's high school diploma would be virtually useless in the modern world because it had been granted so long ago. He grimaced when he noticed Hawker possessed no specialized skills that would stand him in good stead in civilian life.

"You mean there's nothing out there for me," Hawker said.

"I didn't say that," the counselor hurried to correct him. "We'll find something for you, I know it. You'll have triple veteran's preference, which puts you at the head of the line, in front of a lot of other people. You may have to settle for some general type of job, like shoe salesman or supermarket clerk, but we'll get you something, I'm sure of it. The army always looks after its own."

Hawker had to suppress the strong urge to spit.

The counselor cleared his throat and continued, "Now, as to where you'll be relocated. Let's see, it says here you're from Kansas City. Let me check. . . no, Kansas City has no openings. I'll spread the search pattern out a little—ah, there we are: Topeka. I'm sure you'll like it there. We can settle you in there and find some sort of job for you, I promise. What do you say to that?"

"Go fuck yourself," Hawker said, and walked out of the office.

The next day he was stripped naked and facing the

molecular scanner. He was frightened, more so than he'd ever been in his life—more than he was during his first combat with an enemy, more than when he first contemplated leaving the army, more even than when he'd first faced the prospect of being frozen for an indefinite period. All the doubts Green had voiced came back to him, with a few of his own added. The army *said* the process was painless, but how could they really tell? They'd lied to him before, why wouldn't they do it again? And even if it was painless, even if it was foolproof, how safe was it? He would exist only as a pattern inside a computer. What if something happened to the computer? Would he die, then? Without ever knowing he was dead? He'd been raised very strongly to believe in the immortal soul, but where did his soul go during this process? The questions were terrifying.

Then the technician called his name. Closing his eyes and uttering a short, silent prayer, Jerry Hawker entered the molecular scanner.

interludes

The process was indeed painless and seemingly instantaneous. Scarcely had Hawker stepped into the scanner when he found himself lying in a small tub of liquid. It was a bad disorientation, to be standing one moment and lying down the next; he gasped, and accidentally swallowed some of the salty water around him. He choked a bit, just as two men grabbed his arms and helped lift him out of the tank.

Something felt odd about him. His stomach was queasy, as though he were in a falling elevator, and his body felt extraordinarily light. "I think there's something wrong with me," he managed to gasp between chokes. "I feel kind of funny."

"Perfectly normal," one of the men replied. "You're on the Moon, now."

He was led into a room with other resurrectees, without being given much chance to think about the predicament. His steps were light and bouncy, and he felt almost as though he were drunk, except that his mind was absolutely clear. He was given some clothing, a one-piece jumpsuit that zipped all the way up the front, and told to wait for instructions. He mingled with the other men—there were at least fifty of them so far—and listened to their amazed conversations about how they never expected to go to the Moon, and how fantastic this new process was compared to the old freezing method. Hawker, as usual, did not join in any of the conversations; he merely wandered around the room idly, observing.

The room kept filling up as more and more people were resurrected from their shady half-lives in the computer's files, and eventually Hawker saw some familiar faces. Bounding across the room, oblivious to the startled looks of the other men, he threw his arms around Green and Symington and hugged them for all he was worth. The other two were startled, but equally enthusiastic.

"What do you think of the process, Hawk?" Green asked when the glad noises of reunion had died down.

Hawker shrugged. "I don't know. I don't feel any different. It sure beats the freezing and waking up in a hospital bed."

"Yeah, and it's all so sudden," Symington added. "It seems like just this afternoon Dave taped that message to you, and now here we all are—on the Moon, for Christ's sake!"

Their conversation was interrupted by the appearance of a lieutenant who called them to attention for his briefing. First, he told them, they were no longer a part of the United States Army. The United States had been incorporated three years ago into a union with Canada and Mexico, called the North American Complex, or Nacom. They would still be fighting to preserve the land of their births, but it had undergone a change.

The reason they were on the Moon was more difficult to explain. Nacom, along with several other major world factions, was building a series of space colonies, using material mined from the Moon for construction.

Nacom's intelligence service had learned, however, that the Russian-Arab bloc was intending to use its space colony as a military base, from which they hoped to dominate the world. To ensure that their base would be built first, they'd started sabotaging Nacom's mining efforts on the Moon—and that, in turn, had led to the outbreak of hostilities here.

This was a silent, dirty war. For intricate political reasons too complex to explain, neither side wanted the conflict known to the general public; to do so would be to invoke chains of alliances that could have every nation in the world at war in a matter of hours. So the war was being limited to outer space, and particularly to the Moon. The fighting was likely to be on a small scale, but very intense, and the soldiers' bravery here would be unheralded—but much appreciated by their government.

During the next few days they went through a series of exercises—not to get their muscles back into shape, as had been the case before, but to get them used to the one-sixth gravity of the Moon. Using too much muscle in a given situation could be fatal, and the resurrectees had to learn to gauge their strength under the new conditions. They also had to learn quickly how to move in the bulky spacesuits they'd be wearing on the lunar surface. These suits had been quickly made, and fit the men crudely; a well-constructed spacesuit had to be built around an individual, requiring detailed measurements and fittings that time had not permitted in these circumstances. Their instructors repeatedly stressed the fact that the suits would be the only things keeping the soldiers alive outside, and that even a single tear could prove fatal.

During their five days of training in the crowded underground base, the soldiers could feel frequent tremors in the walls and floor. These, they were told, were enemy bombing runs. The Russians were sitting snugly inside their well-fortified base, throwing large chunks of rocks and debris at the Nacom base using a device called a "mass driver," which acted as an enormous slingshot to hurl objects hundreds, or hundreds of thousands, of kilometers. Nacom Base had its own mass driver, which figured prominently in the Nacom strategy.

So far, neither side had been able to do much more than throw rocks at the other. It was assumed that the Russians did not have a system for re-creating soldiers, as Nacom did, and was probably incapable of transporting large numbers of troops to the Moon. Nacom, too, lacked enough troop carriers to ship its soldiers to a position near the Russian base—but there was the mass driver, and Nacom intended to use it.

Having received their training, the soldiers were suited up and placed within their individual padded "buckets." They were told to keep their heads down well between their knees and press themselves as tightly against the back padding as they could. Hawker stood in line with the rest as, one by one, they were loaded into the slingshot and fired off toward enemy territory.

When his turn came, Hawker obediently tucked his head down and pressed back against his padding, nervously wondering what new nightmares technology had cooked up for him. He didn't have to wait long to find out. As his bucket shifted into position, he was suddenly rammed against the back wall as though hit full strength by a giant flyswatter. The force lasted only a few seconds, but it was brutal enough to make him black out for several minutes.

When he came to, he was floating free in space with the Moon "above" him. He felt sick to his stomach and bruised from head to foot, but he was alive and breathing—and in space, those were the crucial factors. He'd been fired like a circus performer out of a cannon, and now he was on a trajectory that would place him down on a plain barely a hundred kilometers from the Russian base. From there, he and his companions were to launch a full-scale assault on the base itself and—hopefully—overwhelm its defenders.

This operation had been in the planning stage for the past month, ever since the decision was first made to resurrect the recorded soldiers, and preparations had been laid with the highest secrecy. Working under cover of the two-week-long lunar night, teams of Nacom construction personnel had built an enormous "net" in the target area to catch the spacesuited figures as they plummeted back to the surface of the Moon after their flight; without the net, the soldiers would simply have crashed into the lunar soil with roughly the same velocity at which they'd been launched. The mass driver's aim was computer-accurate, but Hawker later heard horror stories about soldiers who had missed the two-kilometer-square net and whose bodies were permanently splattered across the lunar landscape.

Hawker landed safely in the net, which was made of some unknown material possessing the strength of steel yet incredible resiliency. The shock of his landing bruised him still more, and he was hurriedly helped off to make room for the next man coming in. It was unlikely that two would land back to back in the same exact place, but the consequences of that were so ghastly that no one wanted to contemplate them.

The Russians realized belatedly what was happening, and took steps to hinder the Nacom effort. The landing area was inside the effective minimum range of their mass driver, but what they did was shoot off a heavy barrage of rocks in a long, complicated trajectory that eventually came raining down on the target field. The hail of moonrocks tore through the netting, but most of Nacom's damage had been done—eighty-three percent of the assault force had been delivered within striking distance of the Russian base. Food, water and oxygen had already been stockpiled there during the nighttime activities, and there were several large tractors to act as tanks and lead the attack. All that remained was to cross the hundred kilometers and destroy the base.

The troops began what was later to be called the Moon March. Each of the men was in peak condition, yet even so they found the trek across the baking lunar plain to be the most arduous of their careers, far surpassing any tortures devised by drill sergeants in basic training. There was no shade, no relief from the damnably bright sun overhead. The spacesuits, constructed hastily, showed the pressure. Twenty-seven men died when their suits overheated; another suit simply exploded for no known reason, instantly killing its wearer; and eleven more people died of tiny rips in the fabric of the suits. The men rested every few hours and the weak lunar gravity helped keep them from becoming too tired. Nevertheless, by the time they were within thirty kilometers of their objective, they were all disconsolate.

Inside this range, the Russians joined nature in working to kill them. The enemy began lobbing "grenades" that were little more than buckets of scrap metal set to explode on impact. On Earth, such things would not have had much effect, but on the Moon— where a small rip in one's suit meant instant death— they took on deadly proportions. All the men could do when they saw the grenades coming was hit the ground, presenting as small a target as possible, and pray that none of the shrapnel found them. In far too many cases, however, those prayers were denied.

Green died during one grenade attack. He and Hawker had been marching together, trying to keep one another's courage up, when word came that another grenade was about to hit. Both dove to the ground, as was now standard operating procedure, and lay still. After a few minutes, when the all clear came, Hawker rose to his feet and Green didn't. Looking down at his friend's prostrate form, Hawker could see no tears in the suit from a shrapnel bit; only when he turned the body over did he see what had happened. Green had evaded the shrapnel, but in falling to the

136

ground he'd torn his suit open on a sharp projection of rock.

For the first time since his grandmother's funeral when he was twelve, Hawker cried. His sergeant came over and helped him to his feet, and Symington put an arm around his shoulder. Between them, the two men helped get Hawker moving again—but something of himself had been left behind there on the surface of the Moon, beside Green's still body. It was the last traces of innocence, the final vestige of any part of him that could claim enjoyment of life. All that was left now was a cold callousness, a machine existing only for its continued survival.

Hawker remembered little of the rest of the conflict. He marched through a blue haze that few things could penetrate. He fought with the rest when the Russians finally sent troops against them, after they'd gotten within five kilometers of the base. He was there in the mob that stormed through the actual base, taking it room by sealed-off room in hand-to-hand fighting that killed eighty percent of the remaining assault team, including Symington. He was standing within three meters of Colonel Gonsalves when the latter announced the base had been secured by Nacom, but he did not celebrate with the rest of the men. Laconically he stood apart, a machine turned off until it received further orders.

There was no agonizing decision to be made this time when the war was over. There was nothing left in this world to live for, so Hawker volunteered to be recorded one more time.

He could tell when he emerged from the protein bath the next time that he was back on Earth; gravity felt right again. He was prepared, this time, for the abrupt transition from one moment to the next, and did not have to be helped from the tub. He nodded silently to the technicians, accepted the clothing they handed him and walked into the next room—where his jaw fell open from shock. Standing there in the center of the room, amid a group of other resurrectees, were Green and Symington, just as naturally as though Hawker had not seen them die with his own eyes. He stood stock still, not believing what he saw, until they finally noticed him and came over to greet him. As Symington reached out one long arm to place around his shoulders, Hawker shrank back from the touch as he would from embracing a corpse.

"Hey, what's the matter, buddy?" Symington said in his usual booming voice. "Ain't you glad to see us? We didn't know whether you'd actually sign up for another term."

"What do you think of the new process?" Green asked. "I told you on the tape—jeez, it seems like just this afternoon I did that, doesn't it?—I told you I had some reservations, but it does seem to work. I sure don't feel any different. It really is instantaneous—what's the matter?"

Hawker had gone white. "You—you're dead. Both of you. You're both dead!"

"Somebody sure forgot to tell me that," Symington laughed, but Green was inclined to take Hawker's upset a little more seriously.

"What do you mean?" he asked. "How can we be dead? The army just resurrected us; we don't even know who we're fighting yet."

"You died last time—on the Moon."

"The Moon? Last time?" Symington's impatience was showing. "What the fuck are you talking about? Maybe this new process has scrambled your brains."

Green turned to Symington. "Take it easy, can't you see something's wrong?" Then, to Hawker, "Take your time, Hawk, and tell us what you're trying to say. We won't interrupt."

Slowly, painfully, Hawker told them the story of the war on the Moon, and of how each of them had died there. The other two listened silently, the expression

138

on Green's face growing more worried by the minute.

When Hawker had finished, Green shook his head slowly and closed his eyes. "Oh my God," he said softly, half to himself. "Oh my God, they've done it."

"Done what?" Symington demanded. "Do you know what's going on?"

"I think so—but I wish I didn't. They really have stolen our souls, and now there's no escape, ever. There's no way out. Damn, why didn't I think? Why didn't I see it coming?"

"If you don't start talking sense, ol' buddy," Symington said, "I'm gonna knock your head right down through your asshole."

"Don't you see? Now that they've got us recorded, they can resurrect us any time they like. If we die in battle, they can still bring us back for the next war—or even later in the same battle—and we'll never know anything is wrong. Even if we quit the program or desert, they can just create another one of us to take the place of the one who left—and that new one will never know that the old one left. They're got us by the balls, now, and they've got us forever. We're slaves, Lucky. We may be immortal, in a funny sort of way, but we're still slaves."

Symington's face clouded with anger. "They can't do that to me! I'll show them!"

"Oh really?" Green gave an ironic laugh. "What are you going to do—mutiny? They don't even have to bother with a court-martial, because you're not a real person. They can shoot you on the spot and make themselves another Lucky Symington, one who doesn't know a thing about what happened to his predecessor and who might be more docile."

"What if we told everyone else about this, organized a sitdown strike or something . . . ?"

Green shook his head. "It wouldn't do any good. Don't you see, our lives aren't worth a flea's fart any more, because they can always make us over. Even if every resurrectee decided to strike along with us, they could come in here with a machine gun, kill every single one of us and simply duplicate the entire herd. They can keep doing that forever until they find a group that goes along with them. Individuals mean nothing any more. Who knows? Maybe if one of us breaks a leg, the army will think it's better to shoot him and make a new one than to take all the trouble to heal the broken leg."

"There's got to be *something* we can do!" Symington said.

"I don't know...."

Green's remarks were interrupted by the arrival of a sergeant who'd come to give them their by now familiar briefing. Hawker was so dazed by Green's observations that he could pay no attention to the lecture. An army of soldiers, turned out like a production line—what an idea. He'd played with little plastic soldiers as a kid, setting them up in various positions to simulate combats. When one soldier "died," he moved it around to another place and pretended it was someone different.

And now he and his friends were the plastic soldiers, no more real in the minds of the generals than Hawker's toys had been to him. If one gets killed in one place, make a new one and stick it someplace else. They were all interchangeable, just pieces in a vast game that had been going on since the beginning of time.

Hawker never did find out very clearly what this particular war was about—but none of the other soldiers seemed to know, either. They just fought where they were told to fight and didn't ask too many questions. Most of the fighting seemed to be in the mountains of Mexico, which had apparently split off from Nacom to be independent once more—and that was all Hawker could ever really pin down. But the spirit of the troops—particularly the resurrectees—had shown a marked deterioration, from which it would never fully recover. Too many of the men were becoming too well aware of what had been done to them, and the trap they had been led into. None of them was happy about it.

Hawker's path crossed Green's several times during the course of the ten-month-long war. The serious young man had done some heavy thinking about their problem and, while he had no solution, he'd at least worked out a philosophy for tackling the situation.

"Memory is the key," he told Hawker once as the two of them enjoyed a leisure moment together in a wartime bar, sipping a beer. "It's the only thing we have left that we can call our own. Don't ever let them take it away from you."

"I don't understand," Hawker said.

Green leaned forward to explain. "Look, we're going to live a very long time, maybe forever, who knows? Somewhere in all that time, an answer has got to appear—and when it does, we have to be ready for it.

"Each time we die they'll resurrect us again—but the person they'll resurrect will be one who's missing the memories of the one who got killed. They'll have to go back to the last time he was recorded to get a new copy. There'll be times when we can't avoid that, obviously, but we've got to try to minimize it. Every fact, every memory may play a crucial role one day in winning our freedom. We can't allow ourselves to forget, we can't give them any opportunity to rob us of even a single item. Don't ever give them an excuse to kill you prematurely and rob you of the memories you've just gained. Be a good soldier, try to stay live, do whatever you must to preserve your memories and keep your mind intact. Good God, if they're going to force us to live forever, then at least let's live with hope that someday, somehow, we can win free."

The battles of this war were particularly fierce, as the Nacom generals threw their troops into combat with suicidal abandon. They, too, had realized how cheap were the lives of their soldiers, and casualty

141

statistics became meaningless to them. Tacticians thought little about a ninety percent fatality rate, as long as the maneuver in question gained its objectives.

Amazingly, all three of the friends survived that war, all kept their memories of the experience intact. None of them was particularly surprised, either, when—at war's end—they were no longer given any choice in the matter; it was just assumed that they would be recorded to serve in future wars. The "merry-go-round," as Green called it, would never stop again, and there was no way for them to get off.

The next war was once again fought in outer space, between two space colonies on artificial worlds in orbit around the Earth. The reasons for the conflict became more abstruse, less comprehensible to the men who came from another time and place. The weapons were constantly being improved and updated, but the dreary business of fighting remained ever the same.

Hawker, however, would have no recollection of this war. A laser beam tore through his spacesuit as he and a boarding party were trying to sabotage the enemy colony's exterior rotation jets. It was his first death, but it was by no means his last.

On the next incarnation, Green and Symington did not mention to Hawker that he had died last time. A new etiquette was growing among the resurrectees, because some of the men reacted badly to the news that they had died one (or more) times before. Some had gone completely crazy and had to be killed and re-created. Now it was completely taboo to mention someone's previous death—and, in fact, it was considered very bad form to even talk about past wars. If it turned out that a person had died in that war he would have no recollection of it, and someone else's talking about it would bring the point home to him most painfully.

With the past taboo and the future a bleak nightmare too frightening to contemplate, the major topics of conversation were all anchored solidly in the present: how tired everyone was, the wretched quality of the food, and successes or failures with women during their infrequent leaves. Society was changing around them, and the men found it hard to keep up. Even the language itself was changing; people who ostensibly spoke English were difficult, if not impossible, to comprehend. Green remarked to Hawker that the entire system would break down soon, at this rate, because the men wouldn't be able to understand their officers.

This war was fought on Earth. It seemed that every nation was set against every other, and alliances shifted so rapidly that it was impossible to tell who was on your side even *with* a scorecard. It was a chaos in its primal form, but that mattered not at all to Hawker. He did his job like a good soldier and refused to let the external world impinge on his personal reality.

The next war was on Mars, and the language spoken was so far from twentieth-century English that the resurrectees had to sit through a basic language course before they could be sent into battle. Green drew some hope from this; if the process of retraining the soldiers became too expensive, perhaps the army—whoever's army it was by now—would decide that the process of reincarnating the soldiers should be scrapped in favor of some other system. It wasn't much to go on, but it was some hope, at least.

Conditions on Mars seemed to be a cross between Antarctica and the Moon, with all the wrong features of each. A rip in one's pressure suit was not automatically lethal here, but it was damned incapacitating. The general staff was belatedly coming to the same conclusion as Green, namely that the memories of its fighters were an asset to be preserved if possible. The more memories a soldier had, the wilier and more cunning a fighter he became; he could remember

143

similar conditions in the past and how to turn them to his advantage. The number of suicide missions leveled off until they became, as they'd been before, merely last-ditch efforts of a desperate strategist.

This was also the first war in which women played a significant combat role on Hawker's side. He'd seen women in battle before, generally as guerrillas, but now they constituted roughly forty percent of his own force. Some of the older men refused to fight alongside the women at first, and had to be persuaded at gunpoint. All the men made lewd and vulgar comments about what they might be doing in the foxholes during breaks in the action—but the truth of the matter was that surprisingly little sexual activity occurred during this war. It was most awkward to engage in such conduct while dressed in pressure suits while the outside temperature was well below zero and the atmospheric pressure almost nonexistent.

There followed several wars that Hawker never knew about, because he died in each of them.

The next war he could recall was on the hell known as Venus, where the atmospheric pressure was hundreds of times that on Earth and the temperature was hot enough to melt tin. To go out on the surface, even in the best spacesuits ever conceived, would be instant death. The war was fought instead inside mobile bases that roamed over the barren landscape like enormous tanks. Each base held a crew of between fifteen and twenty-eight people, and there were long periods of inactivity between battles. Women had been fully integrated into the army by this time, comprising fifty percent of the resurrectees. There *was* a great deal of sexual activity among the troops during this war—but in the cramped confines of the mobile bases, there was very little privacy. Hawker had to learn not to notice when his comrades were intimately engaged, and he hoped they would return the favor.

Then back to Earth, but in a role he hadn't expected. He was part of an expeditionary force from the Planetary League, sent to punish the mother world for its recalcitrance in submitting to the "natural domination" of Geos, the awesome artificial world that controlled the economic life of the Solar System.

Hawker and his cohorts did their job well, and Earth learned its lesson. Never again was it in a position to challenge the leadership of its colonies for control of its own destiny.

Then there came a gap of more than a hundred and fifty years, the largest single hiatus Hawker could ever recall. Since it was unlikely there'd been no wars during all that period, Hawker could only assume he'd died numerous times in the interim. None of his friends, of course, would say anything about it, and he never asked.

Technology had improved markedly during the past few centuries. The resurrection process had been made ever more streamlined, with the nutrient tanks growing smaller and more efficient, until now they were no longer needed. At present it was possible to re-create a person out of "thin air" simply by playing his pattern in a special way that Hawker couldn't even begin to understand. The process had even engendered a new verb: "to duple," shortened from the word "duplicate." Green thought that ironically appropriate since, as he said, they were all dupes anyway.

The language barrier, which had been a constantly growing problem, was also solved by the invention of training caps. Small plastic headpieces were worn for a couple of hours, and all the information the subject needed to know was implanted directly into his brain. After that, he became as fluent in the current language as any native, and was well versed in the theory and practice of all the latest advances in weaponry. Green was vastly disappointed at these developments;

he'd been hoping he and the other resurrectees would become obsolete and gradually phased out. Now there seemed no chance of that.

At the same time, the army dashed another hope of his—that the soldiers would eventually become too old to fight any more. While no time elapsed for them when they were patterns stored in the computer, they did age during the periods when they were let out to fight. Physically, Hawker, Green and Symington were all men in their early thirties by this time; if they aged too much further, even the army would give up on them.

But progress once again decided against them. They were now given treatments to rejuvenate their bodies and prevent the cumulative deterioration that was known as aging. They learned that no one—at least, no one on the advanced, civilized planets—aged any more. Everyone was eternally youthful and, except for accidents and acts of war, no one ever died.

On the surface, it sounded ideal: an age of prosperity when material goods, like the soldiers, could be dupled at will to relieve need, and when people could look forward to many centuries, at least, of useful, active lives.

But this golden age was on the surface only. There were still soldiers, still wars, still a need to fight and kill. The reasons behind the combat had become too subtle for Hawker to comprehend, but they still existed—and as long as they did, he and his friends were doomed to Green's "merry-go-round."

This war was the first one Hawker fought in a different solar system. The planet was a world circling the star Alpha Centauri B, and the enemy was a group of rebel colonists who were trying to declare their independence from the Solar League that had given them birth. Days were long, and very strange. Sometimes there would be two suns in the sky at once, casting odd double shadows on the landscape and playing hell with Hawker's perceptions. Sometimes night never came at all, as Alpha Centauri A would come over the horizon just as B was setting. And even when both stars were down, the night was seldom dark—Proxima Centauri, the nearby companion, often glowed in the sky like a bright red distress flare. Battle strategies had to be considerably revamped to take these ephemerides into account.

Not that it mattered to Hawker. The landscapes might change, the weapons might improve, but war itself remained dismally the same.

The next war was also fought on a world circling a different star, one that didn't even have a real name in human language, just a catalog designation. What made this war particularly memorable was that it was the first time Hawker fought against alien beings. The "Sticks," as they were called, were no more native to this planet than Hawker was; this world had developed no intelligent life of its own, and was being coveted by both races.

The Sticks were tall, thin creatures who looked much more fragile than they really were. They came from a world with a slightly lower gravitational force than Earth, and were probably better suited to this world than the humans. Hawker found the gravity a little too light—though stronger than on Mars—and the air a little too thin for his taste; he was constantly having to gulp for breath, while the Sticks seemed unaffected.

In the end, an agreement was reached. The Sticks settled on two of the three major continents and the humans on the remaining one. Hawker wondered why no one had thought of that earlier.

There was an incarnation, somewhere in this time period, when the army tried an experiment. Someone in Planning decided there was no reason why only one duplicate of a given soldier should be made at a time; why not duple squads composed entirely of a single man? The advantages were obvious. Such a squad

147

would be more coordinated than any other in history. Every member of it would have the same reflexes, the same thought patterns, the same level of skills. There could be no dissension, no arguments, no conflicts of personality—in short, such a squad would be the perfect fighting unit.

The experiment was duly carried out, with Hawker and several of the other resurrectees chosen to be multiply copied for special squadrons. At first, the experiment seemed to be paying off—the "clone squads," as they were called, fought with exceptional precision as long as they received no casualties. But then the experiment fell apart. There was something very demoralizing about seeing *yourself* lying dead or bleeding on the ground beside you. Once a few members of the clone squads were killed, the other members generally went crazy and became useless as fighters. The trauma of seeing "themselves" killed was so deep that these resurrectees were destroyed without allowing their memories to be recorded.

Hawker, naturally, remembered nothing of this, and the experiment was never repeated.

Then there was a war back on Earth itself, but under conditions Hawker would not have believed. The war was between two vast domed cities under the Pacific Ocean, and the soldiers had to fight in pressure suits and odd protective vehicles just as they did in space. Dolphins and porpoises were used extensively on both sides of the conflict. During his few periods of leave, Hawker had a chance to examine the quality of civilian life, and found it totally incomprehensible. People didn't seem to have jobs, yet they kept busy at something. Material objects meant very little, yet— though they seemed immortal—time was very valuable as something not to be wasted. The citizens behaved unpredictably, for motivations Hawker could not begin to understand. These glimpses of life on Earth only made Hawker depressed, because they emphasized how

148

alienated he was from everything he thought he'd known. He was glad when the war was over, because he knew he'd probably end up on some other planet where he *expected* things to be strange.

As it turned out, Hawker never set foot on his native world again.

Technology continued to improve faster than he could keep up with it. Personal force fields were devised to protect the soldiers from most weapons—and then, just as rapidly, weapons were developed that made the force fields obsolete. Even the training caps became outmoded; any necessary information could now be imparted directly into the subject's mind with a mental probe during the resurrection process itself, in a fraction of a second.

Mankind continued to expand into the Galaxy and, as might be expected, the army was at the forefront of the expansion. Hawker fought battles on many worlds, under suns of every hue, against beings of every imaginable description. Sometimes the atmosphere itself was so dense he couldn't see through it, and had to rely on instruments to show him the way. Sometimes the gravity was so high that merely standing up was a major achievement. Sometimes the combat took place in space itself, and Hawker actually found himself *liking* that environment. The dark, silent void ideally matched what his own life was becoming.

Another piece of etiquette that developed through the ages was the mercy-kill. Medical science had made great advances since the days of Hawker's birth, and even lost limbs could be replaced on a wounded resurrectee before his pattern was rerecorded. But out in the field, where medical assistance was often lacking altogether, it was sometimes better to finish off a colleague rather than let him suffer a lingering death.

There was one jungle planet where Hawker encountered Green after the latter's patrol had been

149

caught by an ambush. Most of the soldiers were dead, but Hawker found Green still alive in a pit, impaled on a crudely carved wooden spike. Green was conscious, but in so much pain that he couldn't even speak. He just looked at Hawker with pleading in his eyes.

Hawker took his gun and calmly shot his friend through the head, confident Green would be dupled again.

In their next lifetime, Hawker never even bothered to mention the incident to Green. There was little point. Green would have done the same for him, he knew. Perhaps, sometime in the past, he even had.

Hawker remembered one incident where Thaddeus Connors, the hostile black whose life he'd saved in China, went completely crazy. The soldiers were fighting an alien invasion on a human-occupied colony world, and a group of soldiers were enjoying some leave time in a local bar. Connors, as usual, kept to himself, disdaining to speak to anyone. Several of the bar's customers were civilian colonists of this era, and they got into an involved philosophical discussion on the question of race. Most modern humans were all of a fairly dusky skin, the products of long racial interbreeding, and the civilians could scarcely understand why some people in earlier times had allowed themselves to be all black or all white.

Something in this conversation touched off a spark in Connors. He suddenly went berserk, throwing furniture around the room and lunging at people indiscriminately. He lifted one bar patron bodily and threw her so hard against the wall that her head was smashed in; the rest of the people danced quickly out of his reach and Connors, unable to inflict more damage, left the bar. He was shot and killed a short while later by the robot police.

In relating the incident to Green some time afterward, Hawker wondered what would have caused

Connors to explode that way. "Simple," Green answered. "Those people were attacking the one piece of pride Connors had."

"I don't understand."

"Connors has always kept apart—and he always thought it was *our* prejudice rather than his own. Being black was a convenient excuse for him. He'd say to himself, 'People hate me because I'm black,' and so he turned it around and made it a point of pride: 'People are *jealous* of me because I'm black.' I should know; we Jews have done that for thousands of years, always being different and priding ourselves on it.

"Those people in the bar undercut his entire rationale. They said skin color didn't matter, and it mattered very much to Connors. He's built his whole life around the idea of being Superblack, and he couldn't stand to see himself mocked that way."

Green shook his head. "That's a very dangerous man, Hawk. I try to avoid him whenever possible."

Another duple of Connors was resurrected, of course, one who had no recollection of the incident in the bar. But new man or not, there seemed nothing anyone could do to improve his disposition.

There were a few pleasant memories in all that time. Hawker fondly recalled his first sexual experience with an alien.

He'd been lost and separated from his unit for two days. He'd been wounded slightly in the shoulder—not serious, but combined with hunger and exposure, the injury had weakened him. He came to a farm building and tried to find shelter inside it. Something moved, he glanced up quickly, and there was one of the alien natives staring down at him from a loft.

These beings, the Bimaree, were bipedal and averaged the same height as a human, but those were about the only similarities. Their bodies were completely covered with downy fur, in a wide variety of colors that ranged mostly in the yellows and browns. They had no heads; instead, all their sensory apparatus and their brain cases were in a bony area near the center of their torsos. Their notion of clothing seemed to be lengths of wide, colorful cloth draped tastefully about their limbs, leaving the torso bare. It was rumored they had three, possibly more, sexes. Hawker never knew for certain; soldiers were rarely given such detailed biological data. As long as he knew how to kill them, that was sufficient.

He had no way of knowing what sex this particular Bimaree was, but he always thought of it as female because of its personality—and perhaps, in some little way, that made it acceptable.

The training probe the army had given him on his awakening hadn't included knowledge of the local language—it wasn't anything that the soldiers were expected to know. Consequently, Hawker found himself in an awkward position: he didn't know whether this particular Bimaree was an ally or one of the rebels he was fighting—and his flamer was out of charge. The only other weapon he had was a knife, and his arm was wounded a little too badly to throw it accurately. If this was an enemy, he'd have to wait until it came into range.

But the Bimaree didn't look hostile. She stared back at him with those large green eyes in the center of her torso, and didn't move for several minutes. Then, slowly, she climbed down out of the loft and approached him, careful to make no sudden moves that would alarm him.

An enemy, Hawker decided, would have shot him instantly if it could, and in no case would it approach this timidly. He had probably just stumbled across some hapless civilian farmer tending her chores. He had no quarrel with her. Perhaps she would give him some food and help him find his way back to camp.

He pointed to his shoulder, and even the Bimaree could tell the flamer wound was not a normal part of his body. She said something and backed slowly out of the barn, to return minutes later with a container of salve. Hawker had no idea whether an alien medication would help or hurt him, but, like the other resurrectees, he had developed a philosophical attitude about such things. He might as well try the salve in the hopes it would cure him; if it killed him instead, the worst thing that would happen is he'd be dupled again without remembering this war. Life and death had ceased being matters of high concern.

He peeled off his shirt and motioned the Bimaree closer. She came to him slowly, took a handful of the salve and began rubbing it into the wound. The cream stung at first; Hawker gasped in pain, and the Bimaree pulled back, startled. Hawker beckoned her again, though, and she reluctantly continued the process. After a few minutes the stinging abated, and all he could feel was the coolness of the salve and the warmth of her furry hand caressing his skin.

Hawker had never had sex with an alien before. Some of the other resurrectees had, but he'd always considered them perverted. Now, though, tired as he was he couldn't help recalling some of the obscene barracks chatter about the Bimaree. "They fuck like bunnies," confided one man, who claimed to know. "They got some kind of sexual cycle where they get aroused real easy, and then it don't matter whether you're a man, a Bimaree, or a tree branch, they gotta have you in them. Go for the little slit in the back, where you think the asshole's gonna be—it's really the cunt. Nice and tight, too. They're fantastic." Hawker had been repelled by the idea then—but now, with the Bimaree's hand sensuously caressing his wounded shoulder, he felt himself becoming strongly aroused.

He reached up tentatively to caress the Bimaree. Her down skin was velvet to his questing fingertips, a smooth, sensual warmth that seemed to welcome his touch. The Bimaree did not shy away, but responded to his stroking by rubbing harder against his body—not

153

just his wounded shoulder, but across his chest and neck as well.

It's true, Hawker marveled. *They do arouse quickly.*

He was suddenly more excited than he could bear. He reached awkwardly down to unfasten his slacks and yanked them below his knees, then pulled the alien down on top of him. She came compliantly and he was soon inside her, his only concern being not to grab her eyes accidentally. The feel of her soft fur against his skin added a dimension to the experience that no human female could have matched.

Afterward he felt greatly embarrassed, though she seemed to think nothing of the incident. He dressed again and she brought him into her house—where she apparently lived alone—for dinner. They made love again twice that night, and each time was unique unto itself.

The next morning, a company of soldiers came by the farm, and Hawker joined up with them. He said goodbye to the Bimaree, but he was never sure she understood him. And of course he never saw her again.

He had sex with many other alien females after losing that particular virginity, but he always treasured the memory of that one idyllic encounter. And while other soldiers joked and made obscene comments about the other races, Hawker kept his private relations very much to himself—perhaps out of respect for the "honor" of that one Bimaree who gave so much pleasure to a stranger.

Sex was not always that easily indulged in, however. During one incarnation the resurrectees found themselves segregated by gender once again. This was surprising after so many centuries of sexual equality, but they learned that the culture they were fighting for was a particularly puritanistic one. Sex between a man and a woman before marriage was a capital crime—and even during marriage, it was only permitted during specified religious celebrations.

There was nothing sinful, however, about homosexual relations at any time. The army offered a wide selection of men for Hawker and his comrades to utilize (and Hawker assumed there were women available for the female resurrectees). Somehow, though—despite his experiences with women of other races—the line of homosexuality was one that Hawker could not bring himself to cross. He and most of his fellows decided to abstain throughout the course of this particular war.

Perhaps because of that, or because its defenders lacked the essential enthusiasm, this religious culture lost its war. The society was smashed, its principles crushed, its people scattered to planets all across the Galaxy. The resurrectees never had to face anything quite that strict again.

Through good times and bad, Hawker fought on. He lived hundreds of lives, died hundreds of deaths. He dwelt among the stars and trod on soils that had never before felt the foot of man. He walked side by side with creatures out of a surrealist's imagination, and called them "friend." He killed with the efficiency of his namesake the hawk, and laughed but seldom. He was orphan to the Universe, slave to Chaos and Destruction. He was the ultimate soldier, obeying his orders, marching into unimaginable battles, fighting for causes he could not comprehend.

His soul—if, indeed, he'd ever possessed one—had been lost long ago in the mists of antiquity, when Mankind was still confined to one tiny ball of rock. He pursued his destiny emotionlessly, as though in a dream. He was drained. Nothing in the Universe could matter to him ever again—or at least, that was what he thought when he bothered to think of such things.

Until he came to a world called Cellina.

part 2

cellina

The awakening occurred as it always did, with barely the slightest pause between his last thought and the present, even though, he found later, there had been fifteen years in between. The resurrection machinery was by now quite sophisticated, able to reconstruct the entire army of recorded soldiers at one time in one place, rather than on the piecemeal basis it had been at first.

Hawker was standing in a large blue auditorium with more than a thousand other resurrectees. From the information the training probe had placed in his brain, he knew he was on the planet Cellina, third world out from a G-type star. The inhabitants were all of human extraction, although by this time there had been so much genetic engineering done on the race that "humans" could be as bizarre as any alien. Hawker had generously been given a knowledge of the native language, since it was assumed the army would be doing liaison work with the locals. The dispute was with an alien race who claimed a prior right to colonize the planet, having visited it a thousand years before the humans came and left some esoteric mark to note their presence.

This was all standard stuff, not even worth thinking about. Straightforward, no problem. The only question, deep in the back of his mind, was whether he'd survive the experience and carry the memory forward with him into the future.

Then a woman screamed off to his right, and Hawker—along with the rest of the group—turned quickly to see what was the matter.

At first glance there was an alien in their midst. There was no reason why aliens couldn't be dupled too, and Hawker was certain that there were other computers doing just that; but normally, for the sake of homogeneity if nothing else, each group of resurrectees was of the same race. Still, the mere sight of an alien should not have caused one of their number, battle-hardened as she must be, to scream.

Then Hawker looked more closely at the being, and felt a chill run up his spine. It wasn't an alien, it was a human being—but a human being so twisted and deformed that it was barely recognizable as such. Its face was a putty mask left out in the sun and then attacked by a hyperactive child; the right half of the face was a runny, flesh-colored blank, with both eyes on the left side of the nose and an eyebrow arching crazily upward. The neck was twisted halfway around, so the man was constantly looking over his left shoulder. His spine was bent into an S-curve, and the limbs on his left side were perceptibly longer than those on his right. The fingers on the man's right hand were barely warts growing out of a clublike fist.

Hawker turned away quickly again in disgust. No wonder the woman had screamed. Something had obviously gone wrong with the dupling process, creating a monster instead of the person who was supposed to be there. But Hawker guessed that the real reason

158

behind the woman's scream—and behind his own revulsion—was not the actual sight of the person there; after all, each of them had seen creatures far uglier than that. The really horrifying thought was that this mistake in dupling could just as easily have happened to any of *them*.

He wondered what it would be like to go into the dupling machine as he'd done hundreds of times before, totally confident of the procedure—and then suddenly, between one thought and the next, become a hideous, twisted freak. To become deformed during the course of a lifetime was one thing; everyone in this room had probably lost a limb or been burned beyond recognition, only to be fixed up again, with some degree of success, by army medical technicians. But the suddenness of this transformation hit like a hard blow to the stomach; Hawker had to fight the waves of nausea that threatened to overwhelm him.

Officers in crisp green uniforms pushed their way through the mob of resurrectees to the side of the twisted creature, and Hawker took a second look at the mistake. It was then that he got the second shock in as many minutes. In trying to visualize what that person might have looked like before the accident, he rearranged the facial features—and felt a chill shoot up his spine when he realized who it was.

That pitiful, deformed monstrosity was David Green.

The officers hustled Green out of the room before anyone had a chance to do more than note what had happened. No mention was officially made of the incident, and the army behaved as though nothing out of the ordinary had occurred. But the question burned in Hawker's mind, and he resolved not to leave this incarnation without finding some answer to his friend's horrible transformation.

The war was mostly being fought in space, as the aliens launched wave after wave of attack ships against Cellina's defenses. Hawker served on the crew of one fighter ship, occasionally seeing action by boarding enemy vessels. Everything was totally routine; he'd seen such action a dozen times before. After two months, he received a pass to go on leave back to the planet's surface—where, he hoped, some answers would await him.

As it turned out, Symington was on a pass at the same time. Hawker found him in a bar, drinking with three other resurrectees—two men named Singh and Costanza, and a woman named Belilo. Hawker knew them all vaguely. He joined Symington's party— something he would normally have avoided unless specifically asked—and forced himself to join in the usual bitch session about the duty each had pulled and how rotten the conditions were. After a decent interval of meaningless chatter, Hawker brought the conversation around to the subject of the "accident" at their resurrection.

"Yeah, that was weird," Costanza said with a shiver.

"Do you have any idea who it was, Lucky?" Hawker asked.

Symington scratched his head. "I'm not sure. . . ."

"It was Dave," Hawker said flatly. "He looked pretty horrible, but I recognized him despite the changes."

"Poor bastard," Symington said.

"You mean Green?" asked Singh. "He seemed like a nice guy. I think I served with him once."

"We all did," said Belilo. There was a moment's silence as she took a sip of her drink, and then she added, "It's a damn shame. He sure as hell didn't deserve all this."

"All what?" Hawker asked. "Have you heard anything about him?"

"Well, I spent a part of my time on the base, and I managed to get plugged into the pipeline. A few rumors were leaking around. Nothing much. They just say that something went wrong with the tape, or whatever it is they record our patterns on. It's a total loss, and the guy—Green—can't ever be remade properly.

160

From what I hear, they've got him under observation for tests somewhere on the base. They're studying him like some sort of freak."

"Thanks." Hawker stood up from the table.

"Where are you going?" Symington asked.

"I'm going to see if I can get some answers from the people in charge."

"They don't want to talk much about it," Belilo said.

"They will when I get through with them." Hawker turned angrily to leave.

Singh grabbed his arm. "You think you're going to go in there like that and scare them? They won't take any shit from you."

"You got any better ideas?" Hawker tried to pull his arm away, but Singh's grip was too strong.

"As a matter of fact, I do. We all go in together. Green was our friend too, right?" Singh looked around the table as though daring the others to deny the fact. But there was no thought of disagreement. The resurrectees had been under the thumb of the army so long that the thought of shaking up the bureaucracy was stimulating.

"They'll think twice about crossing us if there's five of us," Costanza said.

"We'd better be ready for trouble, though," Belilo warned. "If we give them too much hassle they can just shoot us down and duple us again—and the new versions won't know anything's wrong."

"I can break into the arms locker, no problem," Symington said.

"Hey, wait," Costanza objected. "Facing them down is one thing; armed revolt is another."

Belilo stared into his face. "Oh yeah? What can they do to us they haven't already done? Come on, Chico, make up your mind—are you in or not?"

Costanza looked at the four determined faces around him. "In," he said with little hesitation. "I just wanted to make sure we all knew what we're doing."

"We know," Hawker said grimly.

By implied consent, Singh took charge of the group. They first "liberated" a floatcar and drove it back to the base, where, as Symington had promised, they had no trouble raiding the weapons storeroom. In addition to two beampistols apiece, which they tucked, hidden, into their trousers, they took a small supply of grenades and rifles. "If we're going to look for trouble," Singh explained, "we'd better be prepared to find it." The grenades were small enough to store in their pockets; the rifles would be left in the floatcar until they met bigger trouble.

Thus armed, they began making their inquiries. They were polite at first, but their tempers grew shorter as they were bounced from office to office, being told at each step along the way that someone else had the information they wanted. Finally, though, they reached a point where the clerks began looking more guilty, and the denials were much too emphatic.

It was Hawker who tired of the runaround first. The clerk behind the desk was a woman with feathered eyebrows and a smooth, downy head of hair. Grabbing her by the front of her tunic, Hawker informed her that he wanted to speak to the officer in charge immediately. The woman looked at him, and then at the determined faces of his four friends. The fighters were usually so apathetic that she didn't know how to deal with them in this aroused state. She decided to pass the problem along to her superior. She coded the door to open and told them they could go in—but Singh insisted that she be brought along, too, so she couldn't give any alarm.

Beyond the door was a spacious office. A flattened computer screen floated in midair like a desktop with no legs, and behind it sat a man who was obviously used to being in charge. He was fat and totally bald, clad in a one-piece gray uniform, and his skin was a mottled green and blue. His breast plate identified him only as "Philaskut."

Rank as Hawker had originally known it had long

162

ago vanished in the army, replaced by a sideways tiered system of authority so complicated he had never fully understood it. Under normal circumstances this caused little problem; everyone not a resurrectee was in principle his superior, and he just obeyed everyone's orders. Soldiers were just pawns in the great cosmic game, and inferior to everyone else. Hawker and his friends had no way of knowing how important this Philaskut was in the chain of command—but at the moment, they didn't care.

"What do you people want?" Philaskut asked. He was neither angry nor indignant at this invasion of his office; if anything, Hawker would have judged him bemused.

Hawker became the group's unofficial spokesman. "We want to know what happened to the man who was accidentally malformed when we were dupled two months ago."

Philaskut steepled his fingers in front of him. "The army would prefer not to dwell on that subject. In view of the process's overwhelming success for centuries, one failure is hardly worth—"

Symington leaned forward, resting his clenched first on the computer screen. His large bulk was satisfactorily intimidating. "He was a friend of ours."

"I see. That is a pity. However, as I said, there's nothing I can—"

"A very special friend," Singh moved around to the other side of the desk, his looming providing a counterpoint to Symington's. He enunciated each word clearly.

"We want to know everything about the problem," Belilo added, taking a menacing stance beside Hawker in front of the desktop.

Philaskut was no longer quite so bemused. "I assure you, there's nothing you could do about the matter, anyway."

"Why don't you just give us the details so we can see that for ourselves?" Hawker allowed his tone to be more reasonable, providing a rational alternative to the blatant menace of the others.

Philaskut leaped at the bait. "It was a total accident, well beyond anyone's ability to either predict or control. Do you know how an object's patterns are stored?"

"No," Singh said slowly, "but I'm sure you'll tell us."

Philaskut licked his lips and considered, reminding himself that he was dealing with people who were, compared to himself, scientifically primitive. "Do you know what molecules are?"

"Basically," Hawker answered.

"Well, the molecules of certain crystals are arranged in an orderly configuration called a lattice. Normally these lattices are rigidly constructed, but under the proper circumstances we can bend them, making some sides infinitesimally longer or shorter, as we choose. There's a complex code for what each slight amount of deviation means, and so wide a possible variation that we can make each molecule hold several bits of information. A crystal large enough to describe an entire human being is only slightly bigger than a grain of salt. The fact that we've kept perfect track of everyone for so long indicates how accurate and efficient our system is."

"But not this time," Hawker persisted.

Philaskut took a deep breath. "No, not this time. Something went wrong in the subject's crystal. . . ."

"Green," Hawker said.

The officer's train of thought was interrupted. "What?"

"He's not just 'the subject.' He's a real person, probably smarter than you and me put together. His name's Green. David Green. Keep that in mind."

"Uh, yes. The . . . the soldier Green had something go wrong with his crystal, so that the information stored in it was distorted."

"What went wrong?" Singh asked.

164

Philaskut turned to answer the question from this new direction. "We don't know precisely. That's why we've been conducting our investigation. We think it may have been an effect of a cosmic ray collision. You see, the Universe is constantly bombarding us with cosmic rays; they can come from any direction at any time, and they've got a great deal of energy. We thought we'd built sufficient shields against them, surrounding the crystals themselves as well as their container. What we think may have happened is that two or more cosmic rays may have hit the same spot almost simultaneously, penetrating the defenses. The high-energy rays struck this one crystal and knocked it slightly out of proportion, causing the deviation you saw."

He shook his head. "Believe me, such an occurrence is so rare it couldn't happen again in a million years. The odds are trillions and trillions to one against it. . . ."

"Can you fix it?" Hawker asked. "Can Green be restored?"

Philaskut cleared his throat. "You have to remember, that was the only such record of him we had. It wasn't the *person* who was damaged, but the complete *record* of him. If it were something in the dupling device itself, or something that happened to the sub . . . to Green *after* he'd been dupled . . ."

"In other words," Belilo said, "there's nothing you can do."

"No. That's what I've been trying to tell you." The officer spread his hands to indicate how hopeless the situation was. "The record itself was damaged—and in fact, the crystal broke apart immediately upon being replayed. We couldn't even duplicate the re-creation. That's why the . . . Green is so important; we must study him thoroughly to learn exactly how the accident occurred, so that in the future we can take steps to see this never happens again."

Hawker felt ill that such a thing should happen to

the closest friend he had in the Universe. "I want to see him."

"Who? Green? I'm afraid that isn't possible. He's in a classified ward; I can't order a video linkage. . . ."

"I don't want to see a fucking picture!" Hawker exploded. "I want to visit him, be beside him, give him comfort if I can. He's my friend, goddamn it!"

Philaskut shrank back from this outburst. "That's even more out of the question. That ward is strictly off limits to anyone without a triple-alpha clearance. . . ."

"I don't think you understand, friend," Symington said, coming around behind the computer screen so that he towered over the seated officer. "That wasn't a request. We didn't say 'pretty please.' That was an order."

Philaskut looked around the room at the five determined faces, and at the look of fright on the clerk's face as Costanza held her tightly. From some unexpected depths of his soul, the officer drew a tiny shred of courage. "Who are you to order me around?"

"Just a group of people who think five to one is pretty good odds." To emphasize his remark, Singh opened his tunic to show the butt of the beampistol tucked into his trousers.

"What will you do, kill me?" Philaskut's bravado was gaining momentum. "Do you think you're the only people who can be dupled? Do you see this little button in my neck? Everyone on Cellina has one. My pattern is being continuously broadcast to Resurrection Central, continuously updated. If you kill me, I'll be dupled exactly as I was the instant before you did it. You'd gain nothing. I'm not scared of you."

"Actually, we weren't thinking of killing you." Belilo leaned down, gently at first, on the computer screen; when it held her weight, despite its apparent lack of support, she sat on it, and leaned over toward the officer. "Killing is so crude, don't you think? Do you happen to know how many bones there are in the human foot?"

Philaskut blinked, confused by her apparent change of subject. "No."

"Neither do I, exactly, but I'm told there's a lot. Twenty or more, I think. All nice, tiny little bones. I wonder if we can set a record for the most broken at one sitting." She looked back at Hawker. "Do you think we should do that before or after we peel the toenails all the way back?"

Philaskut's courage evaporated as quickly as it came. "P-please don't. I'll take you there somehow. But it's all the way across the base. I'll have to get us a floater."

"We've got one downstairs," Singh said. "It's all ready and waiting."

"What about her?" Costanza asked, bringing the clerk forward. "Do I have to drag her around all over?"

Belilo walked over to the frightened woman. "What about it, sister? You got one of those buttons in your neck?"

"Y-yes."

"Good. I'll try to make it painless." With a sudden blow, Belilo lashed out and snapped the woman's neck. The clerk gave just a soft sigh, and fell to the floor as Costanza released her.

Belilo looked at the corpse for a moment. "Somehow it doesn't seem so bad when you know it's not permanent," she remarked.

Philaskut stared nervously at this display, and Symington had to lift him by his collar and deposit him on his feet. "Get moving," he said brusquely. "We've got things to do."

They took Philaskut down to their waiting floater and drove as he indicated to a large building on the far side of the base. Several times they were stopped for ID checks, but Philaskut nervously inserted his clearance card in the appropriate slot and they were passed on to the next checkpoint. Eventually they pulled up beside a door, got out of their floater

167

and Philaskut's card opened the way for them again.

Hawker and Symington walked on either side of the officer, each taking one of Philaskut's arms and locking tightly to it so the frightened man could not escape. The other three walked close behind. They wandered up stairs and through a maze of corridors they could barely keep straight, passing three checkpoints along the way. Each time, Philaskut's card gained them admittance. Had he not been in such an angry mood, Hawker might have been impressed by the importance of the man he'd kidnaped.

At length they came to a door marked "Authorized Personnel Only." Philaskut's card worked perfectly on it, too, and the door opened wide. The group marched silently into the room beyond, and the door slid shut behind them.

They were in a laboratory. Five people in crisp green uniforms moved about the room, checking the wealth of instruments all around, recording the readings and resetting the calibrations. The entire room was bathed in the antiseptic glow of a cool blue light. And there, in the center of the room, lay Green.

He was suspended in midair on an antigravity field, surrounded by dozens of humming machines large and small that poked and prodded at his naked body. If anything, his twisted figure looked even more grotesque than Hawker remembered from the brief glimpse on resurrection day. "Is he awake?" Hawker asked their guide.

"I really don't know. I'm not in charge of this aspect. His mind is as damaged as his body. He slips in and out of awareness. . . ."

The other people in the room noticed the intruders for the first time. One of them, a woman with incandescent orange hair, stepped forward. "What are you doing here? Philaskut, you know perfectly well . . ."

"It's visiting hours," Symington told her, his hand resting lightly on his hip a few centimeters from the butt of his beampistol. "We've come to see our friend."

As Hawker's group strode forward, the scientists parted reluctantly to let them through. Hawker noticed one of the men edging toward the door. "No need to leave," he said as a gentle warning. "We don't have any secrets from you people. Let's just all stay together for now, shall we?"

They lined the scientists up against the wall, along with Philaskut. Costanza kept an eye on them while the other four soldiers approached the body that floated in the middle of the room. Hawker had to force his stomach to remain steady as he glanced down at the surrealist parody that was his friend's face. "Dave," he said quietly. "Dave, it's me. I came to see how you were. Are they treating you all right here?"

Green's face did not change expression; he showed no sign of having heard or understood. Hawker turned to glare angrily at the scientists. "What have you done to him? What drugs have you given him?"

"None," said the woman who was apparently in charge of the scientific team. "We wouldn't introduce foreign substances, because we're not sure how his body would react. We even have to prepare special predigested food, because his stomach has trouble on its own." She was indignant at the very thought.

Symington, more direct, laid his hand on Green's shoulder and shook him gently. "Hey, Dave, it's your buddies. We've come to see you. Can't you even say hi?"

Green's eyes continued to focus on some spot well beyond the ceiling, but his mouth began moving. Saliva dropped out of the side and the sounds, barely audible, were simply nonsense syllables.

Hawker's anger reached new heights. Turning to the scientists once again, he demanded to know, "What have you been doing to him?"

"Just studying him," the woman said. "We run molecular scans of his entire body, recording the pattern and analyzing it to see precisely where the deviations are. We run tests, that's all. We're not trying to hurt

169

him. He was like that when he came to us; we're not to blame for the accident. We're only trying to make some sense of it after the fact."

The fact that her words were reasonable did nothing to mollify Hawker's anger. If anything, it only infuriated him more. What was the good of logic and reason when an unreasonable universe could turn a good man like David Green into a freak like this?

"I can see you cared for him a great deal," the woman continued. "But you'll have to face the fact that the friend you loved is gone forever. We've done what we could to keep the shell alive, but his mind . . ."

"Welcome . . . to Hell."

Those words, even spoken as softly as they were, jerked everyone's attention back to Green. There was awareness of a sort in his face; his eyes, both on the left side of his nose, were now focused on Hawker.

"Dave. Dave." Hawker felt closer to crying now than he had in centuries. "How do you feel?"

"How . . . do I look?"

"Like shit," Symington replied.

"Then that's how mfrtck tablkrt." A cloud passed over Green's eyes as he lapsed into gibberish once more.

"That often happens," the woman scientist volunteered. "There'll be a brief period of lucidness, and then he—"

"Shut up!" Hawker snarled. All his concentration was on Green; he wanted no distractions. Despite the gibberish, Green's face did not look as spacey as it had at first; there were thoughts going on within his mind, but he couldn't connect his tongue to the words.

Seconds passed, with the only sounds being Green's gibbered attempts at speech. Hawker strained, positive that if only he listened hard enough he could make some sense of what his friend was saying. But it continued to elude him, and eventually Green stopped speaking again.

170

It was Singh who broke the spell of silence. "What do you want to do now, Hawk?"

Hawker closed his eyes and tried to think, but it was no good; all his mind could see was Green's twisted body and haunted face. "I don't know, I don't . . ."

"We can't just stand around here forever," Costanza said. "We've got to do something."

Belilo, seeing the pained indecision in Hawker's face, said, "We can take him with us, get him away from these ghouls."

"You can't do that!" Philaskut objected. "He's army property."

"So is this," Symington said, pulling his beampistol from his trousers. With a single shot he blew off the officer's head.

The scientists were cowed, but the woman in charge still had enough courage to speak up. "You don't understand. Taking him away from here is the worst possible thing. He's a freak now. He can't survive in the outside world. You'd only be hurting him, not helping him."

"I told you to shut up," Hawker said. He kept his eyes on Green. "We'll let him decide what he wants."

"He's hardly competent . . ."

Symington's beampistol lashed out again, tearing away the woman's leg. She fell to the floor, moaning and crying in pain.

Hawker looked straight into Green's face. "Dave," he pleaded. "Dave, please concentrate. This is important. Do you want us to take you out of here?"

An eternity passed, then two. Finally, "Yes." The single sighed syllable echoed through the room like a shout.

"That does it, then," Singh said. "I guess he doesn't like the facilities here."

"But where can you take him that's any better?" one of the other scientists asked nervously. "What can he get outside he can't get here?"

"How about freedom?" Belilo suggested.

"The army won't let you get away with this," the woman scientist hissed as she lay on the floor. "They'll hunt you down, bring you back. . . ."

"But we'll have a head start," Symington said.

"What do we do with them?" Costanza asked, indicating the scientists cowering against the wall.

"Well, we can't have much of a head start if they're here to give the alarm the instant we leave, can we?" Singh said.

Costanza nodded, and used his own beampistol to kill the scientists.

"The trouble is, they were probably right," Singh said as he stripped the body of one scientist to get clothes for Green. "We don't know where we're taking him, and we have no idea how long he'll be able to survive away from these machines."

"Doesn't matter," Hawker said brusquely. "You heard him; he wants us to get him out. If he dies, he'll at least die free."

"And for good," Belilo murmured. "Philaskut said his pattern cracked when they dupled him. They won't be able to do it ever again."

They all stopped for a moment to ponder the implications of that. To die for the last time and never face the treadmill of war again. After all these centuries of being trapped in the endless cycle of battle and meaningless death, the idea held a lovely fascination. None of them would admit it—they'd been too highly trained in survival—but the thought was in the backs of their minds.

"Where do we go with him, though?" Costanza asked. "The only time I've been off the base was to go to that bar in town—and it's such a small town we can't hide him there. I don't know anyplace else on this world."

"Let's get him off the base first," Singh said. "We'll figure the rest out later."

Green had slipped back into a trance as they dressed

his unprotesting body, barely able to stand unsupported, in the dead scientist's uniform. Hawker and Costanza carried him to the door while Singh stooped over Philaskut's corpse and retrieved the security pass, hoping it would get them off the base.

They retraced their steps carefully, with Symington and Belilo going on ahead to act as scouts and make sure the way was clear. They made it out to their floatcar and loaded Green into the back. Climbing in after him, they started their vehicle off toward a side gate where they hoped the security would be less rigid. As of yet there had been no alarm about their escape.

The late afternoon shadows were lengthening as they reached the gate. There was only a robot sentinel stationed here, not a living person; that could be either good or bad. A robot could sometimes be fooled more easily than a real person—but if it became too confused, it could activate alarms and bring the entire base down upon them. They would have to proceed cautiously.

They stopped as the robot commanded, and Singh confidently handed out Philaskut's security pass. The robot accepted the pass, scanned it, and handed it back. "Unacceptable," it said tersely.

Singh was sweating. He took the card back and looked at his companions. "Any ideas?"

"Maybe Philaskut wasn't cleared for this gate," Belilo said. "Or maybe the card doesn't work after his death."

"Try it again," Symington said. "Sometimes I'd try a quarter in a candy machine and it wouldn't work the first time, then it would work perfectly the second time. These machines are stupid, sometimes."

Singh handed the pass back to the robot, but the results were the same. In addition, the little light in the machine's forehead that had been blinking green suddenly started blinking yellow. The robot's suspicions were definitely aroused.

In desperation, Singh handed the robot his own

173

personal pass. The machine rejected that, too, and the yellow light blinked faster.

"Oh, fuck it!" Symington said. Pulling his beampistol, he blew the robot to pieces. Immediately the air was filled with the sound of sirens, and the gates ahead of them slammed shut with a blinking red light.

"Wonderful!" Singh exclaimed. "What a perfectly shitheaded thing to do. Now how do we get out?"

"Like this." Symington pulled a grenade from his pocket and flung it at the gates. The massive metal portals blew apart from the explosion, leaving just enough of a gap for the floatcar to ease through. "See how simple?" Symington said.

"Yeah, simple answers for simple minds," Singh said. But regardless of whether he approved of the method, he was not about to pass up the opportunity. He piloted their vehicle slowly through the twisted wreckage of the gates, then gunned forward.

They sped along for more than a minute while the sound of the sirens died in the distance. Then Belilo's sharp eyes spotted something on the horizon ahead of them. "What's that?" she asked.

Singh squinted forward. "Damn. The outer perimeter line went up. Must have happened automatically when we breached the gate."

As they came closer, they could see the walls rising out of the ground, with gun turrets stationed every few hundred meters around the top. The big guns pointed outward, but a few of the smaller guns could swivel in toward the center—and they were doing so now. As they approached the wall, they would soon be coming under heavy fire.

"Even if we get through the wall, we won't be safe," Singh said. "They'll point the big guns at us then and blow us off the map. Our only chance is to take out one of the turrets and hope it'll give us an escape route."

Following his own advice, he steered the floatcar straight for the nearest gun tower. His passengers
174

needed no instructions to get down as low as they could; they were all veterans of countless fire battles.

As the floatcar came within range, Singh began an evasive pattern that he hoped would keep them out of the automated gunsights long enough to reach their objective. His passengers were bumped frantically around against the walls and one another during his maneuvers, and then jolted forward as the car screeched to a halt.

"You can get up," Singh said. "We're at the base of the tower. We'll need a few grenades to bring it down and open ourselves a hole."

Costanza had been on top of the pile, so he was the first one up. Grabbing a grenade from his pocket, he hurled it at the tower and, without waiting to see the effect, took out a second.

Several things happened at once. His first grenade exploded against the base of the gun turret, knocking it off balance and bringing it halfway to the ground, pointing at a cockeyed angle. At the same time, a beam from one of its guns neatly sliced off Costanza's left arm halfway between shoulder and elbow. The soldier screamed in pain and fell out of the floatcar, still holding the grenade in his right hand. Hawker tried to get up to help him—but before he could, Costanza scrambled to his feet once more and charged directly at the wall. Several more deadly beams hit him, but his momentum carried him up to the barrier and the grenade exploded, destroying him as well as blowing a hole in the wall large enough for their craft to fly through.

Singh did not hesitate, but gunned the floatcar through the breach. There was no need to comment on their comrade's heroism; they'd all learned to view death as a temporary phenomenon. Costanza would be resurrected next time with no memory of this incident— and he himself probably wanted to make his death a quick one, rather than suffer the pain from the loss of his arm.

Their destruction of the gun turret seemed to have done the trick; they had a narrow alley of escape through which the base's fire could not reach them. The guns on either side did not overlap their range completely. Singh took advantage of this, racing the vehicle at top speed away from the installation. The other guns along the perimeter continued to fire, sometimes coming dangerously close, but Singh somehow avoided sustaining further damage.

"We've got company," Symington commented. He'd been looking back over the edge of the seat, and was the first to spot the pursuit craft coming toward them. The runaways had perhaps a two-minute head start, but the army had at its disposal vehicles that were much faster than a simple floatcar. Unless Singh could think of a few more tricks, their mutiny would be very short-lived.

The terrain around the base was largely undeveloped, dominated by heavy brush. As they sped outward, the land became more thickly wooded, and there appeared to be a forest up ahead. The floatcar's maximum altitude was no more than a few meters, not nearly high enough to clear the trees—and the woods were dense enough to make passage through them difficult, if not impossible. They would either have to skirt around the edge, thus losing more time to their pursuers, or else abandon the car and continue on foot, hoping to lose the pursuit in the forest. The latter was a forlorn hope, considering the sophisticated sensors the army now had available.

"I'm going to slow the car when I reach the edge of the forest," Singh said calmly. "Then I'll turn and dart off to the right. I want you all to be prepared to jump out when I give the word. If we're lucky, they'll still be too far away to see you leave, and they'll chase after me. You can hide in the woods with Green while I'm evading them. I'll come back and join you after I shake them."

"But . . ." Hawker began.

Singh stopped the protest. "Relax. Without your

weights in the car, I can make this fucker do miracles. Get ready . . . now!"

The car swerved sharply, slowing and banking so abruptly that the passengers were nearly tipped out. Hawker grabbed Green and leaped out with him; Symington and Belilo jumped out on their own. The instant the others were free of the car, Singh raced off to the right without a word of farewell.

Bruised from the rapid exit, Hawker got slowly to his feet, staring at the rapidly departing floatcar until Symington nudged him. "Come on, we can't stand out here all day. We've got to hide." The two men picked up Green's limp body and carried it into the woods without another glance after the vanishing car. Belilo was in the lead, picking a path for them through the woods. All three fugitives knew they'd never see Singh again in this lifetime.

They went just a short way into the forest, deep enough so they couldn't be spotted by surveillance craft outside, and then found places to dig in. They had no way of knowing whether the army knew they were here, or thought they were all still in the floatcar, but they knew there were certain tricks they could use to minimize their chances of detection. Motion was one of the easiest qualities to detect, as was their body heat. By scattering themselves out so they weren't clumped together, each heat spot would be that much smaller and harder to find; and by staying in one place for several hours, a searcher might mistake them for part of the natural landscape.

Hawker stayed with Green, while Symington and Belilo were each a hundred meters away in different directions. As night approached, Hawker huddled with his friend for warmth, whispering quietly the story of what had happened so far. He wasn't sure how much of the tale Green could comprehend, but there were occasional flashes of awareness in the other's eyes that reassured Hawker he was doing the right thing.

With the coming of night, the temperature dropped severely. Hawker's uniform was specially constructed for temperature control, but he could do little for his hands and face. He checked to make sure the controls on Green's borrowed uniform were working correctly; he didn't want to have gone through all this trouble only to have his friend die of exposure.

After about three hours, with the full darkness of night covering them, he heard a rustling in the bushes that turned out to be Belilo. "I think we're probably safe enough for now," she said. "If they'd had any idea we were in here, we'd have seen some sign of them before this. I'll go get Symington and we'll close ranks again. We can stay here for the night and then move out in the morning." She didn't say where they would move out *to;* at this point, she had no more idea of that than Hawker.

She was back a few minutes later with Symington. The three soldiers discussed their situation briefly, and agreed that the best direction for them to go was away from the base. None of them had much idea of the geography of Cellina; they could be heading out into a wilderness with no hope of survival. But that didn't matter at the moment.

They had no idea, either, of what possible dangers might lurk in these woods, so they agreed to keep a watch. Hawker was still feeling too keyed up to sleep after the day's activities, so he volunteered to take the first shift. Belilo and Symington moved off a short way into the brush, and from the noises they made Hawker could tell they were relieving their tensions in other ways than sleeping. He tried to ignore them, but he couldn't help feeling mildly jealous. Belilo was not the most attractive woman he'd ever seen, but she had a strength of personality that was subliminally sexual. He knew, too, from previous experience that deadly peril could be a powerful aphrodisiac.

He shrugged. Maybe later. In the meantime, he had his job to do. The noises stopped after a while, and by

178

the time he went to wake Belilo for her watch, she and Symington were sleeping a meter or so apart on the cold ground. Neither Hawker nor Belilo made any comment; she got up quietly and he took her place on the ground. He thought he might still be too nervous to sleep, but the day's exertions finally caught up with him and he slept until Symington woke him at daybreak.

They were all ravenously hungry, and finding something to eat became their first priority. Belilo discovered some berry bushes whose fruit proved both edible and delicious. Symington shot a small furry animal. At first he and Hawker were worried that they might have to eat it raw, but Belilo showed them how to turn down the intensity of their beampistols to use as simple heat generators. They did not dare build a real fire for fear the smoke might give away their location.

They gave some of the fruit and meat to Green. At first they could just put it in his mouth, but after some time he got the general idea and began eating on his own. His stomach rejected the meal, however, and he threw up almost immediately afterward. This worried his friends, but there was nothing they could do about it now. All they could do was try again later and hope that eventually they would find something he could digest.

Belilo wondered how they would manage to carry Green, but Symington settled the point by hoisting the man over his shoulder and insisting he'd been on forced marches with a heavier pack than this. They set off through the forest at a slow but steady pace.

Hawker and Belilo would occasionally relieve Symington, carrying Green between them. The woods were not so dense that walking was difficult, and the trees kept them out of the worst rays of the sun. They made what they considered reasonable time under the circumstances, and by evening they found themselves at the far side of the small forest facing an open plain of tall, waving grass.

179

They tried once again to feed Green, and again his stomach rejected what they offered. The twisted man looked at them apologetically, but could not speak comprehensively enough for them to understand him. He seemed, at one point, about to cry, but his friends comforted him until he again lapsed into his normal trance.

Symington kept the first watch that night, and it was Hawker's turn to go off into the brush with Belilo. They made love with impersonal passion, both too tired from the day's march to do more than go through the mechanical motions.

Afterward, as they lay side by side, Hawker said, "I'm sorry."

"What for? You weren't that bad. We're both tired."

Hawker shook his head, even though she probably couldn't see the gesture in the dark. "No, I mean about this whole thing. I just wanted to help my friend, and now it looks like it's all been for nothing. I'm sorry I had to get you all involved in this. It's so silly. . . ."

"It's not silly. In fact, it's the first thing I've done in I don't know how many lifetimes that *isn't* silly."

"But it's such a waste. We haven't really accomplished anything except smear our own records."

"So? As I told Costanza, what can they do to us that they haven't already done?" When Hawker didn't answer, Belilo propped herself up on her elbows and looked at him, although the darkness made them scarcely visible to one another. "Look, we've both been the army's slaves for hundreds of years. We've fought for causes we can't understand, against beings we've never even met, on planets where we couldn't even survive without help. We don't even get a single thank-you—just shoved under the scanner to have our patterns copied for the next time, and the next, and the time after that. We live, but we're not alive, if you know what I mean."

"Green said, when this whole experiment began,

180

that we'd be losing our souls," Hawker said quietly.

"He was right," Belilo nodded. "Smart guy; I wish I'd known him better. Makes it all the more tragic that this had to happen to him. But the point I'm trying to make is that now, for the first time, we're fighting for *ourselves*, for something *we* want. It doesn't matter how hopeless the cause is; it's *our* cause, and that makes all the difference. That makes it worthwhile."

She settled back onto the ground, staring up at the sky. "Did you see the expression on Singh's face just as he flew off to lead the army away from us? I did. He was happy, he was alive. I'll bet Costanza felt that way, too. Sure, we're going to die eventually. The army's too big to fight off forever. They'll track us down and kill us, because it's too dangerous to let us roam free for too long. My biggest regret is that I won't be able to remember this episode in my future lives. But the point is that we *are* free—and as long as we are, I intend to enjoy it. So there's no need to apologize."

Hawker lay silently on the ground, also staring at the sky while he tried to assimilate what she'd told him. Her hands were caressing him gently; after a few minutes she rolled over on top of him and Hawker found, much to his surprise, that he was capable again this soon after the last time.

It was during Hawker's watch, just as dawn was lighting the sky, that he first saw the bubbles.

He was sitting with his back to a tree at the edge of the forest, looking over the wide expanse of meadow in front of him. Behind him, hidden in the woods, Symington and Belilo slept, near Green's gruesome body. Hawker had willed his mind to a state of semi-blankness, a private meditation technique he'd taught himself over the years; he merely repeated the word "army" over and over again like a mantra until his mind relaxed in nothingness. It was restful and allowed him to relax, while at the same time keeping him awake in case some emergency should arise.

His eye caught a movement in the sky to his right, bringing him instantly alert. His grip tightened on his rifle, which had lain casually in his lap, but he did not raise the weapon, nor did he cry out to wake his companions. The danger was not imminent yet, and he was too well trained to panic.

A series of translucent bubbles was floating across the sky. They looked like the soap bubbles he'd blown as a kid, drifting several kilometers up in the air and catching the light of the sun, which hadn't even climbed above the horizon yet. It was impossible to tell how big or how high the globes were—but somehow, despite their fragile appearance, Hawker got the impression the bubbles were tougher than they looked.

He searched the memories that had been implanted in his mind by the training probe when he'd been dupled this time. The army had no such weapons or vehicles, of that he was reasonably sure; they moved too slowly to be of any practical military use. Similarly, his experience with the aliens he'd been created to fight told him that this was nothing in their arsenal, either. Whatever these things were, they were probably incidental to the war effort, and thus he'd been given no explanation for them.

He watched them over the course of the next half hour. They posed no immediate threat, and were beautiful to watch. There was some intelligence behind them; that was obvious from the way they interacted. They glided through the sky, perhaps twenty of them—they never held still long enough for him to count them—dancing and interweaving with one another in an elaborately choreographed ballet of the air. The pattern was hypnotic as they spun and danced and glistened. Sometimes the bubbles would touch and merge for a few minutes, only to separate again and fly apart. Sometimes they would join together with a thin connector between them, like giant dumb-bells, and whirl crazily through the sky. Their colors shifted in the changing sunlight, and sometimes they took on unexpected hues of their own. Some turned dark while others glowed so brightly they rivaled the sun itself.

More and more of the bubbles drifted over the horizon to join the ballet. Bedazzled, Hawker could only watch their giddy dance until suddenly he realized there were hundreds of the bubbles filling nearly half the sky, and that the approximate center of the complex dance pattern was moving slowly to a point overhead. Suddenly the bubbles didn't seem quite as innocent as they had before.

Moving quietly and not letting his attention stray from the aerial display, he moved back into the forest and woke his two comrades. He explained in a few words that something unusual was happening, and brought them with him to the edge of the woods to observe the bubbles for themselves.

Symington and Belilo stood awestruck for several minutes by this airborne fantasy, not sure what to make of it. They suggested several possible explanations for the phenomenon, but nothing very convincing. Like Hawker, they were reluctant to use their weapons on the globes unless provoked; opening fire without due cause might give away their position here, and could conceivably incur some counterattack.

The bubbles now were so numerous it was impossible to follow all their intricate movements at once. It was Symington who first spotted the descending globe, drifting softly down from the sky to land in the field near the edge of the forest, barely fifty meters from where the trio stood watching. At this closer distance, they could see that the bubble, while seeming translucent, gave them no indication of what might be inside it. It was considerably bigger than they had estimated, more than twenty meters in diameter, easily big enough to hold several rooms inside it.

Nothing happened for several minutes, and the three

soldiers stood with weapons raised, ready to fight the instant a hostile move was made. Then they saw a crack appear in one side of the bubble, widening to form a doorway. A man stepped out onto the ground—or at least, someone whose ancestors had probably been of human stock.

He was of average height, with a deep chocolate brown skin, but his body was oddly proportioned; his legs and waist seemed much too large for that trunk and head. He was naked except for two wide bands of red cloth, running from shoulder across the chest to opposite hip and up again around the back, forming an X front and rear. He had no body hair, but growing from his head was a full and magnificent set of antlers. Belilo snickered quietly and pointed with the barrel of her rifle to indicate the fact that the man from the bubble had two penises.

The soldiers watched nervously as this being left his bubble and walked into the forest off to their right, apparently not noticing them. The door in the side of the bubble remained tantalizingly open. Hawker suggested they go in and investigate, but Belilo shook her head.

"Too risky. We have no idea what we'd be getting into. Those bubbles are some sort of craft, but we still don't know what makes them go or how to work them. I think we might better try to capture our horny friend and see what information we can get out of him."

The two men agreed, and the trio fanned out through the forest, moving in the direction where they'd last seen their quarry. The man from the bubble made no attempt to conceal himself as he walked deeper into the woods at a leisurely pace, checking the trees as though looking for a special kind. Belilo gave the signal and ran out of her hiding place to tackle him. Hawker and Symington were there a scant second later to help her. Their victim, after his initial moment of surprise, put up no resistance.

"All right, friend, who are you?" Belilo asked him.

The man stared up with wide, calm eyes. "Consakannis," he replied. "And if I really am your friend, you have an odd way of showing it."

The serenity with which he answered, despite the difficulty of his position, was a little unnerving, but Belilo had to tough it out. "You're either our friend, or dead," she told him. "The choice is entirely yours."

"Oh." He paused to consider that. "I suppose I might be your friend for a while. It could be amusing."

"It's anything but amusing," Symington said. "There's a lot at stake here."

"Indeed?" If Consakannis had had eyebrows, one would have been lifted.

Hawker didn't like the way this conversation was turning. "What's that bubble you came down in?" he asked.

"That's my home-sphere."

Symington grabbed Consakannis by the crossing strips of cloth and pulled him roughly to his feet. "Take us in there."

"If you like."

The antlered man led the way back through the forest to the bubble, which rested quietly at the edge of the field exactly as he'd left it. He walked without hesitation through the doorway, and the three soldiers followed quickly after him, afraid he might make the bubble rise into the air once more and get away before they could stop him.

Inside, the bubble was lit with a soothing yellow glow that diffused from the walls. They were in a small compartment barely large enough for all four of them to move around. Holes in the ceiling and the other walls seemed to lead to other rooms. "A little cramped, isn't it?" Symington asked.

"I wasn't expecting guests," Consakannis replied calmly. "I'll just take a second to adjust it."

He reached his left hand out against the wall and tapped his fingers lightly on the surface like a typist tapping out a pattern. The outer wall remained as it was, but the inner walls receded until the room was large enough for them to walk around. "Is that better?" he asked.

"Much," Belilo said, trying to disguise her worries about exactly what sort of person they'd captured. "But doesn't it get boring living in a bare room? Don't you have any furniture?"

"What kind would you like?" Consakannis tapped another pattern on the wall and the material of the floor began shifting, flowing upward and molding itself into the shapes of a long blue sofa and two large green stuffed armchairs. "If the colors aren't suitable," he said, "I can always change them."

"Do you live in here by yourself?" Hawker asked, concentrating on the important questions to take his mind off the disturbing powers their prisoner possessed.

For the first time, Consakannis seemed perplexed. "Of course," he said, tilting his head in puzzlement. "Who else could possibly live in *my* home? People visit from time to time, but . . ." His face brightened. "Would you like to go up and meet them?"

"No," Belilo said emphatically. "We're staying right here until we get all of this sorted out."

"You really are antisocial, aren't you?" Consakannis said. He crossed the room and started to sit down in one of the armchairs.

"No one said you could sit," Symington growled.

"It *is* my home." The prisoner sat defiantly and crossed his legs.

Belilo was sweating. She could feel the entire situation slipping from her grasp, and she didn't like that one bit. "We're giving the orders around here," she said. "You'll sit when we tell you to, and not before."

"This is really getting rather boring," Consakannis said, not moving from his comfortable position.

Belilo pointed her rifle directly at the captive's midsection. "Get up, damn you!"

"And if I don't?"

"Then I'll shoot you where you are."

"Then I'm afraid that's what you'll have to do. You've become too tiresome to bother with."

Belilo glanced nervously at her two companions. If she backed down now, they might as well just surrender, for they would be Consakannis's prisoners within this bubble. Much as she hated to admit it, they'd lost control of their captive. He wasn't afraid of them, and she saw plainly that nothing she could do would bring her any power over him. Reluctantly she squeezed the firing stud and watched the energy beam lash out to devour Consakannis's body.

The man died instantly. Within moments of his death, the three soldiers felt the bubble around them shake as though caught in a massive earthquake. The glow from the walls died, and the walls themselves blurred and turned a dead-leaf brown. The pieces of furniture that had been conjured up through the floor curled at the edges and shriveled into themselves. The bubble, too, began collapsing. Strange indentations appeared in the originally smooth exterior shell, accompanied by a disgusting sucking sound.

Hawker and his friends looked about wildly, but the door through which they'd come had disappeared. The shaking continued, becoming even more violent, and they were knocked off their feet onto the hard floor while the walls around them continued their implosion.

All three cried out, fears of being crushed or suffocated flitting through their minds. As the shell closed in upon them, though, it turned out to be some gooey substance that clung to their skin and clothing like molasses. They reached up their arms, striving to tear holes through the goo to enable themselves to breathe, and just did manage to find the space before the globe collapsed completely, bathing them in a syrupy swamp.

"What is this shit?" Symington asked, struggling to free his arms from the quagmire.

"No wonder Consakannis was confused when we

asked if anyone else lived here with him," Belilo said. "This literally was his house, attuned to his personal pattern. When his body was no longer alive, the house ceased to serve any function and just melted down into this . . . mess." She was struggling, too, to pull herself out of the sticky liquid that had been Consakannis's bubble. "No wonder he wasn't afraid of our killing him. He must have thought we were incredibly stupid."

"He'll be resurrected again anyway, won't he?" Hawker asked.

"I guess so. They seem to have extended that privilege to everyone on this world. They can probably duple his house, too. Not that it helps us any. I'm only glad the bubble was on the ground when I shot him. Can you imagine what would have happened if he'd died while we were floating up there?"

By sheer force she and Symington had begun to pull themselves out of the ocean of goo, and Hawker belatedly followed suit. The viscous fluid clung tenaciously to his clothing and particularly his boots, making walking difficult. "We'd better get back to Green," he panted. "I don't think we'll get any help from the bubble people."

"I'll second that," Symington agreed. He and Hawker helped Belilo climb out of the soup and onto dry land. The slimy mixture flowed slowly down their bodies and onto the ground, leaving the soldiers feeling dirty and somehow tainted. They stomped their feet to shake loose some final vestiges of the bubble, then walked back into the forest, keeping a close eye out for any other bubbles that might descend.

They were in for a surprise, though, when they reached the spot where they'd left their deformed comrade. There was an angel floating in the air above Green's body.

Or at least it looked like an angel at first glance. The being was humanoid, with enormous feathered wings protruding from her back, beating gently to

188

keep herself aloft. Her entire body glowed as though filled with natural phosphorescence. She was naked except for a narrow jeweled belt, and she was quite definitely feminine. Her long flowing hair was a shade halfway between blond and green, her skin a pale coffee color; her breasts were small and firm, and she had no pubic hair. She studied the soldiers as they approached just as curiously as they studied her.

Symington spoke first. "Who the hell are you?"

"My name's Amassa," she replied evenly. "More importantly, who are you?"

"Nobody special," Belilo said warily.

"Really? I'd have guessed you were the escaped soldiers we've all heard about."

Symington raised his rifle, aiming squarely at the angel's midriff. At this range he could scarcely miss.

Amassa looked back at him, unconcerned. "Oh, how primitive! Are you going to kill me, too?"

Belilo reached out and pushed Symington's rifle downward, pointed harmlessly at the ground. "Not if we can avoid it," she said. "We don't want to hurt anybody."

"You could have fooled me," Amassa said. "I was watching the scene in Consakannis's bubble on my own home screen. You sounded awfully mean there."

Hawker felt a chill run up his spine. How many other people had witnessed what went on in Consakannis's bubble? Was everyone on Cellina tuned in? Had their brave—or foolhardy—attempt at freedom been reduced to the level of a TV show to entertain the populace? Were they really free now, or were they merely out on a long leash for the amusement of their masters?

These questions had obviously occurred to Belilo and Symington, too, judging by the doubtful expressions on their faces. But Belilo remained the spokesperson, maintaining her glacial calm even in the midst of this confusion. "We made a mistake," she excused. "We're in a desperate situation and we react largely by instinct."

Amassa clapped her hands, the delight on her face like that of a small child. "Just as I thought. Oh, this could be very good indeed."

Symington's eyes narrowed. "What do you mean by 'this'?"

"Would you like me to help you?" Amassa said, totally ignoring the question.

"Help us?" Hawker asked. "How?"

"I could take you into my bubble and hide you from the army."

"How can we be sure you won't turn us in, instead?" Belilo asked.

Amassa laughed. It was a pleasant laugh, like the tinkle of tiny bells, yet Hawker found it oddly disquieting. "I guess you can't," the angel replied. "But if you don't come with me, I'll definitely turn you in."

It was then that the three on the ground realized just how trapped they were. They stood at the mercy of this strange winged woman, whose body and face radiated with innocence, but whose eyes bespoke depths they could not understand. For a brief moment Hawker thought of killing Amassa too, but realized the futility of that. There were hundreds of other bubbles in the sky, hundreds of other potential witnesses; it only took one to give their location away to the army, and everything they'd fought for would be lost.

No, he decided. Better to go with Amassa now and hope she might really help them. There was no sane alternative. Hawker looked at the faces of his friends and saw that they had come to the same unhappy conclusion.

Amassa, too, could read the expressions on the soldiers' faces. She smiled, and the glow from her body brightened. "Come," she said. "I've brought my home-sphere down just outside the woods. We can retire there." She flew gracefully between the trees; Symington picked up Green, slung him over his shoulder and then joined his friends as the group followed Amassa out of the forest.

190

The bubble looked the same as the previous one from the outside, but Amassa had known to expect company, and had arranged the interior accordingly. The entrance room was large enough to throw a sizable party in. There was a comfortable padded couch on which Green could be set, and miscellaneous other furniture for the guests' comfort. One whole wall acted as a picture window—but the scene it portrayed was not the tableau outside the bubble; rather, it was a constantly changing diorama of views from all over the planet. The other walls glowed with subtle colors that mixed and swirled in no discernible pattern. The eerie lighting only added to the unsettling feeling Hawker got from this unusual captor.

"What are you going to do with us?" Symington asked after setting Green down on the couch.

"I don't know," Amassa said simply. "I haven't thought it out yet. Something interesting will come to mind, no doubt."

"Why are you taking so much interest in us?" asked Belilo.

"Oh, I guess because I'm Consakannis's *nitzah*."

The language lessons that had been implanted in Hawker's mind when he was resurrected reminded him of that term's meaning. A *nitzah* was somewhat less than a spouse, but considerably more than a casual friend. It was not always a sexual relationship, his training told him, but the exact subtleties of the arrangement were beyond his comprehension.

Belilo licked her lips. "Now look, if you want revenge for what we did, you have to remember he goaded us into it. If he'd explained himself at the time and cooperated with us, we wouldn't have had to—"

"Revenge? Oh, how delightfully primitive!" Amassa laughed again. Despite the euphony of the sound, Hawker decided he did not like this woman's laughter.

"No, what would be the point of revenge?" Amassa continued. "Consakannis will be dupled again very

191

shortly, if he hasn't been already. If his death was at all painful, he can excise out that split second of pain; within the next day or so he'll rejoin us, and he'll probably laugh at the pictures of you being caught in his dead sphere."

"If you're not after revenge, why do you want us?" Hawker asked.

Amassa ignored the question. "I suppose you learned some lesson with Consakannis," she said, "but just let me repeat it a little. It's rather foolish to try anything that would make me uncomfortable. I have more powers here than you do."

She didn't need to touch the walls to control her globe, as Consakannis had done; instead, she merely fingered one of the jewels on her belt. Instantly the gravity within the bubble grew so oppressively heavy that none of the soldiers could stand upright. They slumped to the floor, gasping for breath while Amassa, unaffected, floated over them and smiled. "If you'll just remember this one simple fact," she said, "I'm sure we'll get on tremendously." Another touch of the belt, and gravity returned to normal. Hawker and his companions rose slowly to their feet.

"You made your point," Belilo said.

"Good," Amassa said with childlike enthusiasm. "Now, are any of you hungry?"

Thoughts of food had been pushed from their minds by more urgent matters, but the mere mention was enough to spark their appetites. Two days of near-starvation had taken their toll. Despite the soldiers' apprehension over their new condition, they nodded avidly.

Amassa touched her belt again and a small section of the wall became a viewing center. On the screen flashed images of dishes beyond number, each appearing for barely a second before being replaced by another. It was a virtual encyclopedia of foods from a multitude of different planets. "If you see anything you like," Amassa said, "just let me know."

192

The three stared openmouthed at the display, hardly knowing what to answer. "Everything looks so good, it really doesn't matter," Belilo said. She pointed suddenly at random. "How about that?"

Amassa froze the image on the screen. The dish appeared to be a rich kind of stew, and the brief description beside it indicated it was made from four different kinds of meat and two dozen distinct vegetables from three different worlds. The aroma also wafted through the air, making the fugitives' mouths water.

"All of you want that? Fine, you've got it." The angel touched her belt once more and a table rose out of the floor. On the table were three large bowls filled with the steaming stew.

Hawker stared with amazement that a dish with so many complex ingredients could be prepared so quickly —and then he wondered why he was surprised. If people could be dupled exactly, why not a bowl of stew? If, as Philaskut had told them, the pattern for a human being could be recorded in a crystal no larger than a grain of salt, the stew must be simplicity itself—and it was just as easy to re-create it whole as to create the individual ingredients and waste time preparing and cooking it.

He stood transfixed before the table. The implications of all this were staggering. He had never really contemplated it all before, but the matter duplicator was a development that must have changed the entire pattern of human existence. Hunger and poverty could be eliminated; why should anyone go without something when he could simply press a button and have an exact duplicate of it all his own? That would certainly explain the free and easy life-style of Amassa and the other bubble people. They had no knowledge of what it was like to go without something; self-denial was an alien concept.

His imagination soared at the idea of this society, only to crash back to reality with a sudden thud. One thing was still the same: war. The needs and goals of a society might change; they had evolved so far beyond Hawker's comprehension that he seldom bothered to ask what the war was about any more. But the fighting remained—and as long as it did, Hawker and the other "primitives" would still be useful to society.

He stepped forward toward the table, along with Symington and Belilo, then stopped suddenly. "What about our friend?" he asked, gesturing over his shoulder at the still figure of Green.

"What would he like?" Amassa asked.

"I don't know. He can't seem to eat much of anything. The army doctors say they had him on a special diet. His pattern was messed up when they dupled him, and his body doesn't work right. We tried feeding him in the woods, but he just threw up again."

Amassa's perfect face contorted to a thoughtful pout; she was clearly unhappy at this complication. A door opened in one wall and she walked out into the next room, leaving the soldiers along for several minutes. Finally she came back, touched her belt controls and said, "There. That should take care of it."

A transparent dome glowing energy covered Green's body atop the couch. "What's happening?" Hawker asked.

"The house is feeding proteins and digested materials directly into his bloodstream," Amassa explained. "We bypass the eating and digesting stages altogether."

"Sort of an advanced method of intravenous feeding," Belilo said.

Hawker was still a little unsure, but the aroma of the hot stew was weakening his resistance. Unable to do anything further for Green, he turned back to the table and ate his own meal with great relish. Amassa even gave him second helpings, which he wolfed down greedily.

The fugitives ate without much discussion, and when they finished and looked around, they noticed Amassa

194

was gone. "Wonder where she went," Symington said.

"I've given up trying to figure her out," Belilo said. "She'll be back when she's ready, I'm sure of that. In the meantime, let's look around and see what we can find."

"Amassa might not like that," Hawker said.

"She didn't say we couldn't, did she? Besides, I don't quite trust her."

"That's for sure," Symington agreed.

The three soldiers prowled cautiously through Amassa's home-sphere, alert for any further surprises this culture might have in store, but could find nothing of interest other than a semienclosed toilet. The three other rooms within the globe were all small and devoid of furnishings; Amassa probably conjured up her furniture only when she needed it. There was no sign of their hostess, and they could only surmise that she had gone out to visit one of the other bubbles. She could be betraying them to the army at this very moment—but she could have done that quite some time ago, too, without going to this much trouble on their behalf. In any event, there was little they could do about it right now. Disappointed, they returned to the original room.

They found that Green was awake and staring at them with his weird, off-center eyes. They crowded around him, anxious to know how he was feeling.

"Better than I felt in the lab," he replied. "It's no fun living under a microscope. I can't thank you enough for all you've been through for my sake."

"We're not free yet," Belilo said. "Not by a long shot." She proceeded to tell him, with occasional asides from Hawker and Symington, the story of their escape and flight, and their current predicament. Hawker described his hypotheses about the current culture on Cellina, and Green nodded.

"You're really using your brain, Hawk. I'm proud of you." Green coughed harshly and settled back on his couch. "Decadence . . ."

His voice drifted off, and for a few moments his friends were afraid he'd drifted into semiconsciousness once more. But he was only thinking; the look of intelligence never wavered in his eyes.

"A world that's conquered both poverty and death," he mused aloud at last. "It must be decadent beyond our ability to imagine. There's no need to work, no challenge to living. Material goods will mean nothing, so the only thing left of any value is sensation. The only thing they can do to fill their days is experience as many different things as they can."

Again he drifted off into thought, only to snap suddenly out of his reverie. He propped himself up awkwardly on his misshapen elbows and looked at the group—particularly at Hawker. "Be very careful, all of you," he warned. "If these people have no limits, it also means they have no morals. They'll have only one rule of behavior, to stay one up on the next guy. I don't think the rules of human behavior will change that drastically. Power and control, that's what it's always been about. If anything, those drives have probably been amplified since the drive to get enough to eat and enough to own has been eliminated. Amassa's already shown you that she wants to control your actions. She wants to be in charge. Watch out for her . . ."

His voice drifted off again, but this time the luster was fading from his eyes, to be replaced by the glassy stare of incomprehension. Green had slipped out of reality once more, and Hawker clenched his fists in frustration at the thought that a person as good and smart as his friend could have to suffer this terrible tragedy.

Hours passed, and still there was no sign of Amassa. Hawker and his friends talked for a while among themselves, but quickly ran out of things to say. They could make no plans for escape when they didn't know how powerful their enemy was. There was nothing else to do inside the bubble except watch the changing panorama on the picture window, and they quickly tired of that, too. Eventually their boredom led them to the soldier's ultimate recourse—they curled up in the comfortable furniture and went to sleep.

Hawker opened his eyes to find a face staring back at him from only a few centimeters away. The face was bright orange and had three eyes, and at first Hawker thought his own eyes were out of focus from having just woken up. He blinked several times, but the image did not change. Then he felt some hands caressing his shoulders, and he sat up, startled.

The orange face backed quickly away to a more respectful distance, and Hawker noticed with alarm that the face was attached to a body like that of a hairless chimpanzee. The three-eyed orange chimp smiled at him and wiggled its hips seductively. Hawker glanced down its body and saw that it was most definitely masculine. He quickly shook his head and turned away.

The room had expanded out to its full limits, squeezing the other rooms of the bubble into non-existence. Into this vast open space was crowded the most unusual assortment of people Hawker had ever seen in one place. They all had derived from human stock, but they had been so altered that no two of their bodies looked exactly alike. Heights ranged between one and three meters; some bodies were stick thin, others quite well rounded. Hair, eyes and skin colors were of every imaginable shade. Some of the people had more than the standard number of limbs, some had less; others had outré appendages like horns, antlers, wings or lobster claws. Some were clothed, some not, but both sexes were adequately represented —sometimes even within the same body.

Hawker looked for his friends, and spotted them over by Green's couch. Symington and Belilo were equally aghast at this freak assemblage, while Green appeared to be still within his coma. Hawker rose from the chair where he'd been sleeping and pushed his way through the curious crowd to his comrades' side. "What in hell is all this?" he asked them.

Amassa, who'd been standing just a short distance away, came over to them. "I'm glad you're all awake now," she said breezily. "These are a few of my friends. They were so excited when they heard I was entertaining some primitives that they all wanted to come and meet you. I hope you'll be polite to them."

One short female, her face covered with a peachlike fuzz, walked boldly up to the group of soldiers, who crouched back together for mutual protection. She looked over each of the three in turn and stopped in front of Belilo. "I'm Nya," she purred. "You interest me."

"Me?" Belilo said. "But I . . ."

"Don't be so coy. I've heard how savage you primitives can be." Nya ran an exploratory finger down the front of Belilo's uniform, between her breasts. The rest of the crowd watched the scene with delicious anticipation. Belilo tensed and clenched her fists, prepared for a fight. She would show Nya and the others just how savage she could be.

Then Amassa touched Belilo lightly on the shoulder. "Remember, you must behave yourselves. Life can be awfully unpleasant for those who don't cooperate. Nya won't hurt you." She looked over to the woman whose hands were continuing their exploration of Belilo's body. "You won't hurt her, will you? It would be such a waste of such unique material."

"Nothing that can't be fixed," Nya said, her eyes not wavering from Belilo.

"See?" Amassa said to comfort her frightened captive.

But Belilo was far from comforted. She tried to break away, but two other people had sneaked up behind her. They pushed her forward, straight into Nya's arms. Nya laughed as she embraced her prey, and Amassa joined her in the laughter. The general

198

tone throughout the room was one of high amusement.

Symington and Hawker both started forward to help their friend, and fell flat on their faces. Strong anklets had grown out of the floor, wrapped around their feet and held them securely in one spot. They could do nothing to help, and had to watch impotently the fate of their comrade.

Belilo was trying to use her combat training against her attacker. One foot lashed out a vicious swipe that caught Nya off guard. The smaller woman went flying across the room, knocking into several of the onlookers. Amassa clucked and shook her head, then reached down to her belt. Belilo's left foot, still on the ground, was instantly pinioned just as the men's had been. Belilo stood awkwardly poised with her right foot still in the air. She tried to catch her balance and keep the foot away from the floor so it wouldn't be caught like the other one. While she was engaged in that delicate maneuver, other guests came up behind her and grabbed both her arms, while two more grabbed her free leg and held it outstretched.

Nya got slowly to her feet and came forward to face Belilo. Hawker would not have called the smile on her lips cruel; it was merely devoid of any warmth. Nya reached out to touch the struggling but helpless woman again and gently unfastened the front seam of her uniform. "Such passion, such fire," she remarked to herself as she began to peel Belilo's clothing methodically from her body. "Primitive, indeed."

Belilo spit in her face, but Nya kept stripping her undeterred. In just a few minutes, with the aid of her accomplices, she had Belilo standing naked before the crowd. Nya inspected the body, nodding approval of Belilo's muscle tone and admiring the scars she'd acquired during her long military career. Then, as Amassa dissolved the ankle restraint, Nya and her friends carried Belilo through the crowd and out of Hawker's sight.

Amassa released the restraints on Hawker and Symington. "I suppose you should be commended for your primitive impetuosity, but a little of that can go a long way. Let's see if you can be just a little more civilized, shall we?"

"What was civilized about that?" Symington asked as he stood up, but he never received an answer. He was almost immediately encircled by a group of admirers—mostly female, but some male—exploring his large, muscular frame. They began stroking him and tearing at his clothing, sexual hunger naked on their faces.

Amassa came over to Hawker as he knelt, and spread her wings around him protectively. "This one's mine," she announced to the crowd at large. Then, looking into Hawker's face, she said sweetly, "There's nothing to fear. I won't let anything hurt you. Here, try one of these."

Before he knew what she was doing, she popped a tiny tablet into his mouth. He tried to spit it out, but she held a hand over his mouth with more strength than he would have thought she had. He refused to swallow the pill, but it made no difference; the tablet dissolved on his tongue with a fizzy sensation, like the carbon dioxide "exploding" candy he'd had as a child. The fizziness spread outward from his tongue to his cheeks, and finally upward to his eyes and his brain, where it exploded like fireworks on a summer night.

The room did not spin, exactly, but it did go off center, and his every movement to right himself only made the situation worse. The swirling color patterns of the walls, which had seemed so subtle before, suddenly shrieked at him; the red lanced out at his eyes, the yellow threatened him with deadly flames and the blue licked out at his feet like an inviting ocean, tempting him to drown himself in its depths. The noise around him, the talking of Amassa's guests, dopplered in and out of his range like an obscene siren. His skin itched from the feet of a million imagined ants, but his mind was bathed in honey balm and scarcely noticed. His tongue tasted of peppermint and sour apples, while his nose was filled with the musky scent of his own body, unbathed for several days.

His mind moved, his body remained. He was floating well above the tumult, an omniscient but impotent god. Amassa's guests danced and wheeled, just as he had seen their bubbles dancing through the sky. Gravity was no master to them; they defied it at their will, soaring and spinning through the crowded space, their bodies touching and rubbing in sensual patterns as random as they were erotic. His mind pierced the wall, through the other bubbles that congregated around Amassa's, watching the frenetic gyrations of the aerial ballet matching the simulated passions of their creators. He saw Belilo in another bubble, spread-eagled and held helpless by some invisible force, while Nya and a dozen of her minions stroked her and poked her, kissed her and clawed her, laughing at their captive's increasingly hoarse screams. . . .

The sight was repellent, and Hawker left quickly. He floated back to Amassa's bubble, less crowded now that the party had dispersed. Symington was gone, carried off somewhere by his circle of admirers. Green was still on his couch, ignored, his twisted body probably too abhorrent even for this decadent crowd. The Hawker-body was on the floor, stripped naked, center of attention. It was writhing in painful convulsions in reaction to the drug, while Amassa and her friends sat around discussing the phenomenon. The Hawker-mind was too detached, though, and floated against one wall, all uncaring.

When the convulsions stopped he found himself back in his body, but the effects of the drug were far from ended. Time became elastic, stretching out before him like a rubber band, only to snap back with painful abruptness in an instant. Sometimes the actions of the people around him seemed like a speeded-up movie, and he wanted to laugh at the comical antics, while at

201

other times everything around him came to a dead stop and he wanted to shout to get them moving again.

The ceiling, with its changing patterns of light and darkness, became the most fascinating object in the universe. He devoted his entire attention to it. He realized that things were happening to his body; he could tell, in an abstract way, that feelings of a sexual nature were crawling ever so slowly along his nerves to his brain, but they never fully penetrated. He could tell he had an erection, and the tension built to a monstrous orgasm, an ejaculation that went on endlessly through time and space. But those were *distractions,* and he wished they would go away so he could concentrate more fully on the ceiling. That was *really* important.

After a while the ceiling ceased to occupy him, and he found himself floating again—only this time it was the body and mind together. He was naked in empty space, surrounded by ghosts, wraithlike figures he could see right through. They pinched him and tickled him, and when he reached out to defend himself his hand would go through them as though they didn't exist. Then the whole world went blurry, as though seen by a myopic without his glasses. Shapes lost all definition and objects had no distinct edges. Smells tickled his nostril hairs without staying long enough to be identified. Sounds came to him as through the wrong end of a telescope, making no sense whatsoever. He felt that if they would only slow down, and if he could play them backward on a tape recorder, they might just have some meaning—but they kept coming at him without a stop. Putting his hands to his ears did no good; it could not shut out the screaming of some madman in the room, and it wasn't for driftless ages that he realized the screaming madman was himself.

It was not long after that when the shadows crept

up over the horizon of his peripheral vision and engulfed him in a merciful darkness of sleep.

His tongue was fuzzy and his eyeballs ached. Those were the first sensations to hit him as he drew out of the pit into which Amassa's strange drug had cast him. His nose was stuffy and he had to breathe through his mouth. His body was naked but cool, and he felt as though he were floating in a swimming pool. Another body was pressed tightly against his—a female body, soft and smooth and delicate, her slender arms encircling him.

"How did you get your wings?" he heard his own voice ask, as though he'd been in the middle of a conversation and continued on automatically.

"I had them surgically adapted when I was nineteen. Aren't they magnificent?"

Hawker finally opened his eyes despite the throbbing sensation that caused. He was staring directly into Amassa's face, and she was gazing at him with a beatific smile. The two of them were floating in the air in the middle of her bubble; she was holding both of them aloft, with her beautiful feathered angel wings spread wide apart for his inspection.

"I've never seen anything quite like them," he said truthfully.

Her eyes narrowed a bit and she looked at him more critically. "It's worn off, hasn't it?"

"What?"

"The outgo, the drug I gave you."

"I guess so."

"Would you like some more?"

"No!"

He realized instantly, from her expression, that his reply had been much too vehement, and he tried to soften its impact. "That is, I . . . not right now. I'm not used to something like that, I need time to recover. Maybe later."

Amassa smiled and ruffled his hair with one playful hand. "I must remember, my darling primitive, that your body is not as adaptive as ours."

"I'm afraid not." He hesitated. "How long was I . . . under?"

Amassa pouted; time meant little to her, and she hated having to think about it. "Oh, about three days, I think. Does it matter?"

Three days! Who knew what could have happened in all that time? Would the army still be searching for him, or had Singh's ruse put them off the trail? "Where are my friends?" he asked.

"The twisted one is still with me—he wasn't much fun, and no one else wanted him. As for the others . . ." She shrugged. "They're off somewhere. I'm not sure precisely where."

"Will I have a chance to see them again?"

"Perhaps." Amassa's tone made it plain she was annoyed at the direction the conversation was going. "Right now, though, they're no concern of yours. You should be more interested in pleasing me."

To emphasize her point, Amassa rubbed her body suggestively against his. Her smooth bare skin pressed tightly to his own had the desired effect; Hawker came quickly erect, and Amassa moved her hips slightly to allow him to slip easily inside her. She then threw her entire being into a grinding motion that left Hawker gasping with raw desire.

They spun rhythmically through the empty air, and a sudden wave of vertigo almost made Hawker lose his erection. Sensing this, Amassa redoubled her efforts and restored him to full potency. Hawker pushed from his mind the fact that they were floating in midair, refused to think about the spins and somersaults Amassa was putting them through, cleared from his brain every external distraction. Amassa was right: he had to please her if he wanted to escape eventually from this glorious but frightening prison. Hawker concentrated all his feeling into the sexual passion of their union, letting the pressure build until it exploded in a climax so intense it was actually painful.

His body went limp, and Amassa lowered them both to the ground, to which she gave a soft, spongy consistency. Hawker lay panting on his back while she gently traced the muscles of his arm with one long, delicate finger. "Would you mind if I asked you a question?" he said when he'd regained his breath.

He could feel her fingers pause over his skin, fingernails ready to pierce him if he displeased her. "Is it about your friends?" she asked coldly.

"Not exactly. I was just wondering whether the army was still looking for us. Technically we're deserters, and the army doesn't like to let deserters get off too easily. Also, we stole Green away from them before they were finished studying him, and I don't think they were very happy about that."

Amassa relaxed once more. "There have been some bulletins about fugitives, but very vague. Something about your being armed and dangerous." She smiled, as though at a private joke. "But we know better, don't we?"

She was so smug, so superior, and yet Hawker knew there was nothing he could do. She had too much control over the situation. "Are you going to turn us in?"

"Maybe, someday. Not for a while, though." She grinned greedily. "You're much too . . . entertaining."

"I thought you were involved with Consakannis."

"Oh, sometimes," she dismissed casually. "Right now he's over with Nya's group, involved in something or other. He'll wander back into my life, eventually."

Hawker lapsed into silence again, resting in the afterglow of the fantastic lovemaking. His body was coated with sweat, and he felt too weak to do anything. The exertion, following such a long period under the influence of the outgo drug, had worn him down. Right now, he couldn't force himself to care what his future might be.

After a while, Amassa asked, "Why did you do it? Why did you and the others desert?"

Hawker paused and took a few deep breaths while he tried to sort the story out in his mind. "Friendship," he said. "I didn't like what they were doing to my friend."

"I don't understand."

Slowly and carefully, Hawker told Amassa the full story, from Green's malformed duplication through the decision to free him from the laboratory to the actual escape and flight, ending with the story of their "rendezvous" with Amassa and her friends. He was hoping to win her sympathy, thinking that if he told the story in an appealing enough manner he might actually touch her heart and enlist her support in the venture. But even as he spoke, he could see it wouldn't work. Amassa had no soul, no pity—or if she did, it worked along entirely different lines. The very word "friendship" was not the same for her, and the concept of self-sacrifice to help another was alien to her culture. The lack of comprehension was written in her face and broadcast through her eyes; she simply could not understand why Hawker and the others would go to so much trouble and personal aggravation for the sake of someone else.

"I don't know what's going to happen to him now," Hawker concluded sadly. "We got him away from the army, which is what he wanted, but this isn't exactly what we had in mind for him, either. I don't know what we really expected to do. In his condition he could probably never live anywhere naturally."

He shook his head. "Maybe it would be kinder to kill him and put him out of his misery, like shooting a horse with a broken leg. But I just can't do that. He's been my friend forever, it seems. I owe it to him to try everything possible to save him."

"And it wouldn't do any good, even if you did kill him," Amassa said. "The army would just duple him again, and start the whole process over."

"At least that's one thing they can't do."

"Everyone and everything can be dupled," Amassa said firmly.

"You don't understand. Philaskut told us that Green's recording was so badly damaged by whatever happened to it that it fell apart right after they dupled him. That's the whole problem—they can't recreate his pattern."

"It's you who doesn't understand, Maybe his original pattern was destroyed, but they can still make a copy of him the way he is now."

Hawker tensed. "What?"

"I looked at him closely while you were under outgo. He's got a transmitter in his neck, the same as I do." She stretched out her throat to show him the tiny button implanted just below the skin surface.

Looking at the device, Hawker remembered that Philaskut had had one—and had said that everyone on Cellina did, too. Self-consciously he put a hand on his own neck, but felt nothing. "What exactly is that?" he asked, trying to sound much more casual than he felt.

"It's a broadcast transmitter. It makes a continuous reading of my molecular pattern and sends it to Resurrection Central, where my file is recorded and continuously updated. If I were to die, Resurrection Central could duple me exactly the way I was the instant before my death. Or, say, if I had my leg cut off, they could go back in the files to my pattern at the moment *before* my leg was cut off and duple me whole again. It's a wonderful concept, don't you think?"

Hawker did not, could not, answer. He buried his face in his hands and gritted his teeth in frustration. All of this had been for nothing! They had not saved Green from anything. They had perhaps saved this particular edition—but the army could duple him as he was just before he was kidnapped, and poor Dave would have to go through that hell all over again. All this running, all this hiding, all this torture—it was all a study in futility! He wanted to scream at his own stupidity.

Instead, he laughed. The hysteria burst out in loud gales of laughter that had tears pouring from his eyes and his nose running like a faucet. His whole body shook, and he turned over on his side away from Amassa.

"What's funny?" his captor asked.

It took a few seconds for Hawker to bring himself back under control. "It's ridiculous," he said, wiping at the tears with the back of his forearm. "Here I am, worried about the army's tracking us down, and they probably don't even care. They've got Dave in their lab again, conducting the same old tests."

"I don't think so," Amassa said. "In the bulletins I heard, they definitely mentioned they wanted this one back if possible."

"Why? That doesn't make sense."

"I didn't pay much attention. Something about minute differences between the original and the duple. All I know is they wanted to make sure they couldn't get the original before they made a duple. It sounded silly to me, too, but that's what they said."

Her fingers began kneading Hawker's muscles in a sensual pattern, starting at his shoulder blades and working slowly down his body, distracting him from further thoughts at this time.

Some time later, when she went out to visit some friends, Hawker was left alone in the bubble with Green. At first the twisted man was in his unfortunate state of semiconsciousness, but after a while it cleared. He looked at Hawker and smiled. "Hi," he said. "Down from your trip yet?"

"You know about that?"

"I was conscious a few times and saw you. It looked horrible."

Hawker shuddered. "I don't ever want to go through that again. Maybe *they* think it's fun, but I can't take it. You were right about them—they're all heartless
208

bastards." He described what had happened during the "party," and then went into detail about the conversation he'd had with Amassa.

Green was very thoughtful after Hawker had finished. Hawker, not knowing what else to say, ended with the apology, "I'm sorry, Dave, I tried to help, really I did. I guess I kinda fucked up again, huh?"

"It's not all lost yet," Green murmured.

"Huh? What do you mean? Whether they capture us or kill us, they can still make more copies of you."

"But the duple isn't as good as the original. It's like making a Xerox copy of a Xerox copy, it gets slightly fainter each time you do it. The difference might not mean much in practical, everyday terms—they could duple you a million times and there wouldn't be a milligram of difference in the lot. But in my case, they want to study the pattern as it was originally created, and minute differences could be very significant. That's why they haven't dupled me yet—they want to make absolutely sure the original version is unavailable before they work on a copy."

"Big deal. They won't wait forever. If they haven't found you in a couple of weeks, they'll probably take their chances with a duple anyway."

"But if a pattern can be destroyed once, it can be destroyed twice."

Hawker blinked. "What's that mean?"

"They can't use my original pattern to duple me, because that broke. If we could get to this Resurrection Central, wherever it is, and destroy the file they've got on me there, they couldn't use that pattern, either."

Hawker smacked his forehead with his palm. "Why didn't I think of that?" Then, in a more practical vein, "But how can we get in there? If that's where they store the records of everyone on Cellina, it must be a very important place. They'll have thousands of guards all the time."

"Not necessarily." Green smiled, a particularly grotesque expression on his twisted face. "It might even be one of the least guarded places on the whole planet."

"I don't believe that. They'd take good care of it. Just think what would happen if anything went wrong."

"Oh, I'm sure they've kept it safe from enemy attack—probably buried underground or something, with lots of shielding. But as for intruders, why bother keeping guard? Everyone on Cellina is in the same boat—damaging the records might damage themselves. I don't think anyone in the world—or at least in *this* world—would jeopardize his own immortality like that. The way you've described it, this entire culture is based on an implicit faith in the inevitability of resurrection. Nobody would attack Resurrection Central, because to do so would imperil his own welfare. Getting in there is not going to be the problem; finding out which records are mine and destroying them may be a bit tougher."

He paused thoughtfully. "The only thing that bothers me is, why aren't they using this technique on the ordinary soldiers like you? It would seem to be the perfect solution to the problem of people losing their memory of lives in which they die. If they could make a continuous record . . ."

His voice trailed off, and a glazed look came over his eyes, indicating he'd slipped from reality once more. Hawker sighed and moved away again, going to a chair to await Amassa's return.

Over the course of the next two days, Hawker managed to elicit more information about Resurrection Central out of Amassa. Although she had never actually died herself, she had been there on five previous occasions to restore her body after several "accidents" had removed one or more vital parts. Hawker had to be careful to phrase his questions so that she did not suspect he had more than a casual interest in the subject, but he was able to learn enough to draw up tentative plans.

Resurrection Central was an enormous complex

several hundred kilometers away. Its job was so vast—monitoring and recording the patterns of every person on Cellina—that it took an entire mountain to house it. The core of the mountain had been hollowed out and filled with ever increasing data banks and resurrection chambers. The complex was entirely automated; no humans worked there. Amassa had seen no guards or defenses of any kind when she was there—but then, Hawker reasoned, she was not a trained soldier, and had not been planning any attacks on the facility.

Hawker talked the situation over with Green when the two men were alone and Green was coherent. The cripple digested the information and made some tentative plans, and also formulated a hypothesis for why the army was not using this process on the soldiers. "They seem to need a whole mountain to receive the signals from these little transmitters and store the data away. That implies two drawbacks I can think of: it's not very mobile, and it's very vulnerable to enemy attack. They can probably store all our old patterns in something the size of a briefcase, which is easier for them to carry around and harder for the enemy to destroy. What they sacrifice in terms of our continued memory they make up in added flexibility."

Finally there was another party for all the people in this bubble city, and Hawker persuaded Amassa to take him along when she connected her bubble up to the others. She was rather jealous of him, but he argued that unless he had a chance at some variety he might go stale. Actually, variety of the sort this group could offer was the last thing he needed—but he did have to contact Belilo and/or Symington again if he was going to take any effective action to continue their efforts at helping Green.

As he'd feared, he was greeted by swarms of people to whom everything new was an adventure. He was pinched and poked and petted and prodded by men and women who insisted most vigorously that Amassa

211

must allow them to duple this fine primitive specimen. Amassa, knowing full well that she possessed an original in a world of copies, remained noncommittal.

After two hours of encounters, sexual and otherwise, with a strange assortment of beings, Hawker finally found Symington and managed to pry him away from his own circle of admirers. The two men found a quiet corner to talk in, and related to one another their experiences over the past few days.

"It's scary being a slave," Symington admitted, "but I have to hand it to them; they've been able to do things I wouldn't even have dreamed of. Tesaak—she's the woman who has me most of the time—she can think of some of the kinkiest things to do. She can duple up a copy of herself before she lost her virginity and watch while I deflower her—and then she joins in, and we both make love to her younger self. Then she duples a second copy of me, and we—"

"A second copy?" Hawker tensed suddenly. "How do I know I'm talking to the real you, then?"

"What difference does it make?" Symington smiled. "I haven't been the real me for centuries."

Hawker relaxed again. "You're right. This whole thing is so crazy, I keep forgetting." He paused. "Do you know anything of what's happened to Belilo?"

Symington paused, a cloud passing across his face. "No, I, uh, haven't heard anything since Nya took her off."

"Shit." Hawker had been hoping to rescue her, too; her help would certainly be useful in the attack on Resurrection Central. But if they couldn't locate her quickly and easily, they would just have to abandon her and let her fend for herself. The longer they delayed, the more chance there was of the army's dupling Green again, and then all their efforts would have been lost.

"Listen, let's speak in English for a while," Hawker continued, shunting over to his native language—a language they'd hardly spoken in hundreds of years.

"Huh? Why?"

"Because these people have all sorts of monitors, and we can never be sure they aren't watching us or listening in. We can be pretty sure that nobody from this time speaks English, though, so even if they are eavesdropping they won't know what we're saying."

"You've got a plan, then?"

Briefly, Hawker told Symington what he'd learned about Resurrection Central, and about his discussions with Green. When he described their tentative plans, Symington's face grew contemplative.

"Those are pretty wild assumptions you're using," he said.

"What have we got to lose?"

Symington smiled. "You're right. Absolutely nothing."

The two men waited for some hectic action to occupy the attention of the crowd elsewhere, and both slipped away back to Amassa's bubble. Green was still in one of his comas, so there was nothing to do but quietly await Amassa's return.

Amassa finally did come back. She looked at both of them and shook her head. "So here you are. It was most unsocial of you to leave together without telling anyone."

"We wanted to see you here alone," Hawker said. "We thought you might like the idea of having two primitives all to yourself at once."

Amassa smiled, and Hawker could see that his assessment of her had been correct—the concept did appeal to her. She spread her wings wide in a gesture he'd learned was one of sexual preparedness, and stepped forward toward them, arms outstretched.

Hawker moved toward her to take her arms with his. His touch was soft and gentle at first—but then, without warning, Symington dove at her legs, tackling the woman knee-high, and Hawker tightened his own grip as Amassa began falling over. Amassa gasped in amazement at the attack, and started reaching downward to her waist—but Hawker's strong grasp held her firmly.

213

"Her controls are all in her belt," he told Symington. "Get that off her and she's less dangerous."

The bigger man moved to comply, holding onto her viciously kicking legs with one arm while trying to unfasten her narrow belt with his free hand.

Amassa was still far from helpless. Her enormous muscular wings beat furiously against the bodies of both men, battering them with not inconsequential strength. She twisted and writhed in their grip, turning her head to bite Hawker's ear, nearly ripping it in the process. Hawker, though, was a veteran of countless more fights than she was, and held firm to his purpose.

At last Symington succeeded in unfastening the belt—and with its removal, the fight seemed to go out of the captive angel. Amassa let out a deep breath and sagged in Hawker's arms. Hawker held on tightly anyway, suspecting a trick, but this was no ruse; Amassa realized that, without her belt controls, she was at the mercy of the two soldiers.

When she regained her breath, she said, "Very well, you've got my belt. It won't do you any good—you don't know how to use it, and it wouldn't work for you even if you did. Are you trying to frighten me? That won't work with me any more than it did with Consakannis. I'm not afraid of death—and if you kill me, this sphere will just collapse like his did, leaving you powerless once more. My friends and I at least kept you safe from the army—I thought that was what you wanted."

"What we wanted was only coincidental to your plans," Hawker said, still holding her arms tightly. "The only person you really care about is yourself. And I know it's futile to kill you—but there are better ways of getting what we want."

"What do you mean?"

"Do you enjoy pain?" Symington asked. "I know some of your kinky friends do, but I don't think that's your particular fetish." The look on her face confirmed his suspicion. "Good. I think we understand each other, little lady. I know it will be possible later for you to duple yourself starting from before all of this happened, so you can effectively remove all memory of what we do to you—but that's in the future, and I swear to you, Amassa, it's not going to be any fun in the meantime. Hawk and me, we've lived through hundreds of wars, we've been captured and tortured by the best in the business, we learned a lot of useful tricks. Why don't you give her a little demonstration, Hawk?"

Hawker took the woman's right arm and twisted it up suddenly behind her wing until the wrist was almost even with her neck. Amassa screamed, and Hawker heard a satisfying snap at the shoulder.

"Oh, that's such a simple one," Symington said with mock disappointment. "Why not start plucking her wing feathers one by one? What will she think of your expertise?"

"Why give her the whole show at once?" Hawker replied.

Amassa was sobbing with pain now, and her voice was barely coherent. "What do you want of me?"

Hawker considered asking for her help in getting Belilo away from Nya, but discarded the idea as impractical. Much as he wanted to help his friend, it was too risky a business dealing with these strange people. He had one of them at a disadvantage, but he couldn't handle any more—and he had to seize the initiative while he still had it, or he'd never save Green.

He nodded toward the viewscreen wall. "Can you show me a picture of Resurrection Central on there?"

"Not . . . not without the belt," Amassa gasped.

This was a crucial point, and Hawker knew it. They'd never get anywhere unless they could control this bubble, which meant they'd have to let Amassa use her belt. But if she had too much control, she'd destroy them. He would have to maintain a delicate balance.

"All right," he told her. "You can move one finger at

a time, push one control at a time, nice and slow. If anything happens that I don't like, your arm comes the rest of the way out of its socket." He moved around behind her and slid one arm around her waist, holding her tightly before him. "And if anything bad happens, it's just as likely to happen to you as to me."

Symington brought the belt within reach, prepared to yank it away again the instant Amassa got out of line. The woman extended one long finger and pressed a series of jewels around the belt's circumference, slowly and cautiously like a child playing a toy piano. When she'd finished, the view on the screen was of a mountain that looked very much as she'd described it to Hawker before.

Hawker and Symington asked her for other scenes, studying the mountain from all possible angles, close up and far away. They were even able to get images of the entranceway and the admittance hall. They viewed each scene critically, with a professional eye for troublesome details.

"What do you think?" Hawker finally asked in English.

"I don't see anything dangerous there," Symington admitted. "It *looks* like a piece of cake—but I've been wrong before."

"We've got to risk it."

"Yeah, I know."

He changed back to contemporary language. "All right, Amassa, you've been a good girl so far. We've got a few more things we have to do. Can this homesphere be flown to that mountain?"

"Of course."

"How long will it take us to get there, at top speed?"

Amassa considered. "About three, maybe four hours."

"Good. Then start us on the way. Set the bubble to fly the most direct route, avoiding any possible army traps in the meantime."

Amassa pressed a few more controls. "There."

Hawker blinked. "It doesn't feel like we're moving."

"Well, we are. What's it supposed to feel like?"

"Never mind." Hawker realized that these people, with their control over gravity, might easily have control over the simple forces of inertia as well. Moving at a speed of hundreds of kilometers an hour would feel no different from standing still. Such things were taken so much for granted here that Amassa probably couldn't explain it even if she wanted to.

Instead, he changed the subject. "What's their filing system there? How could we find the file being recorded off one particular button transmitter?"

"Everything's listed numerically. Each transmitter has its own number. The first thing anybody learns is his own number."

"But if you die, you can't tell them what your number is," Symington said.

"When you die, your transmitter automatically stops broadcasting, which is a signal to resurrect that pattern number."

"What if someone wasn't told his number?" Hawker asked. "Like our friend David, for instance."

"The number would be recorded somewhere— probably on his army medical file."

"That doesn't help us much," Symington said.

Amassa paused to think. "The number is also inscribed on the transmitter button itself—I think. At least, that's what they tell me; I've never really looked. I know my number."

"I've got your number too," Hawker said. He looked over at Green's unconscious body. "Is that button attached to any nerves or anything?"

"No, it's just a passive scanning system. It's normally buried just below the skin surface of the neck."

Hawker looked to Symington. "Feel like doing some surgery?"

"If I have to. I'll need a knife, though." He looked down at his naked body, and then at Hawker's. "Come to think of it, we'll need our uniforms back, too. I don't cherish the thought of running naked through that mountain."

At the soldiers' insistence, Amassa created duples of their old uniforms, and of the weapons they'd brought aboard with them. Each of the men now had the knives in their belts, plus a beampistol, a rifle and a half a dozen grenades. Thus armed, they felt much better.

While Amassa and Hawker looked on, Symington dug carefully at the skin around Green's transmitter button, prying the small mechanical device out with the point of his knife. It was a tiny flat disc, barely larger than the battery for an electric watch in Hawker's day. It was mindboggling to think that so tiny an instrument could continuously record and transmit the molecular pattern of an entire person—but this was an incredible age.

As Amassa had said, there was a sequence of letters and numbers etched into the bottom of the metal disc. Hawker had to squint to make out the writing, but it was readable. When he reached Resurrection Central, he would know which file was Green's.

He turned his attention back to Amassa. "How will we know when this sphere reaches the mountain?"

"I've set it so a bell will ring."

"Good. You're learning." And to Symington, in English, he said, "I don't think we need her any more. It's too much trouble looking after her all the time."

"What do you suggest?"

"You might try knocking her out. A good blow to the head with your rifle butt might do it."

"Okay."

"Be careful not to kill her, though. We need this bubble to take us to the mountain."

Symington walked casually up to the unsuspecting Amassa and suddenly lifted his rifle, bringing its butt down hard against the side of her head. The woman went limp and slumped forward in Hawker's grasp. Hawker let her fall to the floor, where she lay in an untidy heap.

"Now all we have to do," Hawker said, "is wait."

They settled down in Amassa's comfortable furniture to do just that. Both men were quiet, contemplating the task still ahead of them. Neither had any expectations of living beyond this attack, but if they could at least help their friend they knew they would consider the effort worthwhile.

After half an hour of silence, Symington spoke up. "Hawk?"

"Yeah?"

"I lied to you back there."

"About what?"

"About Belilo. Tesaak did show me on the telescreen what was happening to her."

Hawker did not say anything. He could tell from Symington's manner that the other man was having trouble making this confession; let him make it at his own pace.

"Nya and about a dozen of her friends were using her as some sort of cult sacrifice. They tied her up and gang-banged her all day, tortured her all night, and then killed her in the morning. Then they'd duple her and start the whole thing over again." His breathing was coming in short, quick pants. "I . . . I didn't want to think about it."

"That's all right," Hawker said quietly. "We all knew the risks we were taking when we started out on this job. Besides, there wasn't anything either of us could have done to help her."

They lapsed into awkward silence again. The thought of Belilo being endlessly reincarnated to a life of torture and degradation was a disquieting one. The woman had been a good companion, and she certainly deserved a better fate—but as he'd said, there was little he could have done to help her without jeopardizing everything she and the men had fought for this far.

Another half hour passed before Hawker spoke again. "Lucky?"

"Yeah?"

"What pushed you into all this?"

"What do you mean?"

"Dave had a theory that something pushed all of us into this crazy situation, that some force in our backgrounds made us sign up for the original Project Banknote. We both knew about our own insecurities, but what about you? What pushed you into this mess?"

Symington was quiet for several minutes, and Hawker began to think his friend had decided to ignore the question. Then the other man spoke—so quietly that Hawker had to strain to hear him.

"Cowardice, I guess."

"Huh? You? You've got every medal ever made, and a few I think they invented just for you."

"Yeah. Funny how these things go, ain't it?" He shifted his weight in the chair, and then reshifted, trying to find what was obviously an impossible position of comfort. "But there's all sorts of cowards, and the best ones never let you know it.

"I grew up in the oil fields of Oklahoma. The kids were pretty tough there. I was always big for my age, and I got teased about it. When I was five, a seven-year-old bully picked on me in the playground. I knocked him down and he hit his head on the side of the swings, gashed open a big cut. I heard he needed eleven stitches. I never told anyone about it, and I guess he never told anyone who did it, either—maybe he was embarrassed to be beaten up by a kid two years younger than him. But I remembered what he looked like lying there with his head cut open and bleeding, and I knew I didn't ever want to do that to anybody again.

"All through school, growing up, I avoided fights—and in my neighborhood that took some doing. I learned to be easygoing and I smiled a lot. The kids called me all kinds of names—they thought I was some kind of sissy or queer. That hurt a lot. They tried to provoke me into doing something, but I usually ran away. I got pretty good at running, believe me.

"Then, about two weeks before my high school graduation, a bunch of guys caught me out behind the gym. I couldn't get away, I had to face them." He gave a humorless little laugh. "Naturally I was what you might call out of practice. They beat the shit out of me, and I barely lifted a finger against them.

"I came home with both eyes blacked, my nose bleeding, a rib cracked and bruises over most of my body. I explained to my father what had happened. Maybe I thought I'd get some sympathy. Instead, he took me out in the back and whaled on me for not fighting back. He'd had to put up for all those years with hearing stories about my being a sissy, and I guess this was the last straw. He was disappointed in me, I'd been a failure. I was his only son, and he was ashamed of me.

"I waited that night until everyone in the house was asleep, and I ran away from home. I hitchhiked into Tulsa, got an emergency hospital to patch me up, lied about my age and joined the army. They weren't being particularly fussy then—they needed everyone they could get for Africa. I always volunteered for the toughest jobs they could give me." He shrugged. "I guess all along I've been trying to prove I'm not a coward."

"Your father's been dead a long time now," Hawker said quietly.

"I know. Maybe that's why it's so hard to prove it to the bastard."

Hawker and Symington settled back in their respective chairs, waiting for the bell to tell them they'd reached their destination. Neither man said another word until they arrived.

Hawker had almost dozed off when the bell chimed their arrival outside Resurrection Central. He started, then shook himself to full alertness and stood up. Across the room, Symington was stretching and doing a few quick calisthenics to get himself in shape for the fight ahead.

221

Hawker looked around, and realized his oversight almost at once. There was no door in this bubble at present, no way to get outside. Amassa was still out cold, and they didn't know how to work the belt themselves. They would have to move quickly, though; if the bubble just sat here for too long, it would arouse suspicion.

Symington too saw the problem. He tried using his rifle on the walls, but the powerful beam deflected harmlessly off the material, bouncing almost straight back and barely missing him on the rebound.

"We've got to get out of here somehow," Hawker said.

"I know a quick way," Symington answered. "Get Dave and stand him over here with us. See if he can walk on his own now."

Hawker took Green off his couch and stood him on his feet. The crippled soldier was semiconscious, but not very cooperative. Hawker took Green's right arm and placed it around his shoulder, with his own left arm around Green's waist. "Ready," he said.

Symington took his beampistol and shot Amassa cleanly through the head. Just as happened with Consakannis, the bubble began collapsing immediately upon the death of its owner. The soldiers moved to avoid the worst of the mess, but they were still covered by the noxious goo as they waded away from the puddle that had been Amassa's home.

They found themselves facing a mountain that was much larger than they'd realized just by looking at the pictures of it in Amassa's viewscreen. It was part of a chain that extended left and right as far as they could see, and it must easily have been 3,500 meters high. The front was of craggy rock, into which had been cut a door two stories tall. "Impressive, isn't it?" Symington said.

"What do you think we ought to do?" Hawker asked.

"Let's just walk in and see what happens. Why start

a fight if we don't have to? Maybe they'll just give us what we want."

"And maybe I'm the tooth fairy," Hawker grumbled, but accepted the need to proceed cautiously.

With Symington supporting Green from the other side, the two men walked through the entrance with their friend between them. Inside they found themselves in a large semicircular hall, with at least twenty doors before them going to other places. In the center of the hall was just a giant shining silver globe, so large they had to crane their necks to see its top.

"Come forward," said the globe in reverberating tones, and the men did so reluctantly. "Now, state your names and your business here."

"I'm Joe Smith," Symington said affably. "These are my friends John Doe and Richard Roe. We'd like to see your files, if you don't mind."

"Access to the files is prohibited without specific authorization."

"We have the authorization." Only the way Symington rubbed his right thumb and forefinger together showed Hawker how nervous he was.

The globe was adamant. "Please produce identity card."

Symington fished in his pocket and pulled out nothing. "Here you are," he said, offering the imaginary card.

"There is nothing there."

"Of course there is. Are your scanners functioning properly?"

There was barely a hesitation. "All components operating normally. Furthermore, video correlation identifies you as deserted army personnel Symington, Frank, Hawker, Jerold, and Green—"

"Shit!" Symington exclaimed. He pulled out his beampistol and fired point-blank at the globe, which exploded into a million pieces. "Didn't want to talk to no fucking ball, anyway."

Hawker had his own gun drawn, too, and was looking around for any guards. But the hall remained ominously quiet. "Where do we go now?" he asked.

"Through there, pal." Symington pointed at the wall of doors.

"Which one?"

"What the fuck difference does it make? We've got to go somewhere, don't we?" Symington was not a man to consider the subtleties of a situation. When talk did not work, he believed in charging ahead and figuring it out later. The fact that his instincts were right more often than not accounted for his nickname.

This time was no exception. Unslinging his rifle, he fired at one of the doors across from him. The material was almost as tough as Amassa's bubble, but not quite; after a few seconds of concentrated fire, the door melted into a puddle of slag on the floor. Grabbing Green and, incidentally, Hawker, Symington ran forward and pulled his companions through.

They found themselves in a brightly lit corridor—and still there was no one else in sight. Both men knew one prime rule of survival in these circumstances: keep moving. A moving target was more difficult to hit, and always had more options than a stationary one. They ran down the hallway, half dragging Green between them, looking for an avenue of further possibility. There were closed doors on either side of them, but nothing that seemed right. Doors here couldn't be important—they were still too close to the entrance.

A hundred meters down the corridor they came to a cross hallway—and looking toward the left, they saw what appeared to be a row of elevator banks. They ran toward them, weapons raised, ready to strike down any opponents—but still there was only silence.

They reached the elevators and paused for breath, resting Green, their burden, against the wall for support. "I don't like this," Symington said. "It's too damn quiet."

"And why are there all these halls and elevators if the complex is entirely automated?" Hawker wondered.

"Somebody had to build it," the other man shrugged.

The elevator doors opened unexpectedly, and out came a burst of lethal fire. If the soldiers had been standing directly in front of the elevator when it opened, they would have been fried to perfection. As it was, they barely had time to fall backward out of the line of sight as the beams cut a swath through the air.

Symington grabbed at his belt and pulled loose a grenade. With an expert flip of his wrist he tossed it through the elevator doors, then rolled over and covered Green's body with his own. The explosion shook the floor, and the fire stopped coming from the open elevator.

Symington got to his feet, then helped Hawker lift Green up once more. The men peered inside the still elevator, but all they could see was a twisted mass of wreckage. It had only been machines in there, not people.

"I guess we take the stairs," Symington said.

"If there are any."

"Where's your faith, Hawk? Of course there's stairs. Even today, you always have to have emergency routes in case the machines don't work. Come on."

They started off once more down the hallways, and Symington's luck continued. At the end of the corridor was a door marked "Emergency Only"—and sure enough, there were the stairs. Inside the stairwell, a sign on the wall identified this level as "Ground Floor, Administration."

"I guess we go up," Symington said. "Those records have got to be somewhere. We'll just take the whole mountain apart piece by piece until we find them."

They started climbing. The first five floors were all administration, and Hawker was beginning to worry that they'd taken the wrong path. But the sixth floor bore a sign that said simply "AA." "Does that mean anything to you?" Symington asked Hawker.

Hawker checked the code number on the small disc they'd taken out of Green's neck. "This one starts with 'AE.'"

"Good. Maybe that means we've only got five floors to go."

It turned out to be far more than that, however. The next two levels were also designated "AA," and there were four levels of "AB." Hawker's strength was about to give out. He was in fine physical condition, and by himself would have had no problem with all these stairs. But dragging Green's body up with him and having to maintain constant vigilance against attack were taking their tolls. He was having a harder and harder time keeping pace with the indefatigable Symington.

At the fourth "AB" level they met some resistance. The door to the main section opened and four robots stepped through just as the soldiers were approaching. Each of the machines was armed with a beampistol—but they were no match for the reflexes of Hawker and Symington, honed fine by centuries of combat experience.

"Maybe they'll think twice before trying that again," Symington said.

Hawker leaned against the wall, his vision going blurry. He'd reacted instinctively to the threat, but was paying for it now. Symington noticed his dizziness and came over to check him out. "What's the matter? Get hit?"

"No, just . . . just a little tired. Maybe you'd better go on without me."

"Bullshit. We're in this together. Here, I'll carry Dave. You just worry about carrying yourself." He hoisted their semiconscious friend over his shoulders and set off once more, as strong as ever. Hawker gulped, shook his head to clear it and followed after him, awe in his heart. This was a man who feared he was a coward?

There were two "AC" levels and two "AD" levels

before they finally reached "AE." Hawker's whole body was one huge ache, protesting the torturous treatment it had received. His legs were made of lead. They stopped for breath on this landing. "How do we know if his file's on this 'AE' landing or one further up?" Hawker panted.

"We don't. We work 'em one at a time."

Symington took another grenade from his belt and, opening the door just a crack, tossed the grenade out and closed the door again. The blast, echoing through the enclosed space of the stairwell, rattled their teeth. "That ought to take care of any welcoming committee," he said.

There were indeed the shattered bodies of a few robots lying about the entrance as they emerged from the stairway, proving that an ambush had indeed been planned. This gave the men some hope that they were on the right level; the enemy had probably guessed where they were headed by now, and would have concentrated its forces on the floor that was their ultimate destination.

They found themselves in a forest of pillars, tall white columns reaching from floor to ceiling with narrow pathways in between. Embedded in each pillar were dozens of plastic triangles, lit up with various colors whose significance Hawker could not have begun to guess. Inscribed just below each triangle was a number. These, then, were the files on which people's patterns were continuously recorded and stored. All they had to do now was find Green's out of the thousands and thousands of patterns here.

They checked the pillars at random at first, until they established the order. Serial numbers went in descending order the farther they were from the stairway; Green's should be perhaps three to four dozen rows away.

Symington took the lead, as usual, carrying Green's body slung casually over his shoulder. They ran down the aisles, checking the numbers occasionally to make

227

sure they hadn't overshot their goal, then kept going. They were almost there, and they could feel the flow of time itself speeding up to push them along their way.

As Symington ran across one aisle, the ray from a beampistol cut him down. He stumbled, dropping Green's body, and fired his own gun even as he fell. Hawker pulled up short, looking at the motionless bodies of his two friends on the ground. There was no further fire from whatever source had shot Symington.

He approached that aisle carefully and turned into it with his pistol firing away—but Symington had already done the job for him. The two robots that had lain in ambush there were now smoldering piles of metal. Hawker checked the numbers on the pillars and realized that this was the aisle that would probably contain Green's file.

A quick check showed that Symington was dead, but Green was very much alive and returning slowly to his full awareness. Hawker bent and wearily lifted his friend to his feet, then staggered down the aisle until he found the pillar with the proper number.

He set Green down sitting with his back to the pillar while he searched out the proper triangular plastic insert. It was there, about shoulder height, glowing a bright pink. Hawker tried to pry it from its socket, but either it was embedded too firmly in place or else Hawker had been too drained by his ordeal to take it out; the triangle remained stubbornly in its setting. Taking his beampistol, Hawker fired point-blank at the triangle, and was rewarded by an increasing glow as the plastic heated up, and then finally melted into a useless puddle of slag.

Hawker dropped his beampistol to the floor and then, a moment later, fell to his knees beside Green. He was exhausted beyond all normal understanding of the term, but filled at the same time with a sense of elation he hadn't felt in ages. He closed his eyes, gave a silent prayer of thanks and then looked over to Green.

His friend's lips were moving and, by leaning close, Hawker could hear him repeating over and over again, "Memory is the key. Memory is the key. . . ."

"Dave." Hawker shook his friend by the shoulder, "Dave, we did it."

Green looked blank for a moment, then stared with more comprehension into Hawker's face. "What?"

"We destroyed the record of you. It's melted down into a useless mess."

Green closed his eyes and breathed a long sigh. "Thank God. It's over at last." He opened his eyes again and looked straight into Hawker's face. "But there's still one more thing you have to do for me, Hawk, and it may be harder than anything you've done yet."

Hawker blinked. "What?"

"Kill me."

The words didn't register at first, as though Green were speaking a foreign language. As the meaning penetrated, Hawker shook his head with disbelief. "I . . . I can't do that. I did all this for you. I wanted to help you. That would make it all seem so pointless. . . ."

"You don't understand. That would be the best thing you could do for me. It was all necessary to get to this point. Don't you see, Hawk? My original pattern was destroyed, and now my files have been destroyed. If I die now, there'll be no way they can resurrect me ever again. I'll be free, Hawk, I'll be off the merry-go-round forever."

There was a burning in the corners of Hawker's eyes. "But . . . but you're my friend."

"I know. That's why I asked you. It's not something I could trust to a stranger. Please, Hawk, I'm begging you." He looked up at Hawker with his twisted, off-center face pleading for a special kind of mercy only the two of them could understand.

Hawker looked away. He couldn't meet Green's eyes. He remembered the incident on that jungle planet ages ago when Green had been seriously wounded and

Hawker had administered the *coup de grâce* as a routine blessing. But that was different; he knew Green would be resurrected again next time, healthy as ever. Now, though, the situation had changed radically. After all they had been through together down the centuries of battle, after all Green had meant to him, after all the unspoken warmth of their friendship—how could he possibly end his friend's life, knowing there would be no hope of redemption?

Green's body suddenly tensed as he realized Hawker would not be able to do it. Reaching quickly for Hawker's belt, he grabbed the knife and slashed it across his inner right thigh. The blade cut the major artery he'd been hoping to hit and a fountain of blood spurted out, covering both men with red in seconds.

The malformed soldier slipped forward, his head falling against Hawker's chest. "It's done, Hawk," he coughed. "I saw a guy die once from a leg wound like this—only takes a minute or so to bleed to death. Hold onto me, please. It won't be long. And smile. Remember, I'm free. The bastards can't use me any more."

He looked up into Hawker's face abruptly, as though there were something he'd forgotten to say. He grabbed the front of Hawker's uniform with a death grip. "Remember," he gasped, his voice barely more than a whisper. "Remember. . . ." And that was all.

Hawker held onto the body for a full minute, crying for the first time in centuries. It didn't matter at all that he was coated head to toe in his friend's blood. "Don't worry, Dave," he promised in a whisper barely louder than Green's had been. "I won't forget you. I'll probably live till the end of the Universe, and I'll remember you every day of that life."

He paused for a moment's thought. "If they let me."

The reality of his situation hit him with a sudden frightening impact. With Green gone forever, he was now all alone in enemy territory. The army knew he was here, they would be coming for him. He had deserted, disobeyed more laws than he could count.

What reason did they have to keep him alive? Wouldn't it be far easier for them just to shoot him, then duple another Jerry Hawker, one who knew nothing whatsoever of these events? Green had asked to be remembered—but to do that, Hawker had to live past the next few minutes, live until the next time they recorded him.

They must be coming. They held off for so long, but it couldn't last forever. And they would kill him, unless he could strike a bargain. But what could he offer them? They held all the top cards; what did he have to bargain with?

A grim smile came to his face. He was a dealer in one commodity—destruction. He would deal in that.

He pulled a grenade from his belt, set the control for "contact" and stood up, holding the grenade high off the floor. "Hello," he yelled to empty air. "I bet you can hear me. I know you're coming for me, but you'd better wait for a few minutes and listen to what I have to say."

Silence.

"I've got a grenade here, all set to go off if it hits anything. If you shoot me, it drops to the floor and explodes. It's got a pretty good kill radius; I'll bet it could take out ten, maybe twenty of these pillars. How many people's files is that? A couple hundred, maybe? That's several hundred people whose files will be totally ruined; you'll never be able to get them back. Think about it before anyone takes a shot at me."

More silence for nearly a minute. Then a voice materialized out of the air just above his head, a voice similar to that of the silver globe Symington had shot in the entrance hall. "What do you want?"

It was a deceptively simple question. Hawker opened his mouth and then realized he didn't have an answer. What *did* he want? What in all the Universe could be worthwhile to a man like him? The phrase, "Life, liberty and the pursuit of happiness" climbed out of his childhood memory, but what good were they? He'd had enough life to satisfy ten men. Liberty was illusive; how could he be free when the army could always make another copy of him, a Hawker still shackled to his slavery? The final freedom Green had found was not a path open to him. And as for pursuit of happiness—well, that was what Amassa and her friends were busily engaged in, and it was as hollow as everything else.

Moreover, while he'd made them stop and listen, he was in no position to force them to do anything. He could ask some price—but if they didn't like it, if they thought it too outrageous, they could come in here and wipe him out despite the consequences. Whatever he asked for, it had to be realistic—it had to be within boundaries they might accept.

The one thing he wanted most was to fulfill Green's final request: to remember him. And to do that, he had to live. Even if it made him sound cowardly now, even if it was a betrayal of everything he'd fought for, something deep in the back of his mind told him it was vitally important that he live and remember what had happened here today.

He drew a deep breath and exhaled it slowly. "I want to make a deal with you that I don't think is too unreasonable." He stopped and waited for a reply.

"Go on," said the voice. "You haven't said anything yet."

"I've accomplished what I wanted. I never wanted to disobey the army, I never wanted to desert or commit mutiny. I'm not a troublemaker, I've got a good service record."

"Until now."

"All I wanted to do was help my friend. He was being tortured for something that wasn't his fault, and I thought it was unfair. That's over now; you can't get to him any more. I'm prepared to go back and continue being a good soldier for you."

"You have no choice in that. We could always duple

another of you anyway, no matter what happens here."

Sweat broke out on Hawker's upper lip. He could feel his position slipping. What could he say to rebut that argument? What did he have to offer them that they couldn't get from a duple?

Green had said it, many times, ever since the men first realized the full implications of the resurrection process. *Memory is the key.* "It won't be me, though," Hawker answered. "My memories of the experiences I've undergone during my flight are valuable. Every single one of them goes into making me a better fighter. As bad as this has been for you, it might come in handy sometime in the future. You can never tell."

"If you wish to surrender, we will take it under advisement."

"That's not all," Hawker said, pressing forward a little to gain the ground he'd lost in the bargaining process. "I'll rejoin you voluntarily and go back to being a model soldier—but there's something I want in return."

The voice did not answer.

"I want out," Hawker continued, after a suitable pause. "I want to be free of this life, free of all the fighting. I want to be able to live like an ordinary person, away from the army, and not have to worry about being resurrected into futures I have no say in."

"That would seem to contradict what you've just offered," the voice said, without a trace of irony.

Hawker shook his head. "No, it's a very simple process. Just duple me the way I am right now. One of me is free to go off and pursue his destiny any way he can; the other goes back to the army."

"We can't go around making deals like that, or every soldier would want the same treatment."

"I won't tell anyone about it. It will be our secret. It's a small enough price for you to pay—duples are made all the time, anyway. And if you cooperate with me instead of fighting me, you get a bonus—Green's body. You can probably still learn a lot from it even though he's dead; I think he's past caring now. If this grenade goes off, you won't salvage even that much."

The voice was silent for several minutes, which Hawker considered a positive sign. They must at least be thinking about his deal—which is more than he would ever have expected a few hours ago. When no answer was immediately forthcoming, he prodded them further. "Well, I'm waiting. I'm getting awfully tired after my exertions today; I don't think I can hold this grenade up much longer."

"Stay as you are," the voice answered. "A mobile scanner is on its way to you, and will be there within two minutes."

A mobile scanner! Hawker smiled in triumph. He'd won. It was a small enough victory, after all he'd been through, but he'd faced down the army and gotten concessions from them. He would be dupled, giving him two chances to keep Green's memory alive. It meant a return to slavery for one of him—but that would have been true in any case.

He looked down at Green's still-bleeding corpse. "We know one thing at least, Dave," he said. "They're not invincible."

interludes

Hawker was dupled right there in the aisle standing beside Green's body. There were some very tricky arrangements that had to be developed to make sure the army kept its word. The "original" Hawker stayed in Resurrection Central holding his grenade while the duple was allowed to go free. Only after several hours, when the duple radioed in that he was safely away from the vicinity, did Hawker finally surrender to army authorities.

He half expected them to kill him anyway, as a retaliation for all the trouble he'd caused them—but, to his surprise, they didn't. The conquest of death had made retribution like that a meaningless exercise, and the army was too pragmatic. Green had been right on that score; his memories, even rebellious ones, were too valuable a commodity to be squandered on anything as petty as revenge.

At the same time, the army wanted to make an example of him to prevent future desertions. He was given a showy trial and made to serve a ten-month sentence at hard labor in the stockade—a development that may actually have been in his favor. Had he merely been returned to duty, there was a good chance he might have died in action and his memories been lost anyway; as it was, the war was over by the time he'd finished his sentence. He was simply recorded once more and passed down to the wars of some future generation.

Costanza, Singh, Belilo and Symington were all around at his next resurrection—and of course, none of them had the faintest idea of what had occurred on Cellina. Hawker did his best to avoid them all—particularly Belilo. He still felt guilty about deserting her—and the thought lurked in the back of his mind that one version of her could still be suffering the daily pain and humiliation that Nya and her acolytes loved to inflict. Belilo was puzzled by Hawker's reticence—but the resurrectees had long since learned not to pry into anything related to former lives, and she accepted his behavior without comment.

Hawker learned that twenty-five years had passed since the war on Cellina, and he was naturally curious as to how his duple, anchored in time, had fared during that period. This current fighting, though, was on a world half the Galaxy away from Cellina, and information was impossible to come by. As far as the army was concerned, the other Hawker simply did not exist, and no amount of long-distance investigating could gain him any results.

When the war was over, Hawker was copied once again, his curiosity unabated.

Two more resurrections came and went. Symington was baffled that Green no longer seemed to be with them. He mentioned it once, but Hawker volunteered no information. He could see no point to stirring Symington up again over the matter. Green was gone, that was all there was to it; simply another of the mysteries the soldiers had to face in their centuries of existence. Why tell anyone about the grotesque, twisted monstrosity that had been their comrade? Let Symington remember Green as what he'd really been, not as what some perverse Fate had made him at the end.

Hawker, too, remembered Green as he was. True to his friend's last wish, he would not let that memory die.

On his fourth resurrection after Cellina, the fighting was conducted on a planet near enough for Hawker to hope for information on his duple's fate. It was nearly a century and a half since the events on Cellina, but with modern technology that meant very little. Anything was possible these days—or so it seemed to a man born in the far-off twentieth century. Anything, that is, except hope.

The army still refused him its cooperation, insisting even in private that no such duple had ever been created. Hawker exhausted every legitimate method at his disposal to find out more about his other "free" self, and banged into blank walls at every turn. Finally, with no other recourse left, he went AWOL in his search to find himself.

Alone and undercover, he traveled as a common spacehand to Cellina, only to find that his duple had left the planet less than a year after being created. Thinking to perhaps right an old wrong, he tried to find Nya and Belilo—but there was no trace of either, and he gave up that quest.

Doggedly, Hawker kept in pursuit of his older self. The trail blew hot and cold and hot again, leading him through three different planets in the next seven months. At last, on an insignificant world called Dos, he found what he was looking for—sort of.

Dos was a world founded and populated mostly by religious fanatics who rejected many of the benefits of modern civilization and technology. Its inhabitants lived a simple life, reached an average age of one hundred or so, and then died natural deaths without

237

recourse to artificial resurrections. Dos was considered a backwater where nothing ever happened, a quiet world with little to recommend it.

Hawker's duple had learned about Dos, and was instantly attracted to it—not from any strong religious convictions, but because it was one of the few planets in the civilized Galaxy that remained close to the world of his childhood. He'd had his fill of artificially extended life; one more death would be enough for him. Within five years of Green's death, the Hawker-duple settled on Dos, never to leave it again.

He dwelled there for sixty-eight years, married and had two sons. One of the sons had left the planet for greener pastures, never to return; the other son lived his whole life on Dos, producing one son of his own. That son in turn had a son before his own premature death in an accident—so at present there was only one direct descendant of the original Hawker-duple alive on the planet.

Hawker tracked the man down and found him working as a master potter, teaching his handicraft to a handful of young apprentices. His great-grandson looked to be in his late twenties, but without much family resemblance. Hawker assumed that was due to the various female influences in his genetic background.

Their brief meeting was extremely awkward. Hawker came into his descendant's shop and watched him work for a few minutes. The man stared at him, as though wondering where he'd seen that face before. When his great-grandson finally came out and asked him what he wanted in the shop, Hawker stammered around and finally walked out of the shop without ordering anything. He never bothered to identify himself to the young man who bore, at least in part, his genes. What would have been the point? The two came from different worlds; they had nothing whatsoever in common.

Disillusioned, now, with the whole of life, Hawker returned to the army. He had now gotten a second

238

mark against his record as a troublemaker, and the army seriously debated whether to copy this current version or return to his previous pattern already on file. The convincing factor was Hawker's contention that the previous him, not knowing the fate of his descendants, would probably go AWOL all over again to find them—whereas he now knew there was nothing to find in that direction. That, and the fact that Hawker did have an outstanding combat record, convinced the board of inquiry that he was to be recopied again as is.

And so it went—war after war, planet after planet, century after century. Hawker held on to the memory of Green, but very little else. He became a brutally efficient machine, living without hope of redemption from this eternal slavery. He obeyed orders and did his job, never caring what the fight was about or why he was called on to kill beings he'd never met. Reality for him became a gray blur of fighting, punctuated by the occasional battlefield lulls.

Until he came, at last, to a civil war on a nameless world, to a hopeless siege, to a Spardian woman who spoke to him only in broken Vandik, and to bright blue fireballs that rained death and destruction from the skies. . . .

part 3

eternity

Hawker lay still in the stairwell as the building collapsed around him after the hit from the blue fireball. He covered his head with his hands and closed his eyes to keep out the dust. The ground shook as great chunks of masonry came tumbling down, some missing him by scant millimeters; he was buried instead beneath a pile of fine dust and rubble. His only thought was to keep a breathing passage open, and his chief fear was of suffocating like a miner in a cave-in. A bullet through the brain or an energy beam through the heart were quick ways to go, but a painful death was not his choice.

After a few minutes the dust stopped settling on top of him. He waited a little longer to be sure, then slowly began to dig himself out of the debris, up toward the light and air. He broke through and breathed deeply, taking in great lungfuls of fresh oxygen.

When at last he'd regained his breath, he looked around him at the damage the enemy assault had caused. Almost this entire block had been leveled; not a building remained intact, with just an occasional wall standing here and there. The smoky atmosphere was filled with even more choking fumes than before. There was no sign of his partner, the Spardian woman; the place across the street where he'd last seen her was now buried beneath a small mountain of rubble. He had to assume he was on his own—and the red armband on his uniform might be a definite disadvantage if this area was soon overrun by the side in blue, as seemed likely.

Behind him, his rifle had been shattered by a large piece of falling building, leaving him armed with four grenades, two throwing knives and his wide-dispersion laser pistol. Not much with which to fight off an invading army.

Why bother? he asked himself. *Nobody expects miracles from you any more. Just go through the motions and hope for better luck next time.*

But when the shooting started around him, his instincts took over. He could no more ignore his training than a fish could fly.

No one was aiming precisely at him; the shooting instead seemed to be part of a general barrage intended to keep any survivors in this area under cover. Hawker inched forward, taking advantage of whatever cover he could find, to reach a safer vantage point from which to assess his situation.

He came to a wall that was still standing, with a chink that may have been part of a window to act as a peephole. The wall was at the top of a slight rise, and offered him the best view from a bad neighborhood. From this spot he could look out and see the advancing lines of invading troops, all with their blue armbands neatly in place. They were not far away.

There was a slight noise behind him, and Hawker turned quickly. A figure rose over a pile of rubble, silhouetted against the sky. The blue armband was quite apparent, though the facial features were hidden by the glare from one of the fireballs passing through the sky behind the man.

The enemy soldier had him dead to rights, and yet he didn't fire. Maybe he was under orders to take prisoners, but Hawker was under no such compunction. He raised his laser and fired, hitting the man squarely in the chest. The enemy soldier fell, and as he did so his face became visible for the first time. It was Symington, not quite so lucky this time.

Hawker pounded his fist against the wall. Is this what it all came down to, killing his only real friend in the last few hundred years? What kind of insanity was this, where such things could happen? He did not feel guilt for murdering his friend; how could there be guilt when Symington would be resurrected again next time with no memory of what had occurred here? But Hawker nonetheless felt so frustrated by the lunacy around him that he wanted to scream.

He stood up and walked away from the wall, in full view of anyone who might want to take a shot at him. What did it matter whether he lived or died? He'd only be resurrected again, anyway, to fight some other senseless war on some other world in some further future.

Perhaps because he was so uncaring, no one fired at him as he walked across the street, moving without direction or purpose. His feet trod across the uneven surface of the broken paving and twice he stumbled but did not lose his balance completely. He was heading on an approximate diagonal in the direction of enemy lines, but that didn't matter to him. Nothing mattered very much, it seemed.

He made it almost to the shell of a burned-out building when he saw a movement to his right. Reflex, more than any conscious desire for survival, made him spin that way, gun drawn. He would have shot instantly, but something made him halt in midaction. He stood frozen, staring at the man across from him.

It was Jerry Hawker, wearing a blue armband.

It was a strange sensation, seeing himself like this. A mirror image was something he was used to, but this was an independent entity, someone capable of movement on his own. Left and right seemed curiously interchanged, and Hawker felt dizzily disoriented. Somewhere offstage was the ghoulish laughter of Fate.

The two men stood, suspended in time, no more than five meters apart. Eternity existed in that instant, as volumes of unspoken thoughts flashed through each man's mind. Then the Hawker in blue gave a wan smile and spread his arms apart in a gesture of resignation and friendship. He could not kill himself.

The Hawker in red, because of his experiences here, was more cynical. Looking across at the other him, centuries of rage and frustration exploded in his brain. This was the man who'd been stupid enough to let the army make a toy of him. This was the man who accepted what happened to him and never thought of fighting back. This was the man who'd brought him all the miseries of an eternal damnation in a living hell.

Self-hatred tightened his finger on the trigger. His laser fired at his double's face, and he kept up the fire long after the other Hawker had fallen dead to the ground.

At length the rage passed. Hawker stopped firing and bent down to examine his own corpse. There was nothing left of the face or head, but at least it had been a quick, painless death—there was no point to making himself suffer. He looked over the still body and, after a moment's consideration, ripped the blue armband off the other Hawker's sleeve. Stuffing it into his pocket, he continued along the way he'd started, into the burned-out building.

In this place of comparative shelter, he sat on the floor with his back to one wall and started laughing. He couldn't help himself. This whole war had gone beyond the bounds of insanity; it was now a farce, and he was one of the comedians. This final confrontation had been too crazy for anyone to take seriously, and Hawker's body was shaking hysterically as he collapsed on the floor, tears streaming from his eyes.

After a while the laughter eased, and he sat up again. He thought of David Green, and wondered what his friend would have said about this lunacy. He probably would have been resigned to it, saying something to the effect that their merry-go-round might be passing through the funhouse every once in a while, and they were seeing each other and themselves through those crazy distorting mirrors. But, he would have added, there was no way off the merry-go-round, so they had to accept it and try to deal with it as best they could.

Maybe it should have been Dave with the nickname Lucky, he thought. *He at least managed to break the circuit.*

Hawker suddenly tensed. There *was* a way out; Green had found it. Hawker thought back to his friend's last words as he lay bloody and dying in Hawker's arms. He didn't say, "Remember me." He just said, "Remember."

"He didn't care about himself," Hawker whispered to the empty room. "He was telling me to remember how it was done, how to get off the merry-go-round. He was telling me there was a way, and that I had to remember it to help myself."

His eyes were filling with tears, and he closed them tightly to stanch the flow. "Thank you, Dave," he said. "You were helping me, and I didn't even know it. I thought I was helping you. Thank you. Thank you."

He took a deep breath and wiped at his eyes with the back of his hand. This was a time for clear thinking, something he'd never been too good at. This could be the most important day of his life, and he'd need all his wits about him to do it right.

He pulled himself slowly to his feet, left the shelter of the building and started back toward the underground bunker where he and the others had been resurrected. He moved through the torn-up streets with great caution, now. If he should be killed at this juncture, he'd merely be dupled again with memories of this lifetime gone, and he might never have this insight again. For the first time in longer than he cared to think about, he had a reason to live, a purpose to his existence.

The territory looked considerably different than when he'd first passed through it; the enemy's blue fireballs had done vast damage in their continual barrage, reducing the city to heaps of rubble. He saw very few people wandering about; many of the defenders had probably died in the bombardment, and some of the rest may have fled in despair. Hawker took great care that no one saw him; even though he was in red territory and still wearing his red armband, he didn't want to be shot mistakenly by his own side—not at this stage of the game.

There was a sentry standing at the entrance to the bunker, looking very worried. Hawker approached him slowly, his arms spread wide apart and his red armband in plain view. The guard was nervous, and might fire at anything.

"I've got to make a report," Hawker said. "The enemy has broached the north side. I must get in to headquarters."

The guard didn't understand a word. Hawker ran through all the languages he knew, and still there was no reply. The sentry stood there, not firing at him because he had the proper armband, but at the same time not trusting him enough to let him back down inside the bunker.

Hawker resorted to pantomime. After a few minutes of frantic gesturing, the sentry nodded and stepped aside for Hawker to enter. Hawker did not dare express the relief he felt, and instead walked briskly inside the door and took the elevator down to the command levels.

He wandered for half an hour through the bunker, looking for the particular office he wanted. The air of panic that had been so tangible when he was first here had multiplied several times since then. Everyone knew the cause was lost, and many of the staff were going through the same feelings of apathy he himself had experienced a little while ago. He wandered through normally secured areas unmolested, able to observe things as he pleased. On the few occasions when anyone stopped him, he had the legitimate excuse that he couldn't communicate with them, and they eventually gave up trying. Hawker didn't look like a spy or saboteur, and even if he was—did it really matter at this point?

He came at last to the place he was looking for, the computer in which the soldiers' patterns were filed. The actual stored material was very small, but the machinery to house it filled an entire room. Hawker knew he'd never be able to sort through everything to find just his own pattern and destroy it; he'd have to destroy the entire works. That meant the patterns of all the resurrectees, all the soldiers he'd fought beside down through the ages. He had no authority to make this irrevocable decision for them, but he didn't think he needed it. He knew the soldiers' mood on this matter. None of them enjoyed being slaves; all of them were looking for a way out and would welcome the chance to be free—even if the price were a final, unalterable death.

Hawker took one of the grenades from his jumpsuit, tossed it at the computer and left the room, never looking back. The explosion rocked the bunker and increased the feeling of panic within the headquarters. People began running around without purpose, certain that the enemy had arrived. The confusion only helped his cause; no one paid any attention as he took the elevator to the surface along with twenty other frightened fighters and left the bunker in the general stampede. He was back in the open now, free to move around once more.

Half of his task had been accomplished. This army's copy of his identity file had been destroyed; they could never resurrect him again. But there was one more to go; the other side also had a copy of his pattern—and until that copy was also destroyed, he would never be free.

As soon as he could conveniently do so, he broke away from the panicked mob from the bunker and set off on his own. Staying with the others would be suicide; in their hysterical rush, they would simply be gunned down at leisure by the enemy artillery. He had to be by himself, where he could move with caution and stealth.

He found a deserted spot hidden from view, ripped off his red armband and replaced it with the blue one he'd taken from his dead double. The other Hawker had been wearing a uniform similar enough to his that he could pass as the man he'd killed. The only problem might be language; if the attackers had been better prepared, as it seemed obvious they were, they may have had time to implant a common language in all their soldiers—and if it was one he didn't speak, he'd be spotted as an infiltrator despite his blue armband.

He stopped by a corpse on the ground and ripped off a piece of its uniform, then wrapped it tightly around his head as a bandage. Now if anyone spoke to him in a language he didn't understand, he could pretend he'd gotten a head injury that affected his hearing and left him in shock. He'd seen that glazed expression on comrades' faces thousands of times throughout his career; now he hoped he could emulate it successfully.

He skulked through the ruins until he was well behind the blue lines. The soldiers here weren't nearly as trigger-happy. The slight mop-up action was all

248

being handled by the front-line troops; the job of these soldiers was to occupy and hold against possible counterattack—which everyone on both sides knew was an impossibility. The mood of these fighters was lighthearted, even boisterous. They were triumphant, they were in no danger. There was nothing for them to fear.

Hawker walked through their ranks to the rear, attracting hardly any attention. Once they'd noted the color of his armband and seen the stunned expression on his face, they weren't interested in him any more. They didn't want anything to spoil the feeling of triumph, least of all the knowledge that they, too, had suffered some casualties. The soldiers ignored him as though they hadn't even seen him.

His disguise took him well back into the blue ranks—far enough to see that they'd brought a mobile field headquarters with them. This was something like a floating six-story building, riding majestically across the open ground outside the ruined city on a cushion of antigravity. Hawker was delighted to see it. Such a facility indicated that this army was self-sufficient, with no need to be supplied from the outside; all its services—hospital, mess and administration—could be found in that one building.

In particular, that meant it was much more likely the records of its soldiers were here in the field, rather than many kilometers away at an established base. A mobile field headquarters could travel where it pleased and duple its troops as needed—which, at times, was much better than dupling the troops at one central location and distributing them later. Hawker's pattern would be on file here, simplifying his mission considerably.

The mood back here was relaxed, confident. The blue side had won the battle, totally crushing all red resistance. Their jubilation meant they were less tight with their security than they might have been under more strenuous battle conditions. Hawker walked in plain view to within fifty meters of the mobile head-quarters before receiving his first challenge. "Halt. Where are you going?"

The guard had spoken Arkasan, a language Hawker understood. Relieved that he didn't have to continue his shell-shocked act, he said, "Special mission from patrol five. Our fucking commers went out on us, so they sent me back to get some more. Don't know why we bother, nothing's going to happen out there. We really smashed 'em today."

The guard smiled and pointed at Hawker's bandage. "Looks like *you* saw some action."

"Yeah—slipped on a loose stone and hit my head." Hawker tried to capture the tone of irony that the guard could commiserate with. Only a fellow soldier could truly appreciate these little absurdities life constantly offered—and it would make Hawker's story that much more believable.

As he'd hoped, the guard waved him inside with a slight smile and no further questions. Hawker once again found himself inside a military base with only the vaguest idea of where he was going—but he'd search this entire structure from top to bottom if he had to; he'd come too far and suffered too much to be stopped now.

The mood within this base was the exact opposite of that in the bunker. Here, everything was triumph and calm confidence, the easy feeling of superiority that let the troops relax and take things easier than they otherwise might have. The practical effect, though, was much the same—Hawker was allowed to roam the corridors without much interference, as long as he always pretended to know where he was going and what his specific orders were for going there.

At last, though, Hawker reached an area he was not permitted to penetrate. Relaxation was one thing, but a total breach of security couldn't be expected here. The forbidden area was locked with identity-required doors, and in addition was guarded by two live soldiers stationed out front who told him in no uncertain terms that the resurrection computer was off limits to anyone without specific authorization.

Hawker had come this far; what he was looking for was on the other side of that door, and he wasn't going to let himself be stopped now. He walked back to the first crossing corridor and stepped into it, out of sight of the guards who'd turned him away. The hallway was almost empty, and Hawker dallied innocently until there was no one around to observe his actions. Then, taking one of the grenades from his pocket, he tossed it down the corridor to the end. Just as it exploded he started running back to the guards.

"Quick!" he yelled. "One of their saboteurs got inside. He's that way!"

The guards took their rifles, which had been slung casually over their shoulders, and raced forward to see what the matter was. As soon as they were past him, Hawker took out his own pistol and shot them both in the back, then turned the laser on the security door. The laser's beam was not strong enough to penetrate the door, so Hawker reached into his pocket for another grenade and threw it at the portal. The blast opened a satisfactory hole for him—but it left him with just one grenade. He would have to save that for the final task.

Hawker leaped through the hole, gun drawn. There were more soldiers here, but they were all choking and stunned from the smoke of the sudden explosion; Hawker killed them before they could even shoot back. With most of the opposition gone, Hawker ran down the hall checking every doorway. Most of the rooms in this section were just offices for the battalion staff, unoccupied and unimportant. Twice he came across other people, and shot them down without even caring who they were. Only one thing mattered to him now: finding that resurrection computer. It had to be here somewhere.

Hawker became a demon possessed, a fanatical killing machine with but one goal. Nothing could be allowed to stop him in his quest. All the army's training, all those centuries of combat and conflict, had prepared him for this day, and he was honed to a razor's edge. He would not die before he found the room he sought.

There was a guard outside the computer room when he came to it, but Hawker killed him and ran through the door. Suddenly he confronted his nemesis, the machine that had brought him back to a life of hellfire and damnation time after time. Hawker gave a grim smile, knowing that this time he would even the score forever. He lowered his gun and reached into his pocket to pull out the last grenade.

"Hold it, motherfucker!"

The voice was vaguely familiar. Hawker turned quickly to find himself staring down the sights of a laser pistol. The man behind the pistol was Thaddeus Connors. Hawker's own pistol had been lowered; there was no way he could raise it to shoot before Connors could kill him.

"Hello, Connors," he said. His voice was preternaturally calm, a fact that surprised even him. "Remember me?"

"I remember a lot of people." Connors was wire-taut, only a micron away from murder.

"I saved your life. Remember China, back when this whole fucking mess started? I dragged you across fields at night, and I hid you from the enemy in the daytime."

Connors laughed coldly. "Yeah. If it wasn't for you I wouldn't be here now, right?" No resurrectee could say that and mean it as a compliment.

"I can fix it all now, if you'll let me. If I destroy this computer, all our patterns are gone; they'll never be able to duple us again."

"Cut the bullshit, whitey. There's no way out of

this, never. This is Hell, don't you know? God sent us all here for our crimes. We're all damned souls. It's His punishment, and there ain't nothing no one can do about it."

Hawker's mouth was dry. Thaddeus Connors had been a problem ever since the two men had first met, and he would continue being a problem to the very end. Perhaps some little spark of gratitude way in the back of Connors's mind had kept him from killing Hawker outright—but that margin was rapidly eroding. As bad as the situation was, Hawker would have to do something.

He raised his pistol and fired straight into Connors's stomach. The black man fell back, dying—but even before the beam had hit, his own laser was lashing out, scoring Hawker's body.

Hawker should have died then. Connors's beam cut right through his vitals, missing the heart by no more than a millimeter. The pain was blinding, and Hawker fell to the ground like a lump of lead.

But he was not dead, not yet. He had a purpose that would not let go of him, would not let him stop. As long as the computer still existed, all his lives had been for nothing. He could not die now, or his labors would have been lost.

There was something hard and smooth in his left hand. The grenade. He still held the grenade. He could not turn his head to see it, but he had handled so many grenades that his fingers knew its surface intimately. *Set it,* he ordered his hand, and the fingers moved slowly to obey. First he turned one small dial, then another. A timer fuse. Fifteen seconds. With the last gram of strength in his body, he pushed the grenade away from him along the floor, toward the computer, knowing there were millions of things that could still go wrong. Maybe he hadn't set the grenade right. Maybe there was a third record of him somewhere. Maybe . . .

Jerry Hawker did not live to see the explosion, nor to realize that it produced more than satisfactory results. But that, in and of itself, was a victory.

At long last, and forever, Hawker knew peace.

**From planet Earth
you will be able to
communicate with other worlds—
Just read—**

SCIENCE FICTION

☐ **SPACE MAIL II**　　　　　　　　　　24481　$2.50
　Edited by Isaac Asimov,
　Martin Harry Greenberg,
　& Charles G. Waugh

☐ **EARTH ABIDES**　　　　　　　　　　23252　$2.75
　by George R. Stewart

☐ **ASSAULT ON THE GODS**　　　　　24455　$2.25
　by Stephen Goldin

☐ **GUARDIAN**　　　　　　　　　　　04682　$2.25
　by Thomas F. Monteleone

☐ **FIRE AT THE CENTER**　　　　　　14417　$2.25
　by Geo. W. Proctor

☐ **THE SURVIVAL OF FREEDOM**　　24435　$2.50
　Edited by Jerry Pournelle and
　John F. Carr

☐ **THE X FACTOR**　　　　　　　　　24395　$2.25
　by Andre Norton

Buy them at your local bookstore or use this handy coupon for ordering.

COLUMBIA BOOK SERVICE, CBS Inc.
32275 Mally Road, P.O. Box FB, Madison Heights, MI 48071

Please send me the books I have checked above. Orders for less than 5 books must include 75¢ for the first book and 25¢ for each additional book to cover postage and handling. Orders for 5 books or more postage is FREE. Send check or money order only. Allow 3-4 weeks for delivery.

Cost $_____	Name_____
Sales tax*_____	Address_____
Postage _____	City_____
Total $_____	State_____ Zip_____

The government requires us to collect sales tax in all states except AK, DE, MT, NH and OR.

Prices and availability subject to change without notice.　　　　**8232**

The Legends of the Old West
Live On in Fawcett Westerns

☐ THE LONELY LAW by Matt Stuart	00434	$1.95
☐ WARRIOR CREEK by L. P. Holmes	00444	$1.95
☐ THE CALIFORNIO by Robert MacLeod	14301	$1.75
☐ OUTCAST GUN by Giles Lutz	14079	$1.75
☐ VENGEANCE TRAIL by Dean Owen	04663	$1.95
☐ PAYOFF AT PAWNEE by L.P. Holmes	04671	$1.95
☐ BUCHANAN'S BIG FIGHT by Jonas Ward	14406	$1.95
☐ THE UNTAMED BREED by Gordon D. Shirreffs	14387	$2.75
☐ LITTLE BIG MAN by Thomas Berger	23854	$2.95
☐ HONDO by Louis L'Amour	14255	$2.25
☐ SWEENY'S HONOR by Brian Garfield	24330	$1.95

Buy them at your local bookstore or use this handy coupon for ordering.

COLUMBIA BOOK SERVICE, CBS Inc.
32275 Mally Road, P.O. Box FB, Madison Heights, MI 48071

Please send me the books I have checked above. Orders for less than 5 books must include 75¢ for the first book and 25¢ for each additional book to cover postage and handling. Orders for 5 books or more postage is FREE. Send check or money order only. Allow 3-4 weeks for delivery.

Cost $_____ Name_____

Sales tax*_____ Address_____

Postage _____ City_____

Total $_____ State_____ Zip_____

*The government requires us to collect sales tax in all states except AK, DE, MT, NH and OR.

Prices and availability subject to change without notice.

8231